Trying to Stay Saved:
New Day Divas Series Book Four

Trying to Stay Saved:

New Day Divas Series Book Four

E.N. Joy

URBAN CHRISTIAN

www.urbanchristianonline.com

Urban Books, LLC
78 East Industry Court
Deer Park, NY 11729

Trying to Stay Saved: New Day Divas Series Book Four
Copyright © 2011 E.N. Joy

ISBN 13: 978-1-60162-783-4
ISBN 10: 1-60162-783-1

First Printing May 2011
Printed in the United States of America

10 9 8 7 6 5 4 3 2 1

This is a work of fiction. Any references or similarities to actual events, real people, living, or dead, or to real locales are intended to give the novel a sense of reality. Any similarity in other names, characters, places, and incidents is entirely coincidental.

Distributed by Kensington Corp.
Submit Wholesale Orders to:
Kensington Publishing Corp.
C/O Penguin Group (USA) Inc.
Attention: Order Processing
405 Murray Hill Parkway
East Rutherford, NJ 07073-2316
Phone: 1-800-526-0275
Fax: 1-800-227-9604

Dedication

For the church and the unchurched. For the saved and the unsaved. For the Christian folk and the church folk. For the sinners and the saints. May each of you hear God's voice throughout this series and know that He loves you no matter who you are, no matter what you've been through, and no matter what you are going through. Jesus is Lord!!!

Acknowledgment

I'd like to thank the authors on the Urban Christian imprint, for each of you have taught me more than you will ever know about using the gift of the written Word to please God. I've read some of the best books in the world while editing your manuscripts. But more importantly, under the direction of the Holy Spirit, in editing your manuscripts, I was actually being taught. So God bless each and every one of you for having something to do with the success of this series.

Stay blessed!

Other Books by This Author

Me, Myself and Him

The Secret Olivia Told Me (written under N. Joy)

She Who Finds A Husband

Been There, Prayed That

Love, Honor Or Stray

Even Sinners Have Souls (Edited by E.N. Joy)

Even Sinners Have Souls TOO (Edited by E.N. Joy)

Chapter One

"Are you sure you're ready to jump right back into taking over the business of the New Day Single's Ministry?" Unique asked Lorain through the phone receiver. "I mean, you just got back today, and you've been gone for almost three months."

"Yes, uh, I'm sure," Lorain stated, not sounding too convincing. As a matter of fact, she wasn't sure. She wasn't sure about a lot of things; like why, with this being her first day back from her three-month sabbatical, she'd jumped on the phone and dialed Unique's number. Why hadn't she been led to phone her own mother first? Or even her doctor, who wasn't in favor of her leaving in the first place. Lorain's doctor, who had treated her for her selective memory loss after a bump to the head, wasn't comfortable with Lorain going three entire months without checkups. She made a mental note to make a doctor's appointment for next week.

Lorain couldn't fully explain why she felt so drawn to Unique, the young girl who'd served as her nemesis for the first couple of months they'd interacted. After a while, though, specifically after their pastor forced them to work together on the New Day Temple of Faith Single's Ministry, they sort of grew on each other. Eventually, Lorain learned to respect the God in Unique. But there was a force that was now drawing Lorain so closely to Unique. It was a force she couldn't understand. It was due to something stronger than just having spent time together working on the ministry's affairs.

Had Lorain not have suffered from selective memory loss, she might have recalled her findings after hours of Internet searches. The search was sparked by something Unique had said during an argument between the two at a McDonald's. During this argument, Unique revealed some personal information about her past. It was that information that sent up a red flag in Lorain's head.

Unique had informed Lorain that as a newborn, she'd been thrown away in a dumpster and left for dead by her birth mother. Lorain carefully did the math and compared Unique's age to how long ago her mother had done the awful deed. Lorain realized Unique would have been the same age of the baby girl she'd thrown away as a scared, pregnant teen. But the baby Lorain had thrown away had died in that garbage can and had been carried off to God knows where by a garbage truck. That's what Lorain had thought for years anyway. But after doing some digging, Lorain discovered that the baby had not died. After doing even more digging, she discovered that the baby was Unique.

Lorain had planned on sharing her findings with Unique, but before she could, she had a fateful fall that would cause her to forget certain things. Her discovery of Unique being her biological child was one of those things she'd forgotten.

If only Lorain could regain her full memory, she'd know why the force drawing her to Unique was so strong. The visions Lorain had experienced prior to leaving for her sabbatical was sure to have had something to do with it. Even on her sabbatical, she'd continued to see visions of Unique, documents, and newspaper articles. She kept seeing the words: "Baby girl found in trash can," and "Baby Doe up for adoption." She'd tried her hardest to connect the dots on her own, but couldn't.

The doctor told Lorain that eventually she might recover her full memory, and with God, she knew this was indeed possible. But it was taking too long. Perhaps deep down inside, Lorain truly didn't want to remember everything about her past. After all, the doctor had said that with selective memory, patients usually tend to forget traumatic events. What on God's green Earth could she have experienced that was so traumatic . . . and that involved Unique?

"Well, you don't sound too convincing about wanting to get back into the groove of things," Unique replied. "If that's the case, just let me know, because we'll probably have to talk to Pastor about finding a replacement for you. And before you get to thinking I'm after your title or something, get that straight out of your mind. With my new job and all, I don't know how much longer I'll even be able to—" Before Unique could express how she didn't know if she'd be able to continue to serve as assistant leader, Lorain cut her off.

"You've got a job?" Lorain asked with enthusiasm.

"Oh, yeah, that's right; you don't know." Unique spoke with such pride, like the way she spoke whenever she talked about her three children. "Yes, I've been working with Sister Tamarra for a couple of months or so now. She was willing to give me a chance to work at her catering company. And just before she left the church, she let me handle an event all on my own. It was—"

Once again, Lorain cut Unique off. "Did you say Sister Tamarra left New Day, as in she's no longer a member?"

Lorain couldn't believe what she was hearing. She and Tamarra weren't close, but she'd admired her from afar. She'd always felt as though there'd been some sort of invisible connection between the two of them; like they'd both been in the same place and had experienced some of the same things in life.

Tamarra was one of the people Lorain, during her sabbatical, had made a mental note to reach out to and connect with. Outside of just attending church together, praising and worshiping together, Tamarra had seemed like someone Lorain would have liked to befriend. Lorain shrugged. She guessed now she'd never know exactly what the connection between her and Tamarra could have been, nor would she likely become friends with her. But right now, what worried her most, though, was that she'd possibly never know why she felt the way she did about Unique.

That's why she decided to go on the sabbatical in the first place; she wanted clarity from God. This memory loss thing was making her feel as though she was going insane. It was like certain things were fighting to take their rightful place back in her memory bank. There were just all of these flashes in her head, like paparazzi cameras going off at the red carpet. She wanted her mind refreshed and her spirit cleansed so that she could be wide open to receive the answers she'd been seeking. Answers not only about Unique, but about Broady, her mother's new fiancé.

Lorain had experienced visions about him as well. It was as if she knew him from her past or something. Lorain felt in her spirit that somehow everything connected. How was Broady connected to Unique, or Unique to Broady, or Lorain to Unique . . .?

Surely Unique would think Lorain was crazy if she brought these things up to her and tried to pick her brain. She and the young girl hadn't formed that close of a bond. But maybe she could pick Broady's brain somehow. He hadn't suffered from any type of memory loss as far as Lorain knew, but yet, he acted like he'd never met Lorain in his life. He had to remember something about her, other than the fact that he was engaged to her mother. And Lorain was going to make it her business to see that the marriage between this man and her mother didn't take place until everything was revealed.

"Yep, Sister Tamarra is gone, as in she is no longer a member of New Day Temple of Faith," Unique told Lorain.

"Do you know why she left? Did something happen?" Lorain shook her head. "Was it someone at New Day? You know how some church folks can be. They got tongues that will run a person right up out of there; and I'm not talking about spiritual tongues either. I'm talking about the kind of tongues that talk about a person behind their back—shoot, sometimes right in their face."

Unique felt a little uneasy. She recalled using her tongue to talk bad about Lorain, both behind her back and in her face. But that was in the past. She'd repented to both God and Lorain. Besides, they weren't talking about her and Lorain; they were talking about Tamarra. "I'm not really sure why she left. I really haven't gotten into that with her. We usually just talk business. But if I had to guess, it might have something to do with Brother Maeyl hooking back up with his baby's momma."

"Brother Maeyl has a baby?"

"Yeah, well, she ain't really a baby. Cute little thing though. I took my boys to her birthday party. At first, she and Tamarra appeared to be getting along just fine, but then the little girl started tripping about how Tamarra didn't really want to be her mother. Blah, blah, blah. But anyway, I can't call it. But I bet if you offer to take the church secretary out to dinner, you'll have the entire story from her before you can even finish your appetizer."

Both women chuckled, knowing it was probably true. The New Day Temple of Faith church secretary couldn't hold an ounce of water in a two-gallon pail; she'd find a way to spill it completely.

"Well, I guess all I can do is just keep Sister Tamarra in prayer and hope that she finds another church home."

"Oh, she's attending Power and Glory Ministries International over in Reynoldsburg. I do know that much. She hasn't joined yet, but it's only been a couple of weeks. Who knows, she might even come back to New Day eventually. You never know where you're going to end up when God's behind the wheel. He's the last person you want to be a backseat driver too."

"Well, be sure to tell Sister Tamarra I said hello and give her my love the next time you talk to her."

"Actually, she and I have a catering affair Friday, which is why I wanted to be sure you were ready to jump right back into taking over the Singles Ministry. I'm not going to be able to be there with the catering gig and all."

"Oh, I see." Lorain's voice was laced with disappointment. The only reason why she'd even considered jumping right back into the business of the Singles Ministry was so that she could spend some time with Unique. Quick on her feet, she came up with another plan. "Well, then, perhaps we could meet—you, me, and the kids, one day this week so you can catch me up on what's been going on in the ministry."

Unique sucked her teeth. "Girl, you ain't missed nothing. It's the same ol', same ol'. Ain't nothing changed about the New Day Divas who show up at those meetings just to show out. Some of them refuse to walk in deliverance from the hurts and pain of their past relationships; so they use the ministry as an opportunity to release their frustrations and male bash. And the poor men folk don't know how to act around them," Unique added with a slight chuckle. "We done already lost two of the male members."

"Oh, no," Lorain sighed. She'd been proud to wear the crown of having finally gotten men to join the ministry. That was something her predecessor as the New Day Singles Ministry leader couldn't do. "We'll just have to do something about that, now, won't we?"

"It's no biggie. I'm sure now that you're back, they'll probably come back."

"And what's *that* suppose to mean?" Lorain almost sounded offended.

"Oh, nothing, I'm just saying, you know." Unique had come close to letting the cat out the bag. There had been an inside joke among the women of the Single's Ministry about Lorain joining the ministry. *"Yeah, I bet if that miniskirted-low-cut shirt-wearing Lorain was a member of this ministry, the men would flock here in droves,"* one woman had stated. *"The way they dang near be salivating over the woman is just shameful."*

"Maybe our skirts ain't short enough and V-necks ain't V enough, like the Jezebel spirit that possessed Lorain," another had complained. *"Guess we all can't be spiritual divas like good ol' Sister Lorain."*

Unique continued, being careful to cover her tracks. "I was only the co-leader filling in for you, and you know how some folks are. It's like when they know Pastor ain't preaching on Sunday, they don't come to church. They want the real thing—to hear the house leader give the message."

Now Lorain was slightly flattered. "I'm sure you did a fine job, Sister Unique, but I have to admit that the two of us together make a pretty good team."

"That we do, and who would have thought it?"

"Tell me about it. Anyway, what do you say about us getting together one day this week to go over things? We can meet at my house. I'll come pick you up. I'd love to see the kids."

Unique was taken aback. The last she recalled, Lorain acted like she didn't want her kids nowhere near that cute little condo of hers. Seemed like Lorain always had something slick to say about Unique's three sons. "You sure about that?" Unique double-checked. "I mean, maybe the fact that you were always so funny acting about me and my kids is a part of your memory that you're suppressing." Leave it to Unique to not bite her tongue.

"Come on now, give me some credit. I just spent three months on a sabbatical communing with the Lord. Your mother is a changed woman, Unique."

There was dead silence on the phone upon Lorain referencing herself as Unique's mother. Then finally, Lorain hollered out, "Gotcha!" and brushed it off with a laugh. Unique joined in, recalling how after Lorain's head injury she'd referred to Unique as her daughter. It was funny then. Well, it was funny to everyone else, but it hadn't been funny to Lorain. And although she'd just feigned laughter, it wasn't funny now. Indeed this was a serious matter that she was going to get to the bottom of if it was the last thing she did.

Chapter Two

Although Jamaica had been a beautiful place, Paige was glad to be back home. Surprised couldn't describe how Paige felt the day Blake showed up on her job, swept her out of her office, and rode off with her in the awaiting limousine. They went straight to the airport with nothing but carry-on bags that Flo, their maid, had packed for them.

Blake had taken the liberty of clearing seven days vacation with Paige's company. He'd begun making the plans the day she got out of the hospital after her car accident. Paige's low blood sugar caused her to pass out behind the wheel of her car had almost taken her life. This near-loss had triggered the once emotionally, and oftentimes physically neglectful Blake to vow to never take his wife for granted again. So he'd made it his business to treat her like the queen she was. And Paige was loving every minute of it.

"Home sweet home," Paige stated as she entered their home, Blake trailing behind her, carrying luggage. Although they'd departed the airport with nothing but carry-on bags, after all the shopping they'd done, they now each had a new mini-wardrobe—shoes included.

The two had spent their first few hours in Jamaica shopping for all they'd need on their honeymoon. Paige had to pinch herself several times to make sure she wasn't dreaming back in La-La Land. But it was real. It was all real; God had blessed her with a true king who didn't mind sharing his riches and wealth freely with his queen. Blake, surprising Paige by telling her he was going to be featured in a top financial magazine, made her realize just how much riches and wealth he truly had.

As a commercial real-estate agent, when the recession hit, most folks in real estate began to suffer financially. Blake obviously walked in true favor of God and had the faith of a mustard seed that the God he served wasn't in a recession. The talk, chatter, murmurs, and complaints by some of his coworkers didn't get to him. He didn't walk in fear when it came to his being able to provide for himself and his family. If he learned nothing else from his father before he'd passed away, it was that where there was a will, there was a way. If he'd just hold on, then everything would turn out for his good in the end. After all, everything had turned out good for his father and him.

It didn't look like it would when his father was critically injured on his job and unable to work for the rest of his life. It didn't look like it would when his father's job refused to compensate him fully for the incident. It didn't look like it would when Blake's mother ran off with his little sister, leaving him and his disabled father to fend for themselves. But all had turned out for their good in the end. Yes, it had!

Blake's father finally won a settlement against his job, allowing him and Blake to live a comfortable life. Blake was also able to go to college. It wasn't just the financial blessing of the matter that had turned out good. Having to spend most of his time taking care of his father, Blake was able to form a bond with him that some young men would kill for. He was able to spend the most precious years of his life with his father. He was able to learn how to become a strong willed man through his father's teachings and actions. His father was his hero. His father was the reason why he persevered in life.

Aside from God's favor, it was this strong will that pushed Blake to do his best no matter what the situation looked like. His perseverance in the real-estate market had paid off . . . very well. Because Blake didn't live a flashy lifestyle, no one would have ever known just how financially prosperous he was, including Paige. Blake paid and handled all of their living expenses and finances. This allowed Paige, after taking care of her personal debts, to bank her money. There was none of that going Dutch stuff—all the bills being split down the middle. Paige had landed her a true provider. And now Blake was being recognized by a nationally distributed magazine as one of the top ten commercial real-estate agents in the country: a man able to surf the waves of the recession and come out on top.

"You can say that again," Blake said to Paige as he dropped their belongings on the floor. He was certainly glad to be home as well.

"Home sweet home," Paige abided. She walked over to the couch and collapsed. Then she looked down at all the luggage Blake had brought in and pointed to it. "And you can leave that stuff right there for when Flo comes tomorrow."

"Honey, I know you are *not* going to have that woman put away your drawlz," Blake laughed as he walked over and joined his wife on the couch.

"Shows what you *don't* know." She rested her hand on his knee before spotting something on the living-room table. "What's that?"

Blake followed her eyes to the FedEx package on the table. "Something from FedEx. Flo must have brought it in when she checked on the house for us while we were gone."

"Where's the rest of the mail?" Paige asked.

"Oh, I had the post office hold it. We have to go pick it up," Blake told her as he opened the package. His eyes lit up as he pulled out the contents. "It's here. It hit the stands while we were away."

"Oh my God! Let me see!" Paige exclaimed, knowing exactly what Blake was referring to.

Blake held the magazine where both he and Paige could look at it.

"Cover? They have you guys on the *cover?*" Paige playfully whacked Blake on the shoulder. "And you didn't tell me."

Blake smiled, proud that he'd been able to keep the best part of the secret for last. Keeping the interview and the photo shoot from her had been difficult enough. And it was no coincidence that he'd been out of the country when the magazine hit the stands. Being a very low-key person by nature, Blake knew that once the magazine was published, the local media would be at his doorstep, organizations would be contacting him for speaking engagements, etc. . . . . He'd even been advised to hire a publicist, told he could gain even more notoriety and money as a result. Blake wasn't interested in all of that. He didn't want to be a star. He just wanted to be a hardworking man like his father had raised him to be. So it was his prayer that by the time he returned home, the buzz would have died down some and the media would get the hint when he didn't return any of their calls.

"Oh, honey." Paige's eyes filled with tears. She was so elated. "You have no idea how proud I am to be Mrs. Blake Dickenson right now."

"I'm the one who's proud to have such a loving and caring wife to share this with." Blake stared down at the cover and shook his head. "I just can't believe it. This all seems so surreal."

"Well, believe it. It's all real. This is really happening for us."

Blake stared into Paige's eyes as tears fell. Wiping one away with his thumb he stated, "Yes, honey. This is really happening. And this is only the beginning." His eyes returned to the magazine. "Now I have to work even harder. I can't just live up to this." He shook the magazine. "I have to exceed this. My father always told me to never get complacent. That there's always a higher mountain, a higher peak." Blake stared off remembering his time with his father.

Paige looked down at the magazine again. "Well, don't just sit there; let's read it."

Snapping out of his daze, Blake opened the magazine and flipped to the cover story. He and Paige excitedly read the two-page interview on him. Although he'd made cover, he had to share the spread with the others. Blake's interview covered everything from how he was abandoned as a child by his mother, to his father's accident, to his father winning the settlement that would afford him a college education, to the foundation that catapulted him to where he was today. He was very humble and modest in his interview, giving glory to God and his father. It was a moving article indeed.

"That's my man," Paige pointed to the individual picture of Blake that rested on the first page of his interview. "That's my man."

"I'm your man," Blake agreed.

Paige seductively removed the magazine from his hand and placed it on the table. "No, you are *the* man."

"Oh, I see," Blake nodded with a mischievous grin on his face. "Well, why don't you let *the* man get cleaned up, you do the same, and we'll spend the last day of our vacation curled up together."

"Sounds good to me." Paige licked her lips. "You go ahead and jump in the shower first. I'm going to check the home phone messages."

"You're the boss," Blake said as he headed to their bedroom bathroom to shower.

"And you remember that when I'm calling the shots ten minutes from now," Paige winked as she walked over to check the phone messages.

Twenty minutes later, Blake returned to the living room to find Paige with the phone to her ear still writing down messages. "Geez, is it like that?" Blake asked, standing over her as she scribbled down the information from the last message she'd retrieved.

Hanging up the phone, Paige sighed. "When did that sucker hit the stands?" She nodded to the magazine. "Everybody and they mama called, leaving congratulatory messages. Newspapers and the local news even called." Paige pointed to one message in particular. "And this woman, she called twice. She's some attorney with the law office of Crainbel and Associates."

Blake took the paper from his wife's hand and read the name. "Robin Turner, Esquire. Hmm. Doesn't ring a bell."

Paige took the message back from him. "Well, looks like you're not going to find out until tomorrow, because right now, you have to ring *my* bell, husband." Paige began planting kisses on Blake's lips.

"Umm, hmm, right after you go knock that shower out." Blake sniffed the air and playfully turned his nose up.

Paige turned her lips up and headed to the bedroom. "Boy, quit playing. You *know* you like it funky."

Blake just shook his head, and then turned his attention back toward the message. He looked at the clock. It was four o'clock in the afternoon on a Tuesday. He decided to go ahead and return the attorney's call while Paige was in the shower. He picked up the phone and dialed the number she had written down.

"Crainbel and Associates. How may I direct your call?" the operator answered.

"Robin Turner, please," Blake requested.

"One moment. And may I ask who's calling?"

"Blake Dickenson."

"Thank you, Mr. Dickenson. Please hold."

After a few seconds, Robin Turner came on the line. "Ah, Mr. Dickenson. Attorney Robin Turner, Esquire here. And before we begin, let me first congratulate you on your most recent success. You must be humbled to have appeared in a national financial magazine, receiving such recognition for all of your hard work."

"Thank you, and yes, I am. I'm very humbled. Thank you for sharing in my celebrating."

"You are very welcomed, Mr. Dickenson. But I know someone who would love to really share in celebrating with you."

The next words Robin Turner spoke nearly knocked the wind out of Blake. He couldn't believe what this woman was saying to him. This had to be some kind of joke—a bad joke. After the first few sentences, Blake had tuned Ms. Turner out completely. He was still stuck on those first couple of sentences.

"So, anyway, Mr. Dickenson," Ms. Turner finished up her conversation, "once you receive the papers, just give me a call so we can discuss this further and come to an agreement that will make everybody happy. You take care," Ms. Turner said before ending the call. "And congrats again."

The line went dead, and Blake felt as though he were about to go dead as well. His body turned cold with chills as sweat expelled from his pores.

"Blake? Blake? What's the matter, honey? Are you okay?" Paige began to wipe away the dampness from Blake's forehead. "What is it? Talk to me. What's the matter?" Paige pressed.

Finally Blake was able to gain enough strength to speak. "When you said everybody and they mama had called, you weren't lying."

"Huh? What?" Paige was confused, having just entered the room.

"My mother . . . she called to congratulate me. Well, not personally, but through her attorney, Robin Turner." Blake looked at Paige with horror written all over his face. "She's suing me. My mother, who I haven't seen since I was three years old, is *suing* me."

Chapter Three

"So how was Bible Study last evening?" Bethany asked Mother Doreen as the two of them, along with Bethany's children, Sadie and Hudson, sat at the kitchen table eating dinner.

"Child, Pastor Frey know he taught a mighty good Word," Mother Doreen replied. "The spirit was all up in that place. I thought we were gonna have church for a minute there."

"You know that man always could teach a good Word. Every time he'd fill in for Pastor Davidson he'd have the church . . ." Bethany allowed her words to trail off as every eye in the room penetrated her soul.

She'd said it. She knew better than to say that man's name around her family. After Bethany's affair with the former pastor of her former church, his name was pretty much mud around there. Losing the baby, her lover's baby, had added insult to injury. Hudson and Sadie were having a hard time dealing with the situation on top of the loss of their father after his fatal trucking accident. It was three months now since the death of their father and the miscarriage of their unborn sibling. Bethany knew that eventually, time would heal all wounds, but she needed time to move just a little more quickly. She needed to move on with her life, and in order to do so, she needed her children to move on as well. But something was still holding her back.

Mother Doreen cleared her throat. "You know, you really should come back to Living Word, Living Waters. Pastor Frey deciding to serve as interim pastor while . . . you know . . . everything settles down . . . gets back to normal . . . was the best thing that could have happened to the church."

Bethany gave out a harrumph. "I wish I might show my face up in there. Nobody would be able to keep their eyes on Jesus for having them burn a hole through me. No, thank you." She thought back to the last couple of times she'd returned to the church after suffering from a miscarriage. That's when the rumors, whispering, and gossiping started. Bethany didn't want to subject herself or her children to such viciousness by so-called Christians, so she pulled them, and herself, out of the church. To date, they hadn't been back to that church or any other one.

"You know, it's really not like that," Mother Doreen assured her before taking a bite of corn bread. "Yeah, there was some talk going on for a minute there, but now that's all old news. You know how Christian folk are—*real* Christian folk. They pray for you, they pray for the situation, and then they move on."

"Well, it ain't the Christian folk I'm worried about. It's them church folk. You know, the ones with them religious spirits, acting like they have a heaven or hell to put you in." Bethany shook her head. "Uh-uh. No, thank you. Trust me, Sis; I was a member and had attended that church much longer than you. I know how they are up in there. I can handle it, but the last thing I want is for my kids to be scared by church people."

"So you gonna run from the church for the rest of your life and keep your kids from growing in the Lord too?" Mother Doreen asked.

"Just as soon as the Lord leads me to another church home, so be it."

"Child, they the same way up in Living Word as they are in any other church. Don't you know every church is trying to get it right?"

"Yeah, well, I'm trying to stay saved, so until they get it right, I'll just stick to Bedside Manor on the *Gospel Music Channel*. At least then I know I won't catch a case."

Mother Doreen shook her head. "Ah, bah, ya, sta, yo, saya mo," she spoke in tongues, and then took a bite of her baked chicken. After a couple of chews, she turned her nose up. She'd wanted fried chicken, but opted for baked on her sister's behalf.

Ever since coming to look after Bethany around nine months ago, Mother Doreen had been doing most of the cooking. When she left Malvonia, Ohio to come to Kentucky, her intentions were to make sure her sister walked in her healing. She was going to see to it that Bethany beat this diabetes thing.

She'd helped out by tending to a lot of the house chores; cooking and cleaning. She also kept an eye on the kids, but she quickly learned that keeping an eye on teenagers was not an easy task. At the dinner table was the only time she was ever sure of what those two were really up to. And at the dinner table is also where she could make sure she was helping Bethany keep her diabetes under control. So Mother Doreen had adjusted the preparation of her meals. Every now and then, they would have down-home soul food dinners with desserts made from scratch. She figured Bethany deserved to splurge every now and then. But mostly, she'd replaced her frying with baking, broiling, or grilling.

"Yeah, I'd be speaking in tongues after tasting that chicken too," Bethany teased her older sister.

Mother Doreen shot her a stern look as the children burst out laughing.

"Oh, so you two agree, I suppose." Mother Doreen looked at her fifteen-year-old niece and seventeen-year-old nephew.

"No, Aunti, we're just teasing," Hudson said, shoving a piece of chicken in his mouth just to show her that he thought it was edible.

"But you know I would have loved some of that special battered-fried chicken you be throwing down on," Sadie added.

"Y'all just saying that because y'all love me," Mother Doreen said coyly. "Y'all know just as well as I do that this baked chicken is overcooked. It's a little dry. I gotta watch my timing next go-round."

"It might have helped if instead of being on the phone with Wallace . . . I mean, your *pastor* . . ." Bethany teased.

"That man ain't have nothing to do with this chicken being dry." Mother Doreen stared down at her plate and began to pick at her broccoli with cheese.

"And I suppose he didn't have anything to do with my white socks being pink either," Bethany replied. "That last batch of white clothes you did came out looking like a bottle of Pepto-Bismol."

Once again, the children burst out laughing.

"So that's why Hudson gave me all of his T-shirts," Sadie realized.

"Yeah," Hudson confirmed, "I wasn't about to be caught walking around in no pink T-shirts."

"Besides, now they probably go great with your pink underwear, Sadie," Bethany laughed.

"Why you bunch of ungrateful . . ." Mother Doreen said, playfully pointing her fork at them before stabbing it into a piece of chicken.

"Don't worry about it, Aunti," Sadie told her. "We understand how it is when you get a new boyfriend and start falling in love. You sometimes get distracted and pulled away from things without realizing it."

Hudson nodded in agreement.

"Now just hold on a minute." Mother Doreen dropped her fork on the table. "Who said *anything* about me having a boyfriend?"

Everyone tilted their heads and looked at Mother Doreen like she was crazy.

"Are you *serious?*" Bethany asked her. "Do you *really* not want people to believe that you and Pastor Frey are not seeing each other? That he's not more than just playing the role of your spiritual father? You *can't* be serious."

Mother Doreen paused for a minute. "So it's that obvious, huh?" she finally confessed. It wasn't as though she had anything to hide regarding her and Pastor Frey's relationship. She just knew that with so much drama having taken place in the Tyson household, bringing a new relationship into the midst of everything didn't seem timely. Especially since the man she was seeing had replaced the pastor Bethany had been cheating with.

Pastor Frey had been Pastor Davidson's co-pastor; his right-hand man. He had known about Bethany's affair and had been covering for his pastor by keeping it in the closet. Mother Doreen didn't know how comfortable everyone would be with having Pastor Frey around; how much a reminder of the situation he would be. But now that the cat was out of the bag, she'd soon find out.

"Well, now that everyone knows," Mother Doreen said, "I guess ain't no harm in sharing it with you all." She blushed. "Yes, Pastor Frey and I have grown smitten with each another." She looked at the three of them. "I hope that's okay with everybody."

"Why wouldn't it be?" Sadie questioned, then took a bite of her food.

"Yeah," Hudson shrugged.

"The Lord sure does work in mysterious ways," Bethany said. "You couldn't stand the man at first, and now you're ready to marry him."

Mother Doreen put her hand up. "Hold up, wait a minute. Ain't nobody said nothing about putting marriage in it."

The kids chuckled at Mother Doreen's rhyme.

"Aunti, why are you starting to sound like that Mr. Brown character in a Tyler Perry film?" Sadie asked.

"'Cause that man got her acting all silly like a teenager in love," Bethany answered for her sister.

Mother Doreen looked serious. "You know what, Sis? I think you're right."

There was a hush over the room.

Mother Doreen nodded and a smile spread across her lips. "It's a funny thing when love creeps in. Ain't so easy to ignore or ask it to leave and tell it to come back later . . . at a more appropriate time . . . when you're ready. Nope; love just shows up and knocks you down."

"Uh, oh . . . now Aunti is singing Keri Hilson," Sadie laughed.

Mother Doreen waved her hand. "Uh-uh. I don't know nothing about that secular mess you two young folks listen to." She looked at Bethany. "I don't even know why your mama allows you to play it in her house. As for me and my house—"

"You're right," Bethany said as she sat there with a serious look on her face.

"I know I'm right. Don't nothing about that music glorify God. It just—"

"No, I mean you're right about love," Bethany stated. "It's like this powerful force that you sometimes have no control over."

Bethany was staring off as everyone else was staring at her. She snapped out of her zone once she realized she was the center of attention. The mood was now serious. She knew it was time. Finally it was time that she shared the truth with her family, the real truth about how she'd really been feeling. The whole truth and nothing but. They would understand. They'd have to understand. They'd just agreed themselves that love had a mind of its own. She couldn't help how she felt.

"Sis, kids, there's something I want to tell you." Bethany swallowed hard after clearing her throat. Everyone could tell this was serious by the look on her face.

Mother Doreen shifted nervously in her chair.

"What is it, Ma?" Hudson asked. He'd stopped eating.

The sudden shift in her mother's tone had also caused Sadie to push her plate aside. She had no idea what her mother was about to say, but she knew it was going to be something that would change things. It had already changed the upbeat tone to that of a sour note.

Bethany swallowed. "I know it hasn't been that long since your father passed," Bethany started, but then her nerves set in. She grasped for words, a lie, to cover the truth she was about to tell. Perhaps she'd jumped the gun. It was too soon. It wasn't time for her to reveal her true feelings just yet. But she'd already begun taking the top off the can of worms. She couldn't turn back now.

Bethany fixed her mouth to continue, but before she could say anything, there was a knock on the door. Feeling like divine intervention had just showed up, Bethany jumped up from the table. "I'll get it." She hurried to the door, not even wondering who it might be or that the person had not placed a call first. As she made her way to the door she played with words in her head about how to tell her family what she needed to tell them. She was so focused that she didn't even look to see who was at the door before opening it; otherwise, she might have thought twice about doing so. But it was too late now.

Now Bethany had no choice but to greet her uninvited guest. "Good evening, First Lady Davi—" Before Bethany could finish her greeting, she felt a sting across her cheek.

"First Lady Davidson?" Mother Doreen yelled as she jumped from the table to run to her sister's aid. Before Mother Doreen could even get to the door, First Lady Davidson, the wife of Pastor Davidson, said what she needed to say and then walked off.

"You just couldn't stop sleeping with him, could you?" First Lady Davidson asked Bethany. "Well, there's his stuff." She pointed to bags and loose items that were strewn across the lawn. "He's all yours." And with that, she wiped her hands clean and left just as quickly as she'd come.

But it was obvious that there was much more to come.

Chapter Four

Lorain was filled with such joy to see Unique's three children come trailing out of the house, heading toward her car. Prior to getting to know the three little men, she wasn't much of a kid person. "I don't do the kid thing," she'd always said. But it hadn't taken long for the boys to prick at her heart and burst that bubble. Now, every time she saw kids out and about with their mom or dad, a strange desire would come over her; a desire to actually want to be around kids. It was a desire to maybe even have kids of her own someday.

The gist of this desire had been unearthed during her sabbatical. She didn't know how much of her might have felt this way prior to that. She didn't know a lot of things these days, literally. And she owed it all to the selective memory loss. What she did know was that she was going to have a talk with pastor about working with the youth at the church in one capacity or another. For now, though, she was satisfied with doting on Unique's boys.

"Well, hello, kids," Lorain greeted as Unique buckled her boys in the backseat.

"Hi, Miss Lorain," they replied in unison.

The youngest even tried to reach up to hug Lorain, but Unique held him back.

"Baby, Mommy is trying to buckle you up. Sit back," Unique said, then buckled and kissed him on the head.

Lorain thought she could just cry right there. No one had ever expressed such happiness to see her. Reciprocation of that kind felt good, even if it was from a little person.

"I missed go at your house," the youngest said to Lorain.

"You missed going," the oldest corrected. "You missed going to her house." He then looked at Lorain. "We all did, Miss Lorain." A little smile crept through his always serious face.

"Yeah, and we can't wait to draw you a picture telling you how much we missed you," the middle child added. "You gonna put it on your shine board?"

"Are you going to put it on your shine board?" the oldest now corrected his middle brother. His face was back in its serious disposition.

"Are you going to put it on your shine board?" the middle son asked correctly.

"You know it," Lorain smiled as she looked over and saw that Unique was now secure in the passenger's seat with her seat belt on. "And you know what else?" This time she was speaking to Unique. "I missed you, Sister Unique."

Unique snapped her head back. Had she just heard Lorain correctly? The same woman who used to run to Pastor's office to complain about how much she hated having to work with her now proclaimed to miss her. Unique leaned in and put her hand on Lorain's forehead, checking for a fever. After feeling that Lorain was normal she said, "Just checking," then cracked a smile as they drove off to Lorain's place.

After entering Lorain's condo, everyone took their shoes off.

"You go ahead and get us all set up in the living room," Lorain told Unique. "I'll get the boys situated in the kitchen. I got them some snacks and more art supplies."

Unique paused for a moment. With a serious expression on her face she said, "Look, Sister Lorain, I don't know if it's God or that bump on the head you took, but this new you . . ." She looked Lorain up and down, then allowed a smile to appear on her lips. "I like . . . a lot." She winked and headed over to the couch.

"Thank you," Lorain replied in an inaudible tone before leading the boys into the kitchen. Upon joining Unique back in the living room she asked Unique, "So, what do you think? What type of event should we have in order to try to get some more men to join the Singles Ministry? Not just men, I suppose, but more members, period."

"First things first." Unique stood up and extended her hands to Lorain. "Let's open with some prayer."

Lorain took hold of Unique's hands while Unique led them in prayer.

"Dear Father in heaven, thank you for being you. Thank you for breathing on us. With that breath, Father God, we ask for fresh wind. Fresh anointing. Thank you for this ministry and for blessing Sister Lorain and myself with the responsibility of overseeing it. Thank you for trusting us with your people. Lord, thank you for bringing Sister Lorain back from her sabbatical safe and sound and free from harm. Thank you for the newness you've created in her, O God. Oh sha, bo, so ta ya po. Yes, God, we thank you for the fresh anointing. Oh, ba, ya, to, som, ah ye."

Unique squeezed Lorain's hands a little tighter. "May you continue to do a good work in her. May you fill her up and provide her with an overflow. Um, sha, bo, so ta ya po. May I receive some of that overflow, dear God. Ohhh, I feel the Holy Ghost. Ump, yes, Lord. May you connect us like never before. May you allow our spirits to connect in order to do what you have called us to do.

May we do those things with a spirit of excellence and with love, in a manner that is pleasing to you, Lord in heaven. Oh, God, I know at first Sister Lorain and I were not willing vessels, but now we say, 'Yes, Lord.'"

"Yes! Yes, Lord," Lorain whispered.

"So thank you for changing our hearts, for changing our minds, and for changing our ways. Now use us, Lord, as you see fit. In Jesus' name we pray. Amen."

"Amen," Lorain stated.

Unique opened her eyes only to see Lorain's spilling with tears. She looked around and spotted a box of tissue on an end table. "Here." She extended a couple of tissues to Lorain.

"Thank you." The minute Lorain would wipe one tear, another would fall. She'd been so moved by Unique's anointed prayer. Those words had truly meant so much to her. She wanted their spirits to connect. She wanted their lives to connect. But first, she knew she had to get their stories to connect. So she dried her eyes, cleared her throat, and pulled herself together. A connection was going to take place; Lorain was going to make sure of that as she prepared to execute phase one of her plan.

"So do you have an agenda made up for our meeting this time?" Unique asked, ready to get things started.

"I sure do," Lorain told her, pulling a sheet of paper out of her notebook that sat on the table. But little did Unique know, Lorain had a hidden agenda as well.

Chapter Five

When Paige heard the garage door opening, she rushed to put the final touches on the meal she'd prepared for Blake. Well, actually, Flo had done the bulk of the work prior to leaving for the day, but Paige had insisted on having a hand in the preparation. For the past couple of days, ever since that phone conversation with his mother's attorney, Blake had been on edge. He'd been snappy and restless, tossing and turning all night. And when Paige thought a session of oneness would relax him, he was too tense to even focus on the task at hand.

Now she was bound and determined to do everything she could to see to it that they had a nice evening. Coming off of a honeymoon they'd initially had to cancel and postpone, Paige felt cheated. After spending seven days in paradise, they should have been able to come home with clear minds and spirits. No, it wasn't the sabbatical that New Day members were notorious for going away on, but God had definitely been on that island with them. Only God could have created such beauty, and never would He have left it unattended. So surely He'd been present, keeping watch over His marvelous and wonderfully made creations: the island, Paige, and Blake.

"Baby, I'm glad you're home . . ." Paige's words trailed off when she saw the angry look on her husband's face as he entered the house.

"That witch didn't waste any time," Blake spat as he slammed a set of papers down on the kitchen counter.

"Wha-what's wrong." Paige eased her way over to the papers and picked them up.

"I got served today," Blake barked. "I got served right as the local television station showed up on my job wanting to interview me. I was so embarrassed. Saved me from declining their interview, because they could clearly see that I was in no condition to be interviewed by anybody after that," he rambled on in rage.

"You got served?" Paige questioned, then trying to make light of the situation, she replied, "What did I tell you and Klyde about having those dance offs in the office," she teased with a half smile.

"Huh? What?" Blake was completely lost until he realized Paige was joking in reference to that popular dance movie among youngsters titled *You Got Served.* "This is not the time for jokes." He didn't smile. Not even a half smile.

"Sorry, honey, I just thought—"

"You just thought nothing." He snatched the papers out of Paige's hands. "It's not your money that gold-digging ho is after."

"Blake!" Paige couldn't believe that word had come out of her husband's mouth. She'd never heard him degrade women before. And in less than a minute, he'd referred to one as a gold digging ho; and this was his own mother he was talking about.

"Don't 'Blake' me. The woman deserves to be called worse." He looked down at the papers and began to read them. He'd already read them twice, though, before calling up and faxing a copy over to the company's attorney. "She's got some nerve to have abandoned me and my father, left us for dead, and then pop back into my life bearing court papers. Is this woman serious?"

"Listen, baby, it's going to be all right." Paige walked over to Blake and began rubbing his back. "We've already got the victory in this situation."

"One million dollars," Blake stated as he shook his head and then repeated, "*One million dollars. She's suing me for one million dollars. My own mother. Son of a—!*" He slammed the papers down so hard that it frightened Paige.

Taking a deep breath, now trying to calm her own self down and get her heart rate back on track, Paige said, "Let's just relax. Enjoy this wonderful, delicious dinner, then take a Jacuzzi bath or something. I'll light some candles, turn on some gospel jazz. Afterward, we can go to bed and, you know, comfort each another."

Now Blake was looking at his wife, shaking his head.

"What?" Paige shrugged, wondering why her husband was looking at her like she had a booger hanging out of her nose.

"Is that all you think about? Really? Sex and food?"

Paige put her hands on her hips, highly offended. "*Excuse* me?"

"You heard me," Blake snapped. "I've been busting my butt since the day we got married trying to keep food on the table. And God knows how expensive that can get with a woman your size. Thank God the doctor made you cut back, or else who knows how much I'd still be spending."

Paige swallowed the lump in her throat as she became full of emotions. She was hurt, mad, angry, shocked, and pissed. She wanted to pick up the pan of vegetable lasagna that was cooling on the stove and whack him a good one upside the head with it.

"Look, I'm tired. I'm going to take a shower and go to bed." Blake excused himself and headed for the bedroom.

Paige stood there fighting back tears from the mixed emotions and crazy thoughts still running through her head. Thoughts like her taking the mini-television/ radio off the kitchen counter and throwing it in the shower with Blake. Thoughts like putting something in his dinner that would make him ill. Just then, in the middle of her crazy thoughts, the phone rang. It was perfect timing, because Lord only knows what Paige might have thought up next . . . and then done.

Getting herself together, she walked over to the phone and answered it. "Hello."

"Hey, girl." Paige exhaled when she heard her best friend's voice chime through the phone. "What are you over there doing?" Tamarra asked.

After taking a deep breath, Paige answered, "Trying to stay saved."

Paige talked with Tamarra on the phone for over an hour, sharing the details of everything that had taken place over the last week; everything from their perfect honeymoon of her dreams, to the nightmare that had awaited them once they returned. She told Tamarra how on edge the entire lawsuit thing had made Blake, but she left out the part about the flesh-cutting insults his tongue had wounded her with. She was too embarrassed; besides, she knew that wasn't her Blake talking. That's not how he truly felt about her. He was just angry. It was his mother he really wanted to lash out at. Unfortunately for Paige, she was the only one around to take it. She figured she'd just bear the brunt until they got past everything.

"Honey, you 'sleep?" Paige asked, entering the dark bedroom after ending her call with Tamarra.

At first Blake remained silent, then he let out a sigh and spoke. "No, I'm awake. Can't sleep."

Paige walked over to the bed and sat down on her side. "I know this whole court thing is on your mind—"

"No, it's not that," Blake said, sitting up in the bed. "I can't sleep because of all those awful things I said to you." He scooted close to her and held her face. "Baby, I didn't mean it. You know I didn't mean it. I love you. You are my everything. You are perfect in my eyes. It's just that—"

This time Paige cut him off by putting her index finger to his lips. "Shhh. I understand. I know it's not me you're angry with." She removed her finger.

"But you didn't deserve that from me. You're a good wife. I'm sorry."

"And because I'm a good wife I understand that I have to be there for you. Through the good and the bad; ain't that what Pastor said during our wedding ceremony? So, I'm going to be here for you. And we'll get through this together, okay?"

"Okay." Blake kissed her lips.

"Just try to go a little easy on me, all right?" Paige joked. "Deal?"

"Deal." Blake kissed her again.

"What do you say we figure out a way to somehow seal this deal?" Paige began to slip out of her clothes.

Blake stared at his wife's thick silhouette in the dark. And although he still wasn't really in the mood for lovemaking, he knew he couldn't deny her. After all the awful things he'd just said to her, he knew he had to make his wife feel like a woman again; a desired woman, wanted by her husband. So he performed his husbandly duties, and afterward, he felt they were even. But with the stress of the upcoming court hearings pertaining to the lawsuit, he knew there'd be a lot of "getting even" going on. But neither husband nor wife had any idea of just how bad things were going to get.

Chapter Six

"I can't believe you are still sleeping with that woman's husband," Mother Doreen said to her sister as she dabbed the blood away from her bleeding lip.

Bethany looked up from the couch at her children in embarrassment. "Kids, go to your room."

"We're not babies, Mom," Sadie spat. "Trust me, we've grown up quicker than we'd like to with all the drama that's been going on the last few months. We deserve to know if you're still seeing that man or not."

"Yeah," Hudson jumped in. "Keep in mind that I'm about to be a father."

Bethany had almost forgotten that because of all her neglect and drama that had taken place, her son was about to become a teenage father. Truthfully, that really was something she wanted to forget. Whether she'd been more attentive to her family life may not have affected Hudson having a child on the way, but still, there was a tinge of guilt that told Bethany otherwise.

"I can handle what's going on with you, Mom," Hudson insisted. "You said we'd try to be honest around here from now on; try to hold each other accountable."

Bethany put her head down in shame.

"Look, kids, your mother will come up and talk to you in a minute," Mother Doreen intervened. "Just let me have a word with her for now, okay?"

Sadie sucked her teeth and stomped off, mumbling under her breath, "Here we go again." Hudson reluctantly followed behind his younger sister.

Once the children were no longer in earshot, Mother Doreen started in. "How could you, Beth? Not only are you still seeing the man you disrespected your dead husband with by sleeping with him, a man who disrespected not only his wife, but his entire congregation by taking advantage of one of his church members . . . but a man who could be responsible for the death of your husband."

"Oh, Sis, please don't start that mess up again. You already, against my wishes, decided to take your speculations and the information you dug up on your little witch hunt against him to the police. They didn't even find sufficient evidence in your findings to reopen the case. Pastor Davidson is no murderer."

"Just a liar and an adulterer, I suppose. At least that's all we can prove for now." Mother Doreen sarcastically added, "Guess he's still got a chance at getting into heaven then."

"We all fall short of the glory, 'Reen, and don't you forget it. You're the one gallivanting around here with Pastor Frey like y'all Danny and Sandy from the movie *Grease*."

"But at least we're keeping it holy. And what do you call what you and Senator Edwards there are doing?"

"We're two people trying to follow our hearts."

"Puh-leeze," Mother Doreen stated as she looked frantically around the room. She then spotted what she was looking for, a Bible. She grabbed it, and then threw it down on the couch next to Bethany. "Now, you show me in that there Bible where the Word of God says to follow your heart. Go ahead, show me."

Bethany just sat there.

"Uh-huh. Just what I thought." Mother Doreen snatched the Bible up. "Because it *don't* say nothing about following your heart. But I'll tell you what it does say." Mother Doreen flipped to the book of Proverbs. "Right here in Proverbs, chapter four, verse twenty-three, it says, 'Above all else, guard your heart, for it is the wellspring of life.'" She slammed the book closed. "Guard your heart—*not* follow your heart." Mother Doreen sat down next to Bethany and lovingly put her arm around her shoulder. "Child, you have to follow the direction of the Holy Spirit. You can't lean on or trust your own thoughts and understanding . . . or your heart. Your heart can have you making decisions that will have you all messed up."

Tears began to fall from Bethany's eyes. "Honestly, it's been some time since we were last together. I mean, after I told him about the baby, he became a different person, like he didn't want to be around me anymore. But then after a while, after losing the baby, he came around again and we started talking. But that's it, just talking. We didn't expect it to happen. I just love him, though. I know it's wrong, but I love him. I can't get him out of my heart. And believe it or not, I was going to tell you and the kids about how I was feeling tonight, right before the knock on the door came."

Mother Doreen exhaled. She wasn't sure what needed to be said, so she needed a Word from God to relay. So keeping her fleshly tongue under control, she remained silent while Bethany spoke.

"I must seem so cold that even after the death of my husband I went back into my lover's arms. Even though we've still talked and seen each other on occasion, we've only . . . you know—been together—once," Bethany assured her sister. "I just couldn't turn it off; the feelings I had for the man; the feelings that I still have for the man. I mean, I loved Uriah. God knows I did. My mourning and my grief were real, but I love Davidson too," Bethany confessed. "And I'd be lying if

I said I wasn't happy about his wife putting him out. That could mean I do have a chance with him." A light went on in Bethany's head. "Sis, it could be like a sign from—"

"Don't you dare put this one on God," Mother Doreen snapped. "Child, don't you even fix your lips to say such a thing."

Mother Doreen sat down in the chair next to the couch, speechless. How could this all have been happening right under her nose? Her sister having sex with the pastor? Her teenage nephew having sex, period? She felt as though the moment God had sent her to Kentucky she'd been botching the entire assignment. Obviously she hadn't been in position like she was supposed to be. Obviously she wasn't hearing from God like she should have been. All that had to change. She couldn't let God down. He had to know that He could trust her to do what He'd called her to do. So now it was time for her to start getting to the bottom of things. She needed eagle eyes; eyes that enabled her to see her prey, the enemy, from great distances, long before they ever got a chance to get next to her.

"When did you start seeing him again? I don't understand how . . ." Mother Doreen inquired.

"Whenever you were at the church and the kids were doing their thing or something," Bethany answered honestly. "I mean, I haven't seen him a lot. You guys are hardly ever gone at the same time. I don't know how his wife—"

"Wait just one minute!" Mother Doreen exclaimed as she stood. "In *here?* In *this* house? You and that man . . ." She turned and began pacing. "In the name of Jesus. This house! The house your dead husband's insurance money paid off?"

"Don't try to make me feel guilty." Now Bethany stood. The sudden movement caused a pain, forcing her to caress her wound.

"It shouldn't take me to make you feel guilty. If the Holy Spirit ain't convicted your trifling tail by now, then—"

"How dare you!" Bethany was now in Mother Doreen's face.

"How dare you?" Mother Doreen shot back, standing her ground.

The two sisters were toe-to-toe. If the doorbell hadn't rung when it did, no telling which one of them might have swung the first punch.

"I'll get it." The words seethed through Bethany's teeth as she went and answered the door. This time she looked to see who it was. Upon seeing the caller and the knot that donned his head, she quickly opened the door. "Are you all right?" she asked in a panicked tone. "What did she do to you?"

"Yes, I'm all right. What about you?" he asked, slightly touching Bethany's face.

Mother Doreen couldn't bear the sight of Bethany and Pastor Davidson standing in the doorway displaying their matching wounds. It was evident that First Lady Davidson packed a powerful punch.

"She's a mess," Mother Doreen answered for her sister as she approached the couple. "And so are you."

"Sister Doreen," Pastor Davidson greeted. "I'm sorry about all this."

"As you should be," she spat back at him.

"You don't owe her any explanation," Bethany said while cutting eyes at Mother Doreen. "Come on in. Let me get you some ice or something for that lump on your head."

"No, no. I just came to get my things. First Lady told me I could pick them up here." He looked over his shoulder. "I had no idea they were thrown across your lawn." He turned back to Bethany with hush-puppy eyes.

"So she put you out, huh?" Bethany asked the question to the answer she already knew.

Pastor Davidson nodded.

"Where are you going to go?" Bethany inquired.

"I don't know. She cleaned me out. She went to the bank and withdrew all of our funds today. Cancelled our credit cards. Changed the locks on the doors. She was a busy bee."

"Humph," Mother Doreen mumbled under her breath. "Not half as busy as you've been."

"But how did she find out that we had still been seeing each other?" Bethany asked.

"It seems as though over this past month First Lady's spirit discerned something wasn't right. At first she believed me when I told her you and I were over and that it would never happen again." He looked at Mother Doreen. "Of course, I had to open up and tell her the truth about us when the police came questioning me about Uriah's death."

Mother Doreen rolled her eyes up in her head and crossed her arms. If her actions had forced the man to reveal the truth to his wife, then so be it.

"She believed me," Pastor Davidson continued, "because back then, I was telling the truth. We hadn't been seeing each other. I had no idea it would be so hard to completely cut things off with you. I thought just talking with you, seeing you would ease the loss I was feeling. But that was just a trick of the enemy." Pastor Davidson took a breath. "It seems as though she followed me over here the other day. She's been planning my exit ever since. Already visited a lawyer and everything."

"Oh, honey, I'm so sorry." Bethany rubbed Pastor Davidson's arm.

"Well, if you ask me, you *both* should be sorry," Mother Doreen stated.

"And we *didn't* ask you." Bethany was fed up as she made her way toward Mother Doreen, pointing and waving her finger. "But that has never stopped you from meddling your nose where it doesn't belong, now, has it? Always using the excuse that God sent you here on assignment, all the while you just been here for your own good, to be nosy. And now that Pastor Frey has got your nose all up in the air—"

"Mom! Aunti!" Hudson came rushing down the steps with Sadie behind him. "It's time. The baby is coming. Kells is in labor and headed to the hospital. I'm about to be a dad!"

"Oh, Lord have mercy, child, we've got to go," Mother Doreen said as she began to scurry for her things. She noticed that Bethany wasn't moving. She remained next to Pastor Davidson. "Well, come on, child, get to moving," she said to Bethany. "You're about to be a grandmother."

Bethany looked at Pastor Davidson. "Wha . . . where are you going to go? What are you going to do?"

Pastor Davidson shrugged. "I don't know. I'll figure something out. I'll just clean my things up off your lawn and be going."

"But you don't have anywhere to go."

"Don't you worry about me right now," Pastor Davidson assured her. "You got a grandbaby you got to go see about." He then turned away.

Bethany stood there for a moment. She then looked at Mother Doreen who already had retrieved her purse and keys.

Mother Doreen looked right back at her. "Don't you even *think* about it."

"Sis, I can't just let the man stay on the streets." Bethany then turned her attention back to Pastor Davidson and said, "Pastor, wait a minute. I think I have an idea."

Chapter Seven

"So, when will you be back?" Lorain asked her mother through the phone.

"Oh, Broady and I will just be gone through the weekend," Eleanor told her. "We're leaving first thing in the morning."

"But I haven't really gotten to see you since I've been back. I wanted to invite the two of you over for dinner."

Eleanor almost choked. "*You* . . . invite *us* over there for dinner? What we gon' eat, girl? You ain't never got no food there. And I know your tail ain't been to the grocery store since coming back."

"It's only Thursday. I planned on going grocery shopping and cleaning my house on Saturday morning, figuring maybe you guys could come over after church on Sunday." Lorain ran her fingers across the nightstand next to her bed. "It's amazing how much dust and dirt can accumulate even when nobody's been here to dirty up."

"How about Broady and I have dinner with you when we come back from out little trip? Next weekend? It will be our treat."

Lorain paused for a minute. It really didn't matter to her who cooked dinner. Her mission had nothing to do with food but had everything to do with spending time with her mother and Broady; mainly Broady. She needed to pick his brain. She knew that whatever pieces were missing to the puzzle in her memory, he had at least one of them. "Okay, Mom," Lorain sighed. She didn't want to have to wait until next weekend, but it looked like she didn't have a choice.

"Good," Eleanor replied. "Now let me get off this phone and finish getting packed."

"All right, Mom. You guys be careful."

"We will, honey. I'm glad you're back, and I love you."

"Love you too." Lorain ended the call and then flopped back on her bed. She stared up at the ceiling. "Please, God, help me to keep my mind. In the name of Jesus, keep my mind." The prayer was short, sweet, but definitely to the point. Lorain wanted God's help at making her mind whole again.

Going away on the sabbatical had helped a great deal. During that time of consecration, her mind had stayed focused on God and the things of God. He'd revealed so much to her about her calling and purpose in life. He'd assured her that He'd forgiven her for the mistakes and sins of her past and that she should forgive herself. But how could she forgive herself for things she didn't remember and couldn't see clearly in her mind, but could feel in her spirit?

She couldn't understand for the life of her why God was spoon-feeding her. Why was she still sucking on milk? She could handle the truth—the whole truth. Not just bits and pieces of it, but the whole hunk of meat. But for some reason, Lorain felt God didn't think she could handle it. Thing is, Lorain didn't know how much longer she could wait around on God before she took things into her own hands.

She looked at the digital clock on her dresser. It was going on eight o'clock in the evening. She contemplated for a moment on whether to turn on the television and watch a movie. Even though the night was still young, instead, she decided to go ahead and get some sleep. "Why bother watching a movie anyway?" she said out loud as she pulled the covers over her body. "I probably won't remember what I've watched anyway come morning."

"Who do you think people are going to believe, you or me?" Broady said to Lorain. "Folks aren't going to believe someone like you."

She just sat there confused. She looked around the room, not knowing where she was or how she'd gotten there. "Ya . . . you," she stuttered, figuring that was the answer he wanted to hear. "They'll believe you." She looked around, still trying to figure out where she was. Her eyes landed on the wooden desk, and then to the name plate on the desk that read "Mr. Leary."

"That's right," Broady said as he rose from the chair behind the desk. He walked over toward the chair where Lorain sat.

Lorain's sweaty palms gripped the arms of her chair. As Broady walked toward her, she became frightened and started shifting in the chair. The closer he came, the more he seemed to tower over her, like she was a child. But she wasn't a child. She was a grown woman, but she felt as though she was trapped inside a child's body.

She relaxed a little once she realized that Broady was making his way past her and over to the exit door. She let out a sigh of relief, but then she heard a clicking sound. Lorain turned around to see that Broady had locked the office door and was now making his way back to her. He wore a lewd and sinister smile on his face.

"Oh, God, help me!" Lorain began to mumble, but that was before Broady's huge hand covered her mouth. Suddenly, everything went black. When the darkness was finally filled with light, Lorain found herself laying on hard, cold tile. She was in excruciating pain; pain like nothing she'd ever felt in her life. She began to take deep breaths as the pain subsided, but a few seconds later, it would come back with vengeance. "Oh, God, help me," she found herself crying out once again, this time as she clutched her stomach. The pain was ripping through every fiber of her body, but her stomach seemed to be where it was centered. It was like bad menstrual cramps . . . very bad.

Lorain tried to pull herself up off the floor, but she couldn't, then everything went black again. When there was light, she was still in pain as she managed her way over to a huge dumpster and leaned up against it. The pain was so much. It was too much, too much for her to bear, so she began to black out again. She went in and out of consciousness until darkness blanketed her once again. The next time the darkness dissipated and light surrounded her, she was taking off her jacket and tying it around her waist. She was trying to cover up a stain on her pants. She didn't want people to see. She didn't want people to know. Seeing that the stain was completely hidden by the jacket, Lorain slowly began to walk away from the dumpster. Still in pain, she tried her best to hide it.

As she walked away, she could hear a sound coming from the dumpster. The sound stopped her in her tracks because it sounded like the cries of a baby. With a puzzled look on her face, Lorain slowly crept back over to the dumpster. The cries were louder and harder now. Taking a deep breath, she peeked inside the dumpster. She didn't see anything but trash. Fig-

uring that her mind was playing tricks on her since it had been doing that a lot lately, she assumed she must have imagined it.

Once more, she walked away, but the cries pierced the air and wouldn't let her. So, she returned to the dumpster and began moving the trash around. A cardboard box began to move all on its own. It startled her at first, then she watched it move again. Slowly, she reached for the box, and then moved it. Unique's face stared up at Lorain. This grown woman was lying in a dumpster, her accusatory eyes locked on Lorain's.

"Jesus!" Lorain called out as she rose up from her bed drenched in sweat. It was dark in her room, pitch-black. There was nothing but the light from her digital clock that read one fifty-three A.M.

She knocked over and broke things on her end table as she hurried to turn on the light. Not knowing what was awaiting her once the darkness was filled with light, she frantically looked around her room.

Lorain could barely control her heart rate. She had to take several deep breaths to calm herself down. Sitting on her bed, she replayed everything that had just taken place in her mind. "Why is this happening to me? What does it all mean? Please, God, I'm going crazy. I just want to rest. I just want some peace." Lorain's shoulders heaved up and down as she cried, adding to the pool of water she already rested in.

After a couple of minutes, Lorain decided she needed to refresh herself. She peeled her wet clothes off and then took a shower. She prayed the entire time she was in the shower. She prayed to God and afterward, began calling out orders to Satan.

"Get thee behind, Satan. I have authority over you. You must obey me, and right now, I command you to cancel your assignment on my life, on my mind. In Jesus' name!"

All Lorain wanted was for the devil to get out of her way so that she could get her mind right. So that she could hear from God clearly and be able to figure out what was going on. She had her own interpretation of the visions she'd just experienced. "Unique is my baby," Lorain whispered to herself as she dried off. "I threw her away." A tear rolled down her face. "And her father must be . . ." She could hardly say it, but she did. "Her father must be Broady." She began to weep.

"Folks aren't going to believe someone like you." The words Broady had spoken to her in her vision replayed in her mind.

Lorain knew that he was right. If she did tell anyone about her suspicions, they'd think she was crazy. And she would be inclined to believe them herself. She honestly felt as though she was losing it.

Barely rubbing lotion on her body, Lorain slipped into some dry pajamas. Then she surveyed the mess in her room: the wet, unmade bed and the nightstand with objects in disarray and cluttered. But it could all wait because she had plans to clean her house from top to bottom on Saturday anyway. Making her way to the linen closet in the hallway, Lorain grabbed a sheet and blanket. Then she stopped back at her room and opened the nightstand drawer, pulling out her Bible.

After making a bed on the couch, she began reading the Bible. "Thou wilt keep him in perfect peace, whose mind is stayed on thee: because he trusteth in thee," Isaiah, chapter twenty-six, verse three.

Lorain looked up. "Okay, God, I'm going to keep my mind stayed on thee, now please . . . please . . . keep me in perfect peace. Amen."

Chapter Eight

"Alone in a room, it's just me and you," Paige sang before the choir director interrupted her.

"Hold up. Already I don't believe it's just you and God alone in the room," the director said to Paige as they all stood in the New Day sanctuary at choir rehearsal. "It's you, God, and the million things you have on your mind." The choir director paused, then breathed out loudly. "Sister Dickenson, why don't you go take a break? Get a drink of water or something. Then come back and let the Lord use you for real."

Paige nodded as she exited the choir stands and headed toward the water fountain outside of the women's bathroom. She wasn't even mad at the choir director for calling her out. She knew that when she sang for the Lord, she was always supposed to give her best. Whether it was just rehearsal or Sunday morning in front of the entire congregation, she was expected to operate in a spirit of excellence. As of now, she was operating in a spirit of bondage. Something, so many things, were holding her back from giving her all, from giving God her best. She wanted to be focused on the words she was singing to and for the Lord. She wanted the words to come from her heart straight to God's ear. She wanted it to be a sound that made God smile. This morning, though, all she was doing was making noise with her voice.

Paige leaned over the water fountain and allowed the tiny waterfall to brush across her lips. She wasn't even drinking the water. She wasn't thirsty. Just going through the motions, killing time, and trying to get her mind right.

After a few moments, Paige raised up from the water fountain. "Oh, Sister Nita, you scared me." Paige placed her hand over her heart that had just skipped a beat or two. She had no idea Nita had silently walked up behind her.

"I'm sorry, Sister Paige," Nita apologized as she held a bucket in one hand and a mop in the other. "I was just going to the women's restroom to do my Saturday morning cleaning." Nita looked at Paige's hand that was still resting on her chest and slightly trembling. "You're mighty jumpy. Is everything okay?"

Paige's eyes squinted slightly at Nita. She was trying to read the expression that was on the leader of the Janitorial Ministry's face. Was Nita truly concerned, or was she fishing? It wasn't too long ago when Paige felt that Nita was overstepping her boundaries. Right there in the church sanctuary, Nita had practically alluded to the fact that there might be trouble in Paige and Blake's paradise. She hadn't outright said anything, but the look in her eyes, her facial expression, and the tone of her voice had said it all.

Nita had approached Paige just moments after Blake had handled Paige's arm in a not-so-gentle manner. In truth, he'd had a death grip on it. It had been a discreet act, but obviously not discreet enough. Nita had zoomed in on the physical indiscretion like a hawk, then swarmed down on Paige, questioning her and making little comments. Paige had responded by snapping at Nita. And although afterward she felt bad about it, she would do a repeat right about now if Miss Mop and Broom pulled it again. Paige was simply not in the mood. Not today.

"Everything is just fine, Sister Nita, but I do thank you for your concern." Paige finally allowed her hand to fall down to her side. "But I assure you, there is nothing for you to be concerned about. Everything is fine." On a scale of one to ten, Paige was about a five in the area of sounding convincing. Not everything was fine, especially when it came to her and Blake. Not right now anyway, but Paige had been praying that things would get better.

For a minute there, things had been going great. The first few months of their marriage had been off to a rocky start, but things started to look up after Paige's diabetes diagnosis. Blake had been by her side as she adjusted her lifestyle. But then Paige found herself having to point out to Blake the occasions when he'd been overly aggressive. He hadn't been in denial about it, and when Paige suggested they seek counseling with their pastor, Blake willfully agreed. They immediately started their counseling sessions. To date, they'd only made it to two of the sessions. In those two sessions, though, they'd made great strides, uncovering issues that hadn't been disclosed during premarital counseling.

Upon returning from their honeymoon, the couple had planned on immediately resuming their counseling, but Paige knew better than to bring that up to Blake. He'd been on razor's edge since learning of his mother's pending lawsuit against him. Plus, he'd been trying to play catch-up at work. She knew he didn't need the added worries of trying to manage counseling in the midst of all that.

With it being Saturday morning, today would have been a good day for them to squeeze in a session with

their pastor, but Paige had to leave for work immediately after 9:00 A.M. choir rehearsal. Blake wouldn't
have been able to make it either. With such short notice, this morning was the only time his attorney could
fit him in to go over the lawsuit. The attorney was doing
Blake a huge favor by seeing him on a Saturday. There
was just too much going on right now, way too much.

Paige definitely had a lot on her mind, but she hoped
in time it would get better. It had to. She and Blake
would get through this lawsuit business, get back into
counseling, and everything would be just fine. Then
maybe next time Nita asked her if everything was okay,
she'd rank a ten on the convincing scale.

"If you say so . . ." Nita paused before walking into
the women's bathroom. "You know, I heard you back
in there. I saw you too." She nodded toward the sanctuary. "You barely got the first note out, and I could
tell something had you bound. You weren't singing
like you usually do. You have a voice that can break
off shackles and chains. Sometimes saints can come in
here so heavy with stuff on their mind and their heart,
and then you sing. It's like the windows of heaven open
up, and whatever has been binding people just falls
off them. I bet if you really focused, really spoke those
words to God, whatever it is that has you bound will fall
off you."

Paige smiled at the compliment. "Thank you, Sister
Nita. That's so nice of you to say."

"Well, don't thank me. I'm just speaking things how
I see them. That's a little something I'm working on—
and that pastor is working with me on."

Paige tilted her head, a little lost.

"You know, speaking the truth on what I see . . . what
God shows me," Nita explained.

"Oh, I see." Paige nodded. She really didn't see. Once
again, she was just going through the motions.

"Pastor says I've been hiding behind a mop and broom for long enough now. It's time I begin to operate in my other gifts and callings. Kind of like how you are doing with your singing."

"And what's your other gifts and callings?" Paige asked. "You know, besides doing what you do already."

She shrugged. "I'm not all the way sure. That's why I've been in my Word and in prayer more than ever. I've tried fasting, but for some reason, going all day and all night without eating is a struggle for me. I have tried doing it from six to six, though. I haven't gotten any huge revelation or anything yet, but I know it's coming . . . eventually. It might come much faster if I could afford to miss work and run off on a sabbatical or something like some of the members here can, but my savings won't let me do that just now." Both women chuckled. "But I trust God to speak to me and let me know what I need to know right in my very own prayer closet." She looked up in deep thought. "But I'm almost certain that whatever it is God wants me to do has something to do with my testimony."

"Is that so?" Paige asked. She knew some of Nita's testimony; that she was a survivor of domestic violence. From what Paige had heard, it was real bad. Nita had even lost her children to death as a result. Nita had missed her children's funeral because she had been in the hospital healing. New Day Temple of Faith and the community had stepped up and helped Nita rebuild her life. Paige didn't know all the details because she hadn't been a member of the church back then.

"Yes, it is so," Nita stated. "I think that all that I went through and lived to tell about was so that some other woman doesn't have to. So that another woman will know that no form of abuse is acceptable—not

physical, not sexual, not mental, not verbal insults—
and that—"

"Uh, look, Sister Nita," Paige cut her off. Nita was
driving too close to where Paige lived. "I've, uh, really
got to go. I have to go do this song and then . . ." Paige
looked down at her watch, ". . . I've got to go to work.
But again, I thank you for your concern and, I wish you
the best in finding and operating in your calling. Take
care." Paige rushed back into the sanctuary. She was
walking a mile a minute as if she were running from
someone. She wasn't running from someone, but she
was running from something. She prayed to God it
wouldn't catch up with her. Well, at least, she hoped it
wouldn't follow her back into the sanctuary as she took
her place in the stands and proceeded to belt out her
solo.

"*I open up my heart.*" Paige had hit the last note of
the Yolanda Adams's song as if it were the last note
she'd ever sing. Applause erupted from the choir
stands.

"Now *that's* what I'm talking about," the choir director cheered. "I felt as though I were watching you and
God have a personal conversation."

Paige nodded her head and held back tears. "You
were," she admitted. "You were." This time when Paige
sang, she let every single word pierce her spirit. The
words became a part of her, as if she'd written them
herself. Yolanda Adams had given her a script to read
to God. And as Paige had concluded, she felt as though
God had heard her, forgetting about the fact that everyone else in the room was listening in on it too.

Before Paige got any more emotional, she gathered
her things and rushed out to her car. She'd informed
her fellow choir members that she was running late for
work. So without joining in on the closing prayer, she

made an exit, dang near knocking Nita over on her way out the door.

"Oh, excuse me, Sister Nita," Paige apologized. "Gotta, uh, get to work."

"I feel you," Nita replied. "But just remember, no matter how fast you run, it'll be right there waiting for you when you get there." Nita winked, then walked away.

Chapter Nine

"It's been three days," Mother Doreen said to Bethany.

"I know. It's hard to believe that little bitty thing is just three days old and gets to go home today."

Mother Doreen looked through the glass into the hospital nursery and admired her great-niece. She couldn't believe how much like Hudson the baby looked. "Yeah, I know. She is the cutest baby in the world," Mother Doreen smiled. But as she turned her attention back to her little sister, her smile faded. "But that's not what I'm talking about. I'm talking about it's been three days since that man has been at the house, sleeping in the basement. He's got to go."

Bethany steered her eyes away from the baby and shot them like darts at her sister. "Go where? You heard him; he has no home to go home to. First Lady changed the locks. He doesn't have any money, credit cards . . ."

"Surely he's got a friend though. Someone from Living Word, Living Water who can take him in; one of the brothers, preferably."

"Ever since he stepped down as pastor and the rumors got started about him and I, those so-called church folks act like he's not even alive. They all turned their back on him, including your Pastor Frey. Why do you think he and First Lady stopped attending Living Word in the first place? Same reason as me and mine did." Bethany looked back at the baby and mumbled under her breath. "And Pastor Frey sure don't seem to have any control over his sheep. He just sat there and let it all happen. He probably had this all planned out anyway, waiting around to take Davidson's place."

"I know you are *not* going to try to sit here and blame my pastor for messing up the bed that man made."

"Oh, he's *your* pastor now?" Bethany smirked. "Well, *your* pastor turned on *my* pastor. Won't even take the man's calls."

"Look, it's not because he wanted to cut him loose. Trust me, Pastor Frey loves that man only an ounce less than God. And it's because of that love that God has instructed him to release him from his circle. So, until God says otherwise, Pastor Frey has to separate himself. And if you knew what was good for you, you'd do the same," Mother Doreen spat. "After all, we serve a jealous God, my dear sister. And that pastor of yours had Wallace wrapped so tightly around his collar, he was beginning to do things that went against God—like covering up his affair with you."

"Oh, please. It ain't like Davidson held a gun to the man's head."

"No, but he might as well have. The same way he used his authority from God and as the overseer of the church to manipulate you, he used it to manipulate my pastor as well."

"Oh, chile, please." Bethany shooed her hand and sucked her teeth.

"Look at you; a forty-something-year-old woman acting like a silly, young girl."

"You mean the same way you acted when it came to Willie."

Mother Doreen flinched at the sound of her deceased husband's name.

"Now I loved Willie. He was a fine brother-in-law, but you know darn well the man was no saint. He had his ways, and in spite of them all, you remained steadfast as his helpmate."

"Don't you go bringing my Willie into this." Mother Doreen looked up. "God rest my Willie's soul." She drew an invisible cross across her heart with her index finger, and then continued. "Besides, Pastor Frey already had a helpmate; he didn't need you on the sideline."

"Look," Bethany threw her hands up, "I don't even know why I'm having this conversation with you. You don't have any say as to what goes on in my home. So until *my* pastor can get on his feet and figure something out, he stays."

With hands on hips, Mother Doreen spat, "Well, I'll tell you what; if he stays, then I go."

Mother Doreen's hand had been forced at giving an ultimatum. "I can't stay in that house knowing dog on well the living arrangements go against everything the Word of the Lord says. Next you'll be moving Hudson's baby's momma in there too."

"If she needed a place to stay," Bethany said smugly.

"Umpf, umpf, umpf. Not under *my* watch," Mother Doreen scolded. "You might not mind blocking your blessings, but I've been trying to stay saved far too long to allow him to just stroll up in there and get to blockin' mine. And trust me, it ain't been easy trying to stay saved either. So the ball is in your court, Sis." Mother Doreen crossed her arms and lifted her chin with a smug look on her face.

She knew that after all she'd done for her sister, all she'd given up to come to Kentucky to look after her sister and her children, that Bethany would never choose that man over her.

"Then let me make it easy for you now, Sister." Bethany walked up to Mother Doreen and stood eyeball-to-eyeball with her. "Call me when you get back to Malvonia." Bethany stormed away as she called out over her shoulder, "And be blessed while you're at it."

Mother Doreen couldn't believe the words that had just come out of her sister's mouth. Surely she hadn't just been, in so many words, kicked out of her sister's home. Mother Doreen had the mind to get to marching right behind her sister and tell her that she wasn't going anywhere. *"I'm not going."* She'd sing the words more powerful than either Jennifer Hudson or Jennifer Holiday could ever spit them out. She had the mind to threaten and see the threat through, to put Pastor Davidson's stuff right back on the lawn before she packed up her own things and moved out. But she didn't. Instead, she just took a few deep breaths and tried to calm down. She figured that's something both she and her sister needed to do; calm down. That way, they'd be able to discuss the matter levelheaded.

Besides, they were in a hospital. It wasn't the time or the place to be cutting up. They had a baby they had to get ready to help pack up to go home. This was supposed to be a happy and special occasion. Hudson needed them. He was a teenage father now; a seventeen-year-old child with a child.

To some people, it was such the norm nowadays that they never even looked twice at a teenager strolling around with a baby. But Mother Doreen refused to be conformed to those things of the world. She'd made it up in her mind that now her assignment was to minister to Hudson so that he didn't think that the situation he was in was okay and ended up finding himself in it again. She also had to minister to Sadie so that she didn't look at her brother and think that it was okay to follow in his footsteps and become a teenage parent as well. Brittney Spear's little sister might have been pregnant on the cover of *OKAY* magazine, but the way Mother Doreen saw it, it still wasn't all right. And she'd see to it that her young niece and nephew, and even her new great-niece, didn't think it was okay either.

Yes, indeed, she was sure that was her assignment now, and she wasn't going to allow the devil to use her sister and interfere with it. Unbeknownst to Mother Doreen, though, she'd been wrong about exactly what her assignment there in Kentucky had been before. And she was wrong again. Dead wrong.

Chapter Ten

"I still can't believe Sister Deborah is gone too," Lorain said as she and Unique straightened up the classroom after the Singles Ministry meeting. They'd had a brief meeting after Sunday church service so Lorain could apologize to the members for failing to show up for Friday's meeting. It had totally slipped her mind. And although she hadn't planned on really going over anything on the agenda, the members did discuss a couple of matters.

"At least she was here long enough to help you out with the Singles Ministry while I was gone," Lorain told Unique.

"Tuh! Yeah, *right.*" Unique sucked her teeth. "Some little baller she'd dated back in the day strolled back into town, and he had her nose wide open. The last thing on her mind was this Singles Ministry."

Lorain thought for a moment. "Well, I know the affect of how something from your past can change your life completely."

"Oh, yeah? How so?" Unique asked, sitting down in one of the chairs. In all honesty, she really wasn't all that interested in Lorain's theory; she was just tired. This was her opportunity to take a rest while pretending to be interested in what she had to say. After all, sometimes the Singles Ministry meetings could be draining. Today's meeting, although not nearly as long as the regular ones, had been equally as draining. The

topic of discussion had been how people's relationships with their parents affected the type of relationships they got involved in when it came to the opposite
sex.

It was Lorain who'd added this topic to the agenda.
Little had Unique known, it was part of Lorain's hidden
agenda. This was another reason why Lorain had called
the brief meeting; she needed to get the ball rolling on
her plan.

Lorain wanted to find out all she could about how
Unique felt about her own mother; both the mother
who raised her, and, according to Unique, "the mother
who threw her away."

"Well, I know there must be some things in my past
that were life changing, so much so that my own mind
doesn't even want to keep company with the memories. Hence, it blocks out things." Lorain sat down for
a brief moment too. She needed the rest, considering
she hadn't been getting much rest these past couple of
days. "I'm sure there are some things from your past
that affected you in such a way that it changed your life
completely."

Unique thought for a minute. "Hmm. No, not really;
nothing besides the fact that my no-good biological
mother threw me away like trash so that she could go
on and live her life *la vida loco*."

Unique's words stung Lorain. She'd heard of children being estranged from their parents going through
family matters, but she herself could never imagine
speaking so ill about her own mother. Not even as a
child did Lorain ever say anything against her father
for abandoning his family the way he did. Now it's not
to say that she didn't think up a whole lot of stuff in
her mind, but neither she nor her mother ever bad-
mouthed that man for the decisions he made in life.

"God'll get him," Lorain's mother used to say, and leave it at that.

"Now that I think about it," Unique said, "I guess you could say the effect of that changed my life completely. Since she threw me out like trash, then I was blown around the system like a dirty fast-food wrapper in the wind. I suppose you could say I grew up with the concept that I was trash. That I was litter on God's green Earth that nobody cared about or even noticed. So when guys started noticing me, girl, I lost my mind, right before I lost my virginity."

Unique stared off into the past. "I was twelve years old. I had just gotten my very first training bra for my birthday. You couldn't tell me nothing." Unique stood up and began strutting while poking her chest out. She laughed, and then sat back down and got serious. "My mother's boyfriend had some friends over—"

Before Unique could even finish, Lorain interrupted, horrified. "Oh, God. Don't tell me. He molested you, didn't he? Your mother's boyfriend? Or one of his friends?"

Unique rolled her eyes and shooed away Lorain's words. "Child, no. Ain't no man never took this right here or even tried for that matter . . . shoooot." Unique swished her hand again. "Child, besides, I was too busy *giving* it away." Unique burst out laughing. "Not to no grown men though. I've been blessed in that area, because I know a lot of girls I hung with that suffered incest, rape, and abuse; some at the hands of their very own fathers. I'm talking about full-blown sexual relationships with their father. Mackenzie Phillips, that chick from the old sitcom *One Day at a Time*, ain't the only one. But you know we black folks don't like to talk about *that*." Unique winked. "Incest and molestation don't exist in the lives of black people." Unique was being sarcastic.

Lorain nodded in agreement. She recalled watching the *Oprah Winfrey Show* one time as a little girl and seeing sisters on the stage describing how they'd been being molested by their father for years. The sisters were black. Lorain remembered brushing it off as a talk-show junk episode. Everybody knew that type of thing didn't go on in black households. Black women were supposed to be wiser and on top of things than to allow such a tragedy to go down in their own home. A black mother was more aware of her children and knew when something wasn't right. At this very moment, Lorain had to silently repent for turning the channel, thinking that had it been a white family on the stage she would have believed it. Only a couple years later, the irony of it all would display itself in her own life.

"But anyway," Unique continued, "my mother's boyfriend had some friends over, and one of them had a son he'd brought along. Mama was at bingo and all the fellas were upstairs watching the game. All the kids were in the basement playing video games on the little television. The boy . . . Jay-Jay was his name . . . he kept wanting to play against me. Stupid me was thinking it was because he liked me. He kept wanting to play me because I was the only one he could beat. Eventually the other kids got bored of watching him whoop my butt and decided to go out and play tag. Jay-Jay wanted to stay in the basement and play video games . . . against me.

"Now you know I thought I was the stuff. Had just turned twelve the day before, was wearing a bra. I was grown and someone noticed. Jay-Jay noticed me . . ." Unique's thoughts trailed off for a minute on how good it felt to be noticed for the first time in her life. "I won't go into details. We are in God's house. But we ended up having sex right there in the basement. The physical aspect of it hurt, but the mental aspect of it felt good. I liked feeling good, so from that point on, any boy who noticed little ol' Unique here . . . well, let's just say that I got three sons to show you what happened any time a boy noticed me. So feeling like trash and allowing boys to just lay me down and treat me like trash, we have my biological mother to thank for that."

Unique stood and rubbed her hands together. The so-called break was over. "But thank God I have Jesus in my life. Nobody makes me feel as good as He does." Unique looked around the room. "We better finish up. Sister Helen was kind enough to let my boys stay with her while she got the children's classroom back in order. Besides, I feel good after that Word Pastor preached. The last thing I want to do is ruin this feeling by talking about someone who I couldn't care less was dead or alive. Not Jay-Jay, but the woman who gave birth to me. I know that sounds harsh, but why should I care? Evidently she didn't care about me, but that's all in the past. I'm good. I'm over it. Like I said, I have Jesus in my life now. Who needs her?"

Lorain could barely stand. It pained her to see Unique in so much pain. Yeah, Unique played the hard type, like she was over everything and had moved on in life. But Lorain knew that wasn't the case. She didn't know how she knew; perhaps some might refer to it as a mother's instincts.

Upon arriving home after church, Lorain had attempted to lay down just to take a catnap. A guest pastor was speaking at a special evening service tonight at New Day, and Lorain was going to try to make it back up there. But she'd been so mentally and physically drained lately, that besides forgetting all about the Sin-

gles Ministry meeting this past Friday, she still hadn't
gotten around to cleaning her house.

Fifteen minutes into her nap, Lorain had done nothing but toss and turn. She barely got any sleep at all. It
wasn't because that instead of being in the comfort of
her own bed she was on the couch. It wasn't because
she couldn't drift off to sleep with the sun peeking
through the blinds of the living room. It was because
she really didn't want to find herself in a deep sleep.
Every time her eyelids threatened to stay closed for
longer than a few minutes, she'd subconsciously force
them back open again. She was afraid that the visions
and nightmares that had brought her to a full sweat the
last couple of nights, causing her to have to shower in
the middle of the night and abandon her bed, would
return.

That peace she'd prayed for had not come instantaneously. Chalking her attempt for a catnap as a lost
cause, Lorain now stood in the kitchen sipping on a
bottle of mineral water. She prayed that it would at
least give her the strength to clean her house. After taking a sip of the flavored beverage, Lorain set the bottle
down, walked into the living room, over to her stereo
system.

"I know just the trick to pump me up," she said to
herself as she flipped through her CDs. "Bam," she replied after finding exactly what she'd been looking for.
She took the CD out of its case and popped it into one
of the compartments on her changer. Within seconds,
the intro of Tye Tribbett's "Victory" CD had her on her
way. She danced to her cleaning cupboard and gathered
the supplies she'd need for the next couple hours or so.
Her condo wasn't that big. It was a nice two-bedroom
with two full baths and a basement. But it had been

unattended to for three months. And even before that, Lorain hadn't done any full-blown cleaning.

"Lord, while you clean the cobwebs out of my mind, I'm gonna clean this nasty house," Lorain stated. She decided to start with the bathrooms. That was always her least favorite task; that, and putting away a white load of laundry. All that sock matching and whatnot was tedious and boring. Laundry wasn't one thing she had to worry about today. She washed all her clothes after returning from her sabbatical.

The CD had managed to get Lorain through the cleaning of her kitchen and two bathrooms. Next, she decided to get all of the dusting out of the way. She put in Fred Hammond's CD and listened to him tell her to wait on God while she dusted down the living room. Next, she knocked her bedroom out, and then, lastly, her computer room, which she'd made out of the second bedroom.

She walked over to her computer desk and ran her hand across it. She could see the dust particles getting their praise on to Fred Hammond as well, as they danced through the air. "Lord, this place is a mess," she said. She then chuckled. "Just like my life." She thought for a second. "No, I take that back. My life is not a mess just because I can't remember some of it. Lord, I accept remembering only what you want me to and not what I want to. I know what I think I remember, Lord. One of those things is that I might be the mother of Unique and that Broady might be her father. But unless you confirm it, Lord, I will not dwell on it or let it take over my life. In Jesus' name." Lorain smiled, realizing she'd been making everything about her. And one thing she did remember was her mother once telling her that it wasn't about her. "It's about you, Jesus!" Lorain declared. "Yes, it's all about you."

A sudden peace swept over Lorain. An unexplainable peace. As she dusted, now, instead of thinking about her situation, she thought about the goodness of Jesus. She began to think back on and thank Him for all the things she did remember Him doing for her. "Thank you, Lord! Thank you, Jesus," Lorain cried out as tears of joy dampened her cheeks. She'd managed to dust off and organize her entire desk before she even realized she'd done it.

"All finished," Lorain said as she kneeled down to get the dust rag she'd just dropped. Her eyes spotted some papers that looked as though they'd fallen behind her desk. "What's all this?" she grunted out as she reached back and began to pick them up. Among the papers was also a blue, three-prong folder.

She stood after gathering up the folder and the papers. As she looked at the label on the folder, she read it out loud. "MY LIFE." Quickly, she sat down in the chair at her desk and began reading through them. And good thing she'd sat down too, especially after reading the contents of the folder.

"Oh my God. Oh my God," Lorain whispered as she read through every single document contained in the folder. The more she read, the more she was able to piece together what was in black and white with what had been periodically popping up in her head like an 8 mm film.

Lorain had no clue how much time had gone by as she sat there in her computer room remembering, thinking about, and reliving the past incidents she'd suppressed. And no wonder. Who wouldn't want to forget being molested by their middle school counselor, becoming pregnant, hiding the pregnancy, going into labor, and then throwing the baby out in the dumpster? Not only that, but thinking for years that the baby had died in that dumpster, only to find out that someone had found the baby, turned the baby over to Children's Services, and that the baby had been placed in foster care.

But as if that weren't enough to put a person in a straitjacket in a room with rubber walls, to then find out that the father of the baby, the molester, is engaged to her mother. "Oh, God!" Lorain shouted. "Mother! No! I can't let her marry that man!"

Chapter Eleven

Mother Doreen flung open the front door with suit-case in hand. She was so fired up that before exiting the house, she still had one last thing to say. And she was so glad the kids were at Hudson's baby's mother's house, so that they didn't have to be there to witness all the drama that was unfolding.

Marching right over to Bethany, Mother Doreen told her, "I pray to God that you open up your eyes and see what you're doing to this family. If you choose to live in sin, then so be it, but how could you be so selfish as to force your children to be a part of it? But like I said, I won't be a part of this nonsense—you shacking up with your former pastor, the man whose child you were car-rying before your poor husband met his Maker. You're a saved woman of God, Bethany. I've heard of backslid-ing, but *this* takes the cake."

Mother Doreen looked over at Pastor Davidson who had insisted that he leave instead of Mother Doreen. Bethany wouldn't hear of it, though.

"And you . . . I don't even have the words," Mother Doreen spat out to him. "Well, I have them, but they ain't fit to be coming out of a Christian's mouth, so I'll keep them to myself." She turned her attention back to Bethany. "God's will *will* be done. I'm here for a rea-son, and no devil in hell, nor preacher man, is going to keep me from doing God's will. I might be leaving your house, but I ain't leaving your life." And on that note,

Mother Doreen turned around. But before she could take a step, she froze dead in her tracks, as if she'd seen a ghost. Had she not been a God-fearing woman, she just might have thought it were a ghost. After all, just months ago, she'd been to the funeral of the very person who stood in the doorway.

"After what I've just heard, if you give me a minute, Doreen, and if you don't mind, I'd like to go with you." Uriah looked from his wife, to Pastor Davidson, then back to his wife. "I'm leaving your house and your life too; for real this time."

With arms folded behind her head, Mother Doreen lay fully dressed in her hotel bed staring up at the ceiling. She sighed, and then shook her head. "Lord have mercy, how in the world did it come to this?"

"You tell me," Uriah said from the double bed that sat next to the one Mother Doreen was lying on. He too lay fully dressed with his arms folded behind his head, staring up at the ceiling. He had his own room right next door to Mother Doreen's, but for the last hour and a half, he'd been in her room explaining his . . . "resurrection." They decided that Uriah would stay in the hotel for the night, but then Mother Doreen suggested that they call Pastor Frey in the morning to see if Uriah could stay with him until they got things straight. But in Mother Doreen's eyes, everything was as crooked as a drunk hobo's teeth, and would be just as hard to straighten out.

"My, my, my," she sighed again. Mother Doreen shook her head once more. She thought for a minute. Finally, she sat up in the bed and looked at Uriah. "Now tell me again why you faked this whole death thing? For insurance money?"

Uriah took a deep breath. He knew that when he decided to come clean that he'd have to tell this story . . . a couple of times. But he'd planned on telling it to his wife and children first. They were the ones who he needed to understand. They were the ones who he needed forgiveness from. Then the four of them would decide together on what their next step would be. But after finally deciding to return home and find his wife with his pastor, who was also, from what he'd heard, his wife's lover and father of her baby . . .

"You said something about a baby?" Uriah questioned without first addressing Mother Doreen's query.

"Yes. But it didn't make it." There was silence filled with sympathy for the tiny lost soul. "Bethany miscarried." The silence lingered. "Oh, but guess what?" Mother Doreen got excited, instantly changing the mood. "There *is* a baby; Hudson's baby."

Uriah bolted upright in the bed. "What? Hudson . . . my son? He has a . . . a baby?"

"Yes, a little girl. And my, oh my, is she beautiful. Looks just like her daddy. She's three days old today. Tiny little thing. She came early. As a matter of fact, she came home today. That's where Hudson and Sadie were, over at the mother's house minding the baby. The baby is like honey, and they are like bees. Can't blame 'em though. Wait until you lay eyes on her."

"I'm a grandpa?" Uriah was still in a daze with a smile stuck on his face.

"Yes, you are."

Slowly, Uriah's smile faded. "Oh, my; the kids. What do you think Beth is going to tell the kids? I wanted to tell them. I wanted to explain everything." His body fell back onto the bed. "This is not how my return was supposed to play out. It was supposed to be like in all the soap operas, you know. I come home, the family has been so grief stricken that they are just happy that I'm back. No questions asked, or very few anyway. We embrace, we hug, we laugh, we cry." Uriah closed his eyes. "My kids are probably going to think that their own mama done lost her mind when she tells them that their dead daddy showed up at the house." He paused. "And then left again." Uriah thought for a moment.

"Oh, no." Uriah got up out of the bed and began pacing. "I've got to go back. They're going to think I abandoned them again. Then when I do get to see them, they are going to wish that I really was dead. I've gotta explain all this mess to them myself."

"Just hold up and relax," Mother Doreen stated. "I know that wife of yours, my sister, has dang near lost her mind for real, but I still think she's got enough sense to wait and hear from you before she goes telling the kids anything. There's already enough going on over there at the house without having to drop the bomb to those kids that their father isn't dead after all."

"Ugh. This isn't how things were supposed to turn out," Uriah reiterated, then plopped back down on the bed and buried his face in his hands. "All I wanted was for the family to finally be able to have something. To finally be able to live without worrying about whether the mortgage was going to get paid. I just felt that I was worth more to them dead than alive. So when the opportunity presented itself, that little devil on my left shoulder kept jabbing me with his pitchfork telling me to go for it."

"So when you got into the accident, you say you were ejected from the truck?" Mother Doreen recalled from what he'd told her already.

"Yeah, and rolled down a hill, into some trees and everything. When I came to," Uriah said, "I couldn't move. My legs hurt too bad to move them. I could see my truck up in a blaze. I saw fire crews, ambulances, and police in the distance. I screamed, yelled, and hollered, but I guess they couldn't hear me from up there. After a while, I passed out again. I went in and out of consciousness for a couple of days. When I came to, the dust had been cleared. I couldn't believe no one had come looking for me, but then I remembered him—the hitchhiker, the guy I'd picked up as I headed out of the city. I put two and two together and realized that everyone must have thought that he was me. That he must have burned beyond recognition in the truck and they thought it was me who had burned. Then that's when the devil got to working on me, telling me how all of this was God-ordained. How I'd never picked up a hitchhiker in all my days on that road; never even thought twice about it, but for some reason that night I had. It had all been a divine setup. This was my opportunity to give my family a new life."

"By faking a death?" Mother Doreen questioned.

"I know it sounds crazy. I know it was wrong and against the law. I knew a lot of people would be hurting too. But I promise you, I never intended to be like some of those guys you see on *20/20*, faking deaths so that they can go off and start a new life for themselves, never to return to their families. I just wanted Beth to be able to cash in on the insurance policy and take care of business, our home, and our children."

"So is that what you're going to tell the authorities?" Mother Doreen asked. "You know you're eventually going to have to tell them. You can't continue living this lie. But, of course, I guess you figured that out, which is why you came back."

Uriah shrugged. "I don't know what I'm going to tell the authorities. I know I need to tell them the truth, but I've thought of nothing but lies. Lies like I'd lost my memory and had been living on the streets all this time, then one day, it just came back to me."

"Then you *are* like those other guys on *20/20*, Uriah. You were still going to live the rest of your life a lie."

"I know, I know, Doreen. God, forgive me." Uriah's eyes began to fill with tears.

"God will forgive you, Uriah." Mother Doreen got up out of the bed. "Matter of fact, let's go to the throne and ask Him for forgiveness right now." She walked over to Uriah, took his hands, and led them in the most powerful prayer ever.

"Thank you," Uriah stated after Mother Doreen had finished praying. "Thank you so much, sis. I really feel as though God's forgiveness is upon me." Uriah stared off, and then said, "Now, if I could only forgive my wife just as easily . . . and if she could forgive me."

Chapter Twelve

The special Sunday evening service at New Day Temple of Faith had been awesome. Too bad Lorain hadn't been there to experience it. Technically and physically, she had been there. As a matter of fact, she'd practically had a courtside seat; the second row from the front. Mentally, though, she'd been absent. Her mind was too busy anticipating her mother and Broady's return from their little weekend excursion. She'd tried calling her mother's house all evening but hadn't gotten an answer. She wished she'd asked her mother what time on Sunday she planned on returning home. The wait was difficult. So although she was late getting there, Lorain had decided to go ahead to the evening service to keep from going stir-crazy. There was no way she could sit at home alone waiting on her mother.

She didn't care about dinner. Her concerns were no longer about picking Broady's brain for answers. The truth had come to her. Her full memory had finally returned, with no lingering doubts this time. The visions weren't just visions anymore; they were vivid recollections that she recalled as if everything had happened just yesterday. The nightmares were more than nightmares; they'd actually happened to her. And the documents; the folder she'd found while cleaning was her proof of the reality of everything. That folder had been the safe haven for the documents she'd accumulated after hours of Internet searches. Some of the searches were even paid searches she'd received hits on just by inputting Broady's and Unique's name, city, and state of residence.

That folder had held all the answers. No telling how many more sleepless nights Lorain might have had had she not discovered that folder that had fallen behind her desk. The folder was now found, as had been a piece of Lorain; the missing piece . . . missing pieces. It contained the truth she'd been trying to put together. It contained the proof to those truths. Truths that she now had to share.

She knew once she confronted her mother and Broady with the truth that they'd dismiss her, saying that her memory had been affected by the fall. That her mind was playing tricks on her. But she could back everything up now. She had it tucked safely away in her folder. It was all in black and white, and she planned on using it to bring color, some light, to the situation.

Her intentions were to drive to her mother's house after church. Hotel checkout time was usually 11:00 A.M. Late checkout was normally no later than 4:00 P.M. Depending on how far her mother and Broady had driven, certainly they should be home by the time service was over.

She wasn't quite sure where her mother and Broady had planned to stay. She hadn't even bothered to ask. But since they were just gone for the weekend, she figured it wasn't too far. They just had to be home by the time church let out. They just *had* to. The confrontation that would soon take place was all Lorain could think about.

Her favorite scripture had been read after the service's opening prayer. The choir had sung her favorite praise and worship songs. The dance ministry had even ministered to one of her favorite songs. And the guest pastor preached the Word of God so tough that five people got a breakthrough and a revelation. And during altar call, two individuals turned their lives over to Christ. And if God hadn't already moved in the place, the pastor opened the doors to the church and a family of four joined. All this had taken place, and Lorain had missed it.

Before walking out the door of her condo to drive to the evening church service, she had prayed that God would give her some type of confirmation that her means and methods of what she was about to do were in order. Had Jesus Himself been seated next to her in church, she wouldn't have noticed, let alone heard a Word from God. But in her spirit, she felt it was the right thing to do. She had to tell her mother the truth about her fiancé. She could not allow her mother to marry a man who molested her as a child. A man who fathered the baby that she'd thrown in the garbage and left for dead. Only the baby hadn't died. The baby lived; she grew up to be a healthy, beautiful young woman with three boys . . . who just happened to attend the same church as Lorain did.

"Sister Lorain? Sister Lorain?" Unique was calling out to her church sister as loud as being inside God's house would allow. Folks were already looking at her like she was crazy for even using the tone she was. Evidently it wasn't loud enough, because Lorain just kept it moving as if Unique hadn't said a word. But everyone else seemed to hear her loud and clear.

On a mission, Lorain kept walking, heading straight out the church doors. Unique didn't go after her. It was no biggie. She didn't want anything; just to say hello was all. She still had to go get her children from child care.

Once in her car, Lorain looked at the time on her dashboard. It was almost nine o'clock. Service had been projected to end at eight-thirty. Church had gone over a little. "Wow," Lorain said to herself. The service hadn't seemed that long at all. As a matter of fact, it had felt pretty short. But that was because Lorain hadn't really been focused on the service.

Realizing that her mother and Broady should have had more than enough time to make it home by now, she pulled out of the church parking lot and drove straight for her mother's house. When she pulled up in the driveway, she couldn't even recall having driven there. Jesus must have definitely taken the wheel. *Thank you, God, for your angels that kept me on the highways and byways,* Lorain silently prayed, for she knew only God could have gotten her there safely. And only God knows how many red lights or stop signs she might have run getting to her destination.

Lorain turned her car off, and after taking a few deep breaths, she walked to her mother's front door. Once her wobbly legs were on the porch, she rang the bell. There was no answer. She knocked. Still no answer. It was apparent that they still had not arrived back home. Or maybe they'd gone to Broady's place. No, her mother had never spent the night at a man's house.

"Darn it," Lorain groaned as she stood there contemplating whether or not she should go home and come back in the morning or just wait there. She had a key to her mother's house. She could go inside and wait. Lorain opted to just wait in the car. No one wanted to come home from a mini getaway and find someone waiting for them in their living room. It was bad enough she was even there at all, bearing the news she needed to share.

After getting back into the car, she just sat there twiddling her thumbs. A few minutes passed by and she decided to rehearse the exact words she would say to her mother. After all, how does a girl tell her mother that the man she is engaged to is the man who molested her daughter as a young girl? A few lines went through Lorain's head. After rehearsing them a couple of times, Lorain decided to say them out loud. She pulled down the sun visor and looked at herself in the mirror. As her lips began to move, the woman who she was today seemed to fade away. Before Lorain knew it, staring back at her was a little girl; a scared little girl.

Drenched with sweat and eyes full of tears, the little girl looked to be in so much pain. "Oh, God, what's happening to me?" the little girl cried out as she stared at herself in the mirror. Then all of a sudden it was like an electric shock flowing through the child's body. "Oh, God! Oh, God! Make it stop. Please make it stop."

She'd never been in so much pain in her entire life . . . and she'd thought her menstrual cramps were bad. This felt like bad cramps to the one-hundredth power. Suddenly the young girl had a look of fear in her eyes as she heard voices getting closer and closer. Someone was coming. She panicked. She couldn't let anyone see her like that; not in the condition she was in. They'd ask her what was wrong, and then she'd have to tell them. And then she'd be in a world of trouble. She had to hide.

Walking away from the bathroom mirror, she made her way to a stall. There were no toilet lids on the toilets, so she just sat down on the ring. Just as the crowd of girls entered the bathroom, another sharp pain ripped through her body. She quickly placed her hand over her mouth to muffle the moan that was bursting at the seams of her voice box. As bad as she wanted to yell out in pain, she had to swallow the sound. It was like swallowing razor blades.

In order to tune out all of the pain she was in, she decided to focus on the chitchat of the girls who were just touching up lip gloss and straightening their hair before their next class.

"Have you noticed Miss Thing ain't been playing dress up here lately?" one of the girls said. "Coming to school in one thing, but then changing into something else once she steps inside the school."

"That's probably because she can't fit in anything anymore," another girl chuckled.

"Word. Homegirl is getting large and in charge."

"Wouldn't surprise me if she's pregnant."

"I overheard Ms. Garrison talking to one of the other teachers one day when I went into her office. She said she'd bet anything that Viola is going to be one of those girls who gets pregnant and drops out of school before she even reaches her junior year in high school."

"Nah . . . I don't agree with that," a new voice stated. "I say before her sophomore year."

All the girls burst out laughing as the warning bell rang.

"Come on, let's go. We don't want to be late." Soon the voices vanished, and the young girl was in the stall alone.

More tears were pouring down her face than before. She was now in excruciating pain. Only now, it wasn't just her stomach that was hurting; it was her heart too. She had heard through the grapevine that girls talked bad about her. She knew not many of them liked her anyway. None of them walked to and from school with her. None of them ever invited her to come to their table and eat lunch with them. None of them ever picked her first to be their study partner in class. They treated her like she didn't even exist. But

Mr. Leary didn't treat her that way. He told her she was special. He treated her special. He wanted to do things with her, lots of things. He wanted to do special things with her—because she was a special girl. And she let him. And now, because of all the things she'd let him do to her, she was hiding in the girl's restroom, in a bathroom stall, at the peak of labor.

The pain that shot through her body this time was so powerful, that even with her hand trying to muffle it, a screech escaped, right at the same time the tardy bell rang. Then that's when she felt as though something had just dropped out of her.

"What the . . ." she questioned as her pants became drenched. Then she felt as though her entire insides were dropping out of her. From that point on, it was like she was matted to the bathroom ceiling looking down at herself. There was water, there was blood, there was pain, then there was a baby.

"Shhh. Shhh." The girl rocked the baby. "Shhh, before someone hears and catches us, baby. Shhh," she cried. And then what happened next is something she never thought she'd forget. It's something she never imagined a fall and a bump to the head would ever make her forget.

The scissors in her book bag had come in handy. The book bag itself had come in handy. It's what she would use to tote the baby from the bathroom to the dumpster. The scissors were what she would use to detach the baby from her. It was the scissors she used when she realized her teeth weren't sharp enough. But that was after she'd used up practically every paper towel to clean up the mess she'd made delivering her baby in the bathroom stall.

She was so scared, so afraid, and there was no one she could turn to. Mr. Leary wasn't around anymore.

He'd packed up and left once her belly started to grow, leaving her to bear the cross alone. But now, as the young girl, now a full-grown woman, waited outside of her mother's house, Mr. Leary—Broady—was finally going to carry his weight.

Slamming close the sun visor, Lorain ran her hands across her forehead. She was soaking wet. Just thinking back about that day had made her feel as though it was happening all over again. She had to get herself together, because she knew she'd have to relive it at least two more times; one time when she told her mother, and the other time when she told Unique.

"I gotta get myself cleaned up," Lorain said to herself as she exited the car. She'd use the spare door key to her mother's house to let herself in so that she could use the bathroom.

With keys in hand, Lorain unlocked her mother's door and went in, heading toward the first-floor bathroom. Suddenly, she heard a noise coming from the upstairs that made her heart skip a beat. Stopping in her tracks, Lorain paused to see if she could hear the noise again. There was silence, so she continued on her way. Right before she made it to the bathroom, she heard the noise again. This time, she made a quick detour into the kitchen. She shuffled around looking for a makeshift weapon. During the process, she heard the noise again and grabbed the iron skillet that always sat on her mother's stovetop. With the skillet gripped in her hand, she closed her eyes and said a quick prayer.

"God, cover me in the blood of Jesus. Send your angels to fight for me and protect me right now in the name of Jesus." She opened her eyes and cautiously crept toward the staircase, but once again she was stopped in her tracks at the vision that appeared at the top landing.

"Lorain, what are you doing here?" It was her mother. She was wrapped in a silky white robe trimmed in lace and was tying the belt around the robe as she spoke.

"Mom? You're . . . you're home. But I thought . . ." Lorain's words trailed off once she realized that perhaps her mother had been inside and simply hadn't heard her knock at the door. Maybe the trip had tired her out just that much. On top of that, Lorain hadn't even thought to check the garage to see if her mother's car was parked inside.

"Honey, is everything okay?" Eleanor asked her confused-looking daughter. "What's wrong? Why are you here?"

"Well, I was . . . I was waiting for you and Broady to come back, but I see you're already here." Lorain swallowed. "I wanted to talk to you both, together, and what I have to say, Mother, it really can't wait."

"Then it won't have to." Eleanor looked at her bedroom door and signaled with her hand. Seconds later, Broady appeared next to Eleanor, tying his robe. "As you can see, Broady is here." She looked up at him with a huge grin on her face. "As a matter of fact, he's here to stay." Eleanor turned back to Lorain. She lifted her hand to display a beautiful wedding band to match the engagement ring that had already rested on her finger. She then exclaimed, "We got married!"

Chapter Thirteen

Paige practically had to peel herself from the leather seat of her car and drag her body to the door. She was beat; worn-out. Two employees had been out with the swine flu, so today at work, she had to go above and beyond the call of duty. She did everything from inventory to selling tickets at the ticket window to popping popcorn. It was days like this when she felt she was being gypped by being a salaried employee.

When she walked into the house it was dark, but she could smell the delicious aroma of whatever it was that Flo had prepared and left warming on the stove. Only thing was, Paige was too tired to even eat. The kitchen's ceiling lights were off, but the overhead stove light was on. Paige followed the glow to the simmering pot. She lifted the lid and found a concoction of turkey, green beans, peas, corn, carrots, and potatoes, all in a creamy juice.

"Must be that turkey hash Flo was telling me about," Paige said to herself as she inhaled the aroma. "Mmmm. Smells good enough." She decided that maybe, after her shower, she'd have to try some.

Before moseying to the bedroom, Paige made a pit stop in the living room to look at the mail. There were no lights on in the living room at all. She made her way over to the table where they always placed the mail and turned on the lamp. Then she picked up the four envelopes and flipped through them, took one out and placed the other three back on the table. They were bills. Blake handled all the bills.

With her single letter in hand she turned around to walk to the bedroom. "Jesus!" she yelled out in fear. "Wha-what are you doing sitting here in the dark?" she asked Blake.

Her blood was pumping through her veins rapidly and her heart was trying to keep up. She'd ordered a blood pressure machine. Her doctors had told her that sometimes high blood pressure goes hand in hand with diabetes. As preventative maintenance, she'd decided to keep tabs on her blood pressure so she'd ordered a machine. It hadn't arrived yet, but she was sure that if it had and she'd taken her blood pressure at that very moment, they'd have to take her to the ER.

"I . . . I didn't even realize you were home," Paige stuttered. "I guess I was just so hell-bent about getting in here and resting that I didn't even pay attention to the fact that your car was parked in the garage."

"That's because it isn't," Blake said in a dry tone. "It got towed. I had to double park downtown because I was running late for the mediation; you know, the one we had set at a special evening hour so that both you and I could attend? The one where we'd meet with my mother's attorney and convince them how absurd this entire lawsuit is? You were supposed to meet me at my office. We were going to go together."

Blake remained seated in the chair he'd been sitting in like a statue. He didn't even look up at Paige while he spoke. He was utterly disgusted. "I waited for you a half hour in the parking lot at my office. I called your cell."

"You know I don't keep my cell on at work," Paige reminded him. "It sets a bad example for all the younger kids who work there—"

"I called your job. I hit zero after the long drawn out recording and was transferred to your line. I got your voice recording. I left you a message."

Paige sighed. "Baby, I am so sorry." She made her way over to Blake. "I didn't have time to sit down and check my messages. You wouldn't believe the kind of day I had." She approached him and went to rest her hand on his shoulder. "Two of my employees were out with the—"

SWAT!

Paige's words were immediately halted by the sting she felt across the backside of her hand.

"The day *you* had? I wouldn't believe the day *you* had?" Blake mocked as he stood.

Paige was looking at him as if he'd lost his mind. Had that man just smacked her hand off of his? Hard?

"How about you think about somebody else besides yourself for once?" he spat. "My day was pretty jacked up too, and you not showing up to support me made it even worse." Blake paced back and forth as he spoke what was on his mind. "You knew that if I didn't show up to that mediation the trial would move forth. What? Do you want to see me risk losing all that money to that no good . . ." Blake tightened his lips, balled his fist, and shook his head. "Ugghhh."

"So you didn't make it to the mediation?" Paige was afraid to ask because she could pretty much tell by her husband's mood what the answer was going to be.

"I was almost an hour late. The traffic on 70 was horrific. I couldn't find any parking meters, the lot across from the courthouse was full, and I couldn't risk running three blocks from the parking garage, making me even later than I already was." He shook his head. "By the time I got in the building, my attorney was down in the lobby waiting on me. He'd just walked Miss Turner out."

"Baby, I'm so sorry. I don't know what to say." Paige was sincere. Despite the fact that she wanted to be angry as her hand throbbed, she felt bad. Blake could possibly lose everything he'd worked so hard for all these years, and all because he'd been sitting around waiting on her. Waiting on her to be the supportive wife she'd promised him she'd be. How could she expect him to be the type of husband she wanted him to be if she couldn't even be the type of wife he wanted her to be? The type of wife who couldn't even follow a simple request?

Perhaps he had every right to be angry with her. He could only get better if she got better. "Let me make it up to you," Paige said as she placed her arms around Blake. She prayed that the love and warmth of her embrace melted the coldness he was feeling toward her at the moment.

Blake took a deep breath, and then paused for a minute. "It's okay. It's not your fault. This is just too much for me right now."

"I know, and that's why I promise from now on that I'm going to be here to help you bear some of it."

Blake exhaled. "Thank you, sweetheart." He kissed her on the forehead.

Although Paige was willing to accept his apology, something inside of her needed clarity on just exactly what Blake was apologizing for. Was he apologizing for snapping at her? For slapping her hand? Or everything?

"Babe, I'm willing to accept your apology . . ." she looked him in his eyes, ". . . if you mean it and promise to never do it again."

Blake pulled away. "Honey, you know I get a little edgy sometimes. I'll try to watch my tone and not come off on you so—"

"That's not what I mean," Paige interrupted. "Babe . . . you hit me." She held up her hand.

Blake let out a nervous chuckle. "I didn't hit you. I was . . . I was just merely pushing your hand away. I was agitated, that's all." He threw his arms around Paige. "I'd never hit you; not intentionally. I'm sorry." He took her injured hand and began planting kisses all over it. "I'm so sorry if I hurt you." Eventually his kisses went from her hand and up her arm. "Do you believe me? Do you forgive me?" Now his kisses were on her neck.

Paige rolled her head back in ecstasy at the kisses being planted on her neck by her husband. And just like that, any anger, bitterness, or hesitation she'd felt toward him disappeared.

Leading the way to the bedroom, Paige felt that if making up made her feel this way, then what harm could a little fighting be? Taken in by the rapture of her husband's body taking over her, a very sick pattern was beginning to form, but Paige was too caught up in physical bliss to even realize it.

Chapter Fourteen

"It's good to see you two back in counseling," Pastor stated, welcoming the couple into the office.

"I hope you didn't give up on us, Pastor," Blake said as he embraced the New Day Temple of Faith pastor.

"Oh, no, sir. God didn't give up on me, so I'm not going to give up on you, Brother Blake. How are things going with you two anyway?" Pastor sat down in a chair across from the couch while motioning for the couple to sit. "And by the way, congrats on the magazine article."

"Thanks, Pastor," Blake nodded.

"And to answer your question, things have been going great, Pastor," Paige said while smiling like a schoolgirl in love. She still had the way Blake had loved on her last night on her mind. And although they'd made up, Paige still felt it necessary in her spirit to resume counseling. Fortunately, Pastor had been able to squeeze them in during the lunch hour.

"Well, praise God. Oh, I guess before we get started, we better open up in prayer," Pastor suggested, then stood back up. Blake and Paige followed suit.

The pastor extended both hands to the couple. Still smiling, Paige extended one hand to Blake and the other to Pastor. "Ouch!" Paige immediately flinched upon Pastor grabbing her hand.

"Oh, my, I'm sorry," Pastor apologized. "Did I shock you or something?" That's when Pastor lifted Paige's

hand and noticed the slight bruising. Because she was
a thick girl to begin with, the slight swelling was hard
to detect. "What . . . what happened here? Do you need
some ice?" Pastor was very concerned.

"I hit it against the . . ." Paige had started.

"She slammed it in the . . ." Blake had started simul-
taneously with Paige.

They both looked at each other nervously.

"I slammed it in the . . ." Paige had started to validate
Blake's lie.

"She hit it against the . . ." Blake had started to validate Paige's lie.

They both stopped and looked at each other nervously.

Pastor shot them each a peculiar glare. "Let's pray."
After praying, Pastor caught both Blake and Paige off
guard. "Uhh, Blake, do you mind if I counsel you guys
separately? I'll start with you first." Pastor looked at
Paige. "Daughter, could you just step out for a few minutes?"

"Uh, well, uh," Paige stammered. "Pastor, we really
don't have much time. We're both on our lunch hour.
And I thought we were doing couple's counseling, not
individual counseling."

"Go on, sweetheart. It's fine," Blake said to his wife
with a reassuring nod. "Why don't you go to the church
kitchen and ice that hand that you just slammed in the
car door on the way in here." Blake smiled while his
eyes told Paige to play along.

Pastor wasn't missing a beat.

"Oh, uh, yeah, right. Ice . . . for my hand . . . yes, that
I slammed. Yes, slammed just now . . . on the way in
here."

"Go on now." Blake did everything but push Paige
out the door before she blew their cover.

"Okay, I'll see you in a minute." Paige closed the door behind her. With her hand still on the doorknob she took a deep breath. "Oh, God," she sighed. She looked down at her hand. Pastor had just ignited a pain in it by squeezing it. She walked toward the church kitchen for ice.

On her way, it dawned on her that she and her husband had just told a bold-faced lie to their pastor . . . in God's house. But what really had her stumped was why? Why was she lying about what had happened to her hand? Why did she even feel the need to lie in the first place? Blake hadn't meant it. That's what he'd told her. Besides that, he'd apologized, and she'd forgiven him just like the Bible had told her to do. People lie when they are trying to cover up something. So what was she trying to cover up?

Paige found a plastic grocery bag in one of the kitchen cabinets and filled it with ice. She then placed the bag on her hand.

"You shouldn't put the bag of ice directly on your skin," a voice said to Paige. "Put something in between it, like a paper towel or something. Here." Nita tore off a paper towel from the holder and handed it to Paige.

Paige hesitated before taking it. "Thank you."

"No problem. You see, I got a lot of experience covering up bruises."

Paige immediately took offense. "Who said I was covering up anything? I'm not trying to cover it up. It was an accident. I slammed—"

"Whoa." Nita put her hands up as if to halt Paige's words. "I never said you were. I said *I* got a lot of experience covering up bruises."

Paige cleared her throat. "Oh." She turned her attention to her hand, feeling a little embarrassed for letting loose like she'd just done.

Nita looked down at Paige's hand as well. "So you were about to say you slammed your hand?"

"Uh, yeah, uh, in the door. The car door. Just now—on my way here."

"That happened to me before too. I slammed my hand in the car door. I opened the door and hit myself in the head. I burned my hand on a hot pan. I fell from a ladder. Let's see, what other excuses did I make up for all the times my husband hit me?" Nita quickly looked at Paige. "Again, I'm just talking about me here. Not you." She twisted her lips and stared up as if thinking. "Oh, yeah, I fell on a rake. I dropped a box on my foot. I fell down the steps. I—"

"Sister Nita," Paige interrupted, "is there a point to all of this? I mean, I'm not trying to be rude or anything, but . . ." Paige shrugged.

"No, I guess there really isn't a point to it. I just felt led to talk about it all of a sudden. I guess seeing you there with that ice pack on your hand brought back memories."

Paige sighed. She closed her eyes. She took a deep breath. She counted to five, and then opened her eyes. She was hoping that Nita would be gone because she was tired; she was tired of her popping up, sticking her nose in her business. She was tired of her indirect accusations. But she was really hoping that Nita would be gone so that she wouldn't have to say to her what she was about to say.

"Look, Sister Nita. I'm saved, not stupid. I know what you're thinking, making all your little slick and snide comments. But you're wrong, dead wrong. Now I know you are a . . . what do you call it . . . domestic violence survivor. But you can't run around thinking that every time one of the sisters shows up with a bump or a bruise that their husband did it. Don't get me wrong, I appreciate your concern. I really do. But like I told you before, there is nothing to be concerned about. Blake is—"

"Blake is what?"

The bass in Blake's voice startled Paige. She jumped, dropping the bag of ice. Nita, on the other hand, was unmoved as both she and Paige turned their attention to the doorway.

"Oh, uh, nothing," Paige said in a poor attempt to hide her nervousness. "I was just telling Sister Nita here that you were, you know, in the office talking with Pastor. She was asking how you were and all. That's all."

There was silence as the lie bounced off the walls, never really finding a place of belief to land.

"Anyway," Blake said to Paige, "Pastor is waiting for you. I gotta head back to work. Walk me out before you go to Pastor's office, okay?"

"Oh, yes, sure." Paige went to pick up the ice pack, but Nita beat her to it.

"Don't worry about it. I'll get it." Nita picked up the ice pack and walked over to the freezer. "I'll just put it in the freezer so that it will be waiting for you the next time." She placed it in the freezer, then left the kitchen, brushing past Blake. She looked back at Paige and said, "And trust me, nine times out of ten, there *will* be a next time."

Chapter Fifteen

"I really appreciate you coming over here these past couple of days checking on me and making sure I get a decent meal," Uriah stated as he pushed his plate away. "But I just haven't had an appetite. Especially not today."

"You gotta eat," Mother Doreen told him as she pushed the plate back toward him. Instead of silence, there was the clinging of a fork hitting a plate, then the slurping of juice.

Both Mother Doreen and Uriah turned in the direction from where the noise was coming. It took a few seconds before Pastor Frey realized two sets of eyes were fixed him. He continued to stuff his face with the split polish sausage, jelly toast, scrambled eggs, and cheese grits, washing it all down with freshly squeezed orange juice. Coming up for air, he noticed Mother Doreen and Uriah staring at him.

"Oh, pardon me." Slightly embarrassed, Pastor Frey picked up his napkin and wiped his mouth.

"But this one, on the other hand," Mother Doreen pointed at Pastor Frey, "I suppose is eating enough for the both of yous."

"I'ma single man. Before Uriah showed up here and you came over to cook for him, I was living off bread alone, and you know what Jesus had to say about that." Pastor Frey took another drink of orange juice.

"Forgive me, Pastor," Mother Doreen replied, "but I don't think this is exactly what our Lord and Savior had in mind when He made that statement about man not living on bread alone. Nonetheless, I'm glad you're enjoying it. It's the least I can do for you for allowing my brother-in-law to stay here until he and Bethany get things situated." Mother Doreen turned to Uriah. "I spoke to her; let her know we'd be there in about an hour or so. She wants to make sure you two have plenty of time to talk before the kids get home from school."

Uriah nodded to let her know he was listening, although he wasn't making eye contact with her.

"Oh, and she said she hasn't said anything to the kids. She didn't know what to tell them. She wanted to talk to you first," Mother Doreen told him.

Uriah nodded, then he asked, "Is that man still staying in my house?"

"No. He hasn't been there since the day you came back," Mother Doreen replied. "But like I told you, he'd only been there for a couple of days since his wife put him out, and he didn't have any place to go."

Uriah shook his head. "And that's my Bethany; always willing to take in a stray dog." He slammed his fist on the table. "The nerve of that man! He had me fooled. Loaning me that money so I could buy my truck because he knew I'd always be on the road. That gave him all the time he needed to impregnate my wife. He basically bought her, so you know what that makes her, don't you?" Uriah's veins nearly popped out from the side of his head. "That's it! I can't do it. I can't go over there and talk to her. I don't even think I can stand to look at that woman. I should have just stayed gone, living from hand to mouth like the homeless man I was. With the pain I'm feeling, I would have been better off dead."

"Now come on, son," Pastor Frey interrupted, putting his fork down. "That's the devil talking, and I rebuke him in the name of Jesus."

"I'm sorry, Pastor Frey." Uriah calmed down, regretting indirectly calling his wife a prostitute. "You and I both know that ain't nothing but a bunch of crazy talk," Uriah admitted. "I'm just feeling so much pain right now. And I thought I was in pain lying on the side of the road after the accident. That was a cakewalk compared to what I'm about to face." Uriah looked at Pastor Frey. "What do I say to her?"

Pastor Frey stood. "Well, first off, son, you have to admit your own faults. You have to set her free first by apologizing to her for this whole death-faking thing. Then I'm sure the Holy Spirit will lead you from there."

"But that's the thing," Mother Doreen chimed in, "you have to let the Holy Spirit lead you."

Taking a deep breath, Uriah nodded his understanding. "Well, you 'bout ready to go, sis?"

"Yes, sir," Mother Doreen stated, holding her purse and keys in hand.

Pastor Frey patted Uriah on the back. "Just remember, Brother Uriah, I don't know how things are about to turn out, but know that you have a place here for as long as you like."

"Thank you, Pastor Frey," Uriah said, shaking his extended hand. "I hope you really mean that and are not just saying it because you want Doreen to come back and do some more cooking."

The three let out a chuckle.

"No, son, I really mean it," Pastor Frey confirmed.

"Thank you, Pastor, for being the man you are," Uriah stated, "and not some jackleg preacher man like Pastor Davidson."

"Now, now, son. I had my part in all of this too. I knew what was going on between your wife and our pastor."

"I know, and I thank you for sharing that with me and being honest."

"Well, I didn't want to have you staying here up under my roof not knowing everything."

"And like I said, I appreciate that, and I forgive you."

"Thank you." The two men shared a brotherly hug.

"Come on now, Uriah," Mother Doreen said, walking to the door. "We better get going."

And on that note, they exited the house. They got in Mother Doreen's car and drove off to meet with Bethany. Mother Doreen planned on dropping Uriah off and allowing him to talk with his wife while she stayed outside and interceded in prayer, no matter how many hours it took. Then afterward, she'd go inside because she still had a word or two for her little sister. If Bethany thought she could just put Mother Doreen out of her house and be done with her, she had another thing coming.

Chapter Sixteen

Lorain, calling in sick after being gone from work three long months, did not make a smart move. Due to her fall and memory loss thing, her job understood and had granted her a temporary medical leave of absence. Now, not only had she called in sick, but she'd left the message in her boss's voice mailbox, a major no-no in corporate America, right next to having your boyfriend or mother call in sick for you.

Lying in bed, she looked over at her makeshift makeup counter of Mary Kay cosmetics. She hadn't even pushed a tube of lip gloss since she could remember. So right about now, that side gig alone definitely wouldn't pay her bills. Her job was her bread and butter, and no matter what was going on in her personal life, she couldn't afford to jeopardize it. So, on second notion, Lorain decided to drag herself out of bed and go on to work. She couldn't risk her livelihood even though right about now she didn't feel much like living anyway.

She didn't know why, but all of the guilt and shame and insecurities Lorain had felt back in middle school, she felt all over again now. It was heavy, weighing her down something awful. Why was it that that man could still make her feel that way? It was like she could still hear him telling her how the way she dressed had something to do with what he'd done to her. His words had made her feel so dirty. Just thinking about them

made her feel dirty, so much so that even though she'd
taken a shower last night before going to bed, she felt
she desperately needed another one.

As Lorain got out of bed and hopped in the shower,
there was something else that worried her the most.
Why did she not only feel bad about having to tell her
mother about her past with Broady, but she almost felt
even worse for Broady. She'd heard more times than
she could remember since getting saved that God pulls
the covers off of people. And maybe that was true. So
did that mean that she should sit back and wait on God
to do it instead of doing it herself?

"God, I need to talk to you," Lorain began to pray as
the shower water pellets pummeled her body. She'd
set the showerhead massager on high. "I need your
guidance, Lord. In the name of Jesus I need a word
from you, Lord. Every time I feel as though you are
laying the red carpet out for me to move forth in this
thing, doubt creeps in. I don't know if you are really
in control, orchestrating this entire thing, or if Satan
is trying to confuse me. God, I know you are not the
author of confusion; therefore, the enemy must be trying to infiltrate the matter. So in Jesus' name, Satan, I
command you to move out of my way. Take your dirty
tricks with you to the pits of hell where you belong. In
Jesus' name."

Feeling confident that her words had saturated the
atmosphere and had begun to work, Lorain felt victorious as she washed up, got out of the shower, and dried
off. With the towel wrapped around her size twelve
frame, she walked out of the bathroom and over to
her bedroom phone and made a quick call to her job,
letting her boss know that she was feeling better and
would be in.

After getting dressed, Lorain used a foam mousse
to spike up her edgy haircut that was tapered at her

neck. Before she knew it, she was almost out the door. She'd forgotten all about how she'd learned that her mother had already married the very man she'd gone over there to keep her from marrying. She'd forgotten about how she had to feign happiness; how when she broke out crying she had to lie to her mother and tell her that they were tears of joy. She'd forgotten how she'd rushed out of her mother's house, afraid she'd lose the contents of her stomach right there in her mother's living room. But what she'd told her mother is that she felt awful for interrupting their honeymoon and wanted them to have time alone. She hadn't heard from her mother again until this morning.

"I called your job, and they said you weren't there," Eleanor had said into the phone receiver, worry etching her tone. "They said you were home sick. Do you need me to do anything for you? It's not your head, is it?"

Lorain had assured her mother that she'd be just fine, that she'd probably just overdone it with the cleaning this past weekend and needed to rest her body. Eleanor had insisted that she come tend to her daughter, but Lorain forbade her, telling her that she just needed the rest.

So now as Lorain grasped the doorknob, ready to step outside and face the breezy April weather, the ringing of the doorbell didn't surprise her. She knew just how persistent her mother could be.

"That mother of mine . . ." Lorain huffed as she made her way to the door and opened it. "Ma, didn't I tell you—" Lorain started after flinging open the door, but then realized that it wasn't her mother at all. It was Broady.

"Lorain," Broady said as he stood on her porch. "Can I come in? We need to talk."

Chapter Seventeen

Paige got out of the shower and wrapped the towel around her body. There was a time when she couldn't get the towel halfway around her body, but in the past couple of months, she'd been averaging a seven- to eight-pound a month weight loss. It was starting to show. She walked over to the mirror and that's when she realized that more than just her weight loss was starting to show. There was now a visible bruise on her left arm. With her skin being as dark as it was, she was surprised that a bruise had even shown up. It looked as though Blake had punched her in the arm. But he would never hit her. He'd just yanked at her arm a little too hard the other day at church. He'd gripped it too tightly. Paige knew he hadn't meant to. He was just anxious to find out what she'd been saying and who she'd been saying it to, if anybody. He hadn't realized, as they stood in the church kitchen, that he was gripping and yanking at her arm so roughly.

"What did you tell her? What were you saying to her about me?" He'd grabbed Paige's arm and asked her once Nita was out of sight. *"What were you saying about us? Did you tell her I did that to you?"* He pointed to her hand, the one he'd smacked the night before. *"Is that what you're going to tell Pastor? Let me guess, you've already said something, haven't you? That's why Pastor wanted to counsel us separately, huh?"*

Paige wanted to reply, but Blake didn't give her a chance. In addition to that, she was in too much pain to think clearly. His fingers clutched around her arm felt like the jaws of death. Even now she flinched at just the thought of how painful it had been.

"You almost ready?" Blake's voice boomed as he peeked his head into the bathroom.

Paige nearly jumped out of her skin.

"Oh, honey, I didn't mean to scare you." Blake came inside the bathroom and walked over to her. He placed his hands on her arms to comfort her and gently rubbed. But his touch made her jump out of her skin once again.

"Owee!" she yelped, then rested her hand softly over her bruise to protect it.

"What is it? Let me see." Blake examined the bruise and swelling on Paige's arm. "Baby, I'm so sorry. I didn't know." He kissed her on the forehead.

His kiss was a nice apology. It made Paige feel better.

"I didn't know you had a bruise," Blake told her. "How in the world did you do that? You need to be more careful."

Paige was in complete disbelief. Had he *really* just asked her that question? Was he *really* in that much of denial?

Realizing that his wife was staring at him like he had two heads and three legs, Blake innocently asked, "What?"

"Are you serious?" Paige asked. "*You* did this; yesterday at the church . . . in the kitchen."

Blake thought for a minute while shaking his head, a sign that he clearly didn't recall his manhandling of her. It had been the action that was responsible for the bruise on her arm.

"Remember, when you were questioning me about what I might have told anyone about you. You stood right in the kitchen and squeezed my arm."

"Yeah, but I didn't realize I was holding it so tight that I'd bruised it."

"Well, you were." Just thinking about it, Paige copped an attitude and created some space between her and her husband. "Anyway, we have to meet your mother and her attorney. I don't want to make you late this time, so I need to finish getting dressed." Paige made an attempt to brush by Blake, but he blocked her path.

"I . . . I'm so sorry. I can tell you're upset." Blake fished around in his mind for words. "I don't know what to say."

"Forget it. It's nothing." At least that's what Paige kept telling herself—that it was nothing. Even when she was alone in Pastor's office and Pastor asked her what was going on between her and Blake, Paige's response had been, "Nothing." But she couldn't help but following it up with, "Why do you ask?"

"No reason in particular, I guess," her pastor had replied. "You and Blake were both just acting a little strange is all. I figured maybe something might have been going on that neither of you wanted to discuss in front of the other. Sometimes couples get uncomfortable or embarrassed discussing certain topics in front of their mate. Subject matters like sex, for example."

"Oh, well, Pastor, I guarantee you that everything is just fine in that area," Paige had been proud to say, considering at the beginning of her marriage, Blake barely touched her. He'd kept himself super busy with work in order to make a nice little nest egg for the two of them. This was the same nest egg his estranged mother was now threatening to take. But at the

thought of almost losing Paige in the car accident and to diabetes, Blake had reprioritized things. He'd made great strives in tearing himself away from his job in order to spend more time at home with her.

At first, Paige greatly appreciated his efforts. She loved having Blake home more, but now, with him always being on edge, she'd almost rather he stayed at the office. There was so much tension in the home. He was so unpredictable these days. Disagreements came so easy now. Paige hated that part of their marriage and prayed that with the counseling things would get back on track . . . and soon. She didn't want to get into the habit of hiding bruises or lying to her pastor, for that matter. After all, what good would counseling do if she wasn't going to be honest?

Pastor had expressed such by reminding Paige, "You know this whole counseling thing only works if both spouses are honest about their feelings and what's going on in the marriage. And if you can't be honest with each other, well, I'd hope you'd at least be honest with me. That way, I'll know what to seek God for on your behalf and hear from Him clearly regarding His word about your situation. I'm not God, just one of His vessels that He's called to do His work here on earth."

Paige believed her pastor heard from God. That was evident by the Sunday sermons and her pastor's Christian walk, period. But on the same token, her pastor wasn't married, and to her knowledge, had never been married. So there was a little part of her that doubted whether it was worth it to share everything about her marriage; at least the thing in her marriage that was starting to bother her, even scare her to some degree. That thing being Blake's temper and his "accidentally" grabbing her and hitting her too hard.

Would Pastor truly understand or jump to conclusions? To Paige, it felt impossible for someone who wasn't in her shoes to relate to what she was going through. At least for now, Paige decided to hold back. And if all went well, things would get back on track and it would all be water under the bridge. Blake would be back to his old self in no time. And hopefully, so would the bruised patch of skin on her arm.

"Well, let me at least kiss your arm and make it better," Blake had said, leaning down and planting a kiss on Paige's bruised arm. "How was that?" Before she could answer, he kissed her again. And again. And before she knew it, he was kissing her in places that only a husband should kiss his wife.

How was it that the same man who'd hurt her could make her feel so good? Could make her forget about the hurt altogether and just focus on what made her feel good? And that's just what happened. Blake apologized to her over and over again as he kissed every crevice of her body. Easily caught up in the rapture of love, Paige accepted his apology. He told her that he'd never hurt her again. He said it with such sincerity and conviction. Paige could have even sworn she saw a tear in his eye. She believed him. She believed that he never meant to hurt her and that he would never hurt her again.

Who was in denial now?

Chapter Eighteen

"So I'm glad to see that Pastor Davidson is no longer staying here." Mother Doreen looked around Bethany's living room as if to make sure there were no remnants of that man left behind.

"He left the day Uriah came home," Bethany stated, "or didn't come home . . . or left again." She huffed. "You know what I mean." Bethany walked over to the couch and sat down, in preparation of entertaining whatever thoughts were on her sister's mind. "You said you wanted to talk to me?"

"Yes, that's true." Two hours or so after Mother Doreen dropped Uriah off at Bethany's, he came back out to the car ready to return to Pastor Frey's. After taking him back to Pastor Frey's, Mother Doreen drove back to her sister's house to talk.

"I can only imagine what it is you want to talk about." Bethany rolled her eyes.

"Look, Sis, I don't want to bicker and fight with you. I just want to talk like the two civilized, God-fearing adults that we are." Mother Doreen took a seat next to Bethany on the couch. "You're my little sister, and I love you. You're the only family I have left, and I'll be darned if I allow Satan to destroy that."

"I hear you, but can't you see that the devil doesn't have anything to do with what's going on between you and me? It's you." Bethany stood. "Ever since you moved here to Kentucky, you've been snooping around me, my church, my children like you're some type of private detective."

"But I told you from jump that's what I came here to do," Mother Doreen reminded her. "I told you that my sole purpose for being here was to watch over and take care of you all."

"What you've been doing crosses the line of just 'watching over' us." Bethany took a deep breath. She'd made up her mind when agreeing to have a talk with her sister that she wouldn't cut the fool. She'd stay calm and listen to what her sister had to say. Mother Doreen was in her sixties; over two decades Bethany's senior. How Bethany saw it was that Mother Doreen couldn't relate. She was old-school; *too* old-school, and had no idea how marriages and relationships operated nowadays. "I feel as though you're sitting on the right hand of the throne, just waiting to judge me."

"I'm sorry you feel that way," Mother Doreen apologized sincerely. "I promise you that I never meant to make you feel as though you were being judged. I guess ever since my newfound so-called holy boldness has taken affect, I have been overdoing it a little bit. It's just that I strive to please God in everything I do. I just don't want to fail Him in any way."

"And I understand that about you, 'Reen, really I do. I know that you are a true woman of God, but that doesn't mean you have to be the perfect Christian. And it certainly doesn't mean that you should expect for everyone around you to be perfect either."

Mother Doreen nodded her head in agreement.

"I know I messed up with Pastor and Uriah and everything," Bethany continued. "But in spite of what you think, I'm still leaning on God to help me through this. I still trust God. I still love God, and I know He loves me because His Word says nothing can come between His love and me."

"Speaking of Uriah, when are you going to tell the kids about him now that he's back?" Mother Doreen asked.

"I'm not."

Mother Doreen was stunned. "What? So you're just going to let them think—"

"He's going to tell them himself, tonight," Bethany said. "See? There you were about to do it again; go off on one of your judgmental tangents. You have to realize that God gave man free will. People are going to make the choices they make, and they are not always going to be the right ones. But you have to realize, 'Reen, that you are not the only somebody who hears from God. God speaks to me. No, I don't always listen and do the right thing. Sometimes my flesh gets the best of me, but you have to trust me and trust the God that we both serve that everything is going to work out for the good in the end."

Mother Doreen took in her sister's words with such admiration. "Oh, Sis, I underestimate you sometimes, and I'm sorry. I'm so, so sorry." Mother Doreen embraced her sister with a warm and loving hug.

"Aunti!" Sadie came through the door excited to see her aunt and glad to see that her mother and aunt were embracing.

Mother Doreen was also glad; glad that for once, Sadie had caught her and her sister doing something besides arguing. "How's my bestest niece?" Mother Doreen asked, releasing Bethany to hug Sadie.

"I'm doing good now that you're back." Sadie looked at her mother, then back at Mother Doreen. "You *are* back, aren't you?"

Now it was Mother Doreen's turn to look to Bethany. Her eyes silently posed the same question Sadie had just asked out loud.

After a moment or two, a smile crept across Bethany's lips. "That's if she wants to be back." Now Bethany looked at Mother Doreen and with her eyes, posed the same question.

Mother Doreen didn't hesitate. "If you all will have me back, I'd be honored to come home."

"Yes!" Sadie cheered. "I don't know what I'll do if I have to eat one more bowl of Beanie-Weenies."

All three laughed.

"So you just want me back for my cooking, huh?" Mother Doreen teased her niece.

"Aunti, I'd be lying if I said that didn't play a big part," Sadie admitted. She then kissed her aunt on the cheek. "That, and the fact that I miss you."

"Aw, now, that's more like it." Mother Doreen returned her niece's gesture with a kiss on the cheek. "Now, go get moving." She playfully slapped Sadie on the rear end. "Go get your studies done while I check out of that hotel and stop at the grocer. I know just what I'm going to make for this special occasion." Mother Doreen winked at Bethany, alluding to the fact that later on this evening, they'd be celebrating a far more special occasion than just her coming back. Uriah would be back as well.

"Okay, Aunti. I love you." Sadie ran off.

"Wait, where's Hudson?" Mother Doreen asked.

"Oh, he went to see the baby," Sadie replied stopping. "He said he'll be home at around seven."

"Isn't that something?" Mother Doreen stated. "Most teen fathers would be running as far as they could from the responsibility of being a daddy, but Hudson is running to it."

"Can you blame him?" Sadie's eyes lit up. "I mean, my niece is the most beautiful and perfect baby in the world." Sadie stared off starry-eyed. "I can't wait for Justice and I to have a baby of our own."

"Justice?" both Mother Doreen and Bethany exclaimed loudly.

"Baby?" Mother Doreen spat even louder. "Oh, ba-ba-bo-bolska." The tongues got to rolling as Mother Doreen approached Sadie. "In the name of Jesus, child, there will be no talk about babies. You just turned fifteen last month. And who is this Justice anyway?"

Sadie brushed off her mother's and aunt's apprehension with a hand swish and a smile. "Oh, I don't mean now. Justice and I have to finish high school at least. He's only in tenth grade like me." She rolled her eyes up in her head. "He's new here in town. Been here about a month."

"The boy has only been here a month and you're talking about having a baby with him?" Mother Doreen asked in disbelief.

"We've only been officially 'talking' for a couple of weeks. But we have so much in common that it ain't funny."

"Well, I'd like to meet this Justice and his parents," Bethany stated.

"His father is a bishop. He's here scoping out a church scene or something; kind of like an undercover mission or something."

"Well, I hope that's the only thing under covers, if you know what I mean," Bethany said sternly to her daughter.

Sadie chuckled and shook her head. "Mom, if you're asking if Justice and I are having sex yet, the answer is no. Besides, he's one of the good ones. You can trust him. He's a preacher's kid, for Pete's sake." And on that note, Sadie galloped to her room.

Mother Doreen looked over at Bethany. "A preacher's kid, huh?" she said, shaking her head. "And you know what they say . . . sometimes there's only one thing worse than a preacher's kid."

"Who is that?" Bethany asked dumfounded.

"The preacher himself."

Chapter Nineteen

Lorain stood erect and stiff like a Russian toy soldier. She couldn't believe he was at her door—Broady, Mr. Leary. Her mother's new husband. Her stepfather. Him standing there in her doorway was like déjà vu, only this time, he didn't appear from behind her mother. This time, Lorain wasn't popping a grape in her mouth. She wasn't caught up in the element of surprise to the point where she choked on the grape, ultimately needing the Heimlich maneuver to save her life. But there was more than just an element of surprise this time. There was complete shock. She never expected him to come to her. She'd been trying to figure out how she would go to him, confront him about the past—their past. That way, the ball would be in *her* court. This was clearly a flagrant foul and the ref had made the wrong call, because now Broady had possession of the ball. It was in *his* court, a home game, and he stood there dribbling, every bounce getting louder and louder, taunting Lorain's very being.

Not wanting to be defeated, Lorain had to try to make a steal. She needed to get control of the ball again. She began her fake out.

"Broady . . . uh, please . . . come in." Getting those words out of her mouth was not as easy as it sounded. Without saying a word, Broady accepted Lorain's invitation and entered the house. "Please," Lorain said, extending a hand toward a chair, "sit down." Once again, without saying a word, he accepted Lorain's offer and took a seat. "Water?" she offered.

"No, thank you," he finally spoke.

His voice, for some reason, was so menacing to Lorain. All of a sudden, she felt as though the walls were closing in on her. The room was becoming as small as an office—Mr. Leary's old office back at the middle school. She couldn't breath. She had to get out of there. She called a time-out. "I need some water," Lorain managed to get out, grabbing her throat as she rushed out of the living room and into the kitchen.

She ran over to the kitchen sink and turned on the cold water. She didn't even bother to get a glass. She just bent over and scooped the water in her mouth straight from the faucet. After gulping down several handfuls of water, Lorain stood up and took several deep breaths. She still felt suffocated. Water always seemed to help out the people in movies whenever they were feeling anxiety. Obviously, that only worked in the movies . . . or just not for her.

For a second she thought about trying the brown paper bag trick; the old exercise of breathing in and out of the bag. She'd seen that in movies as well, but felt now she was being ridiculous. So, instead, she tried something that she knew worked. She began to pray.

"Heavenly Father, I come to you as humble as I know how to be right now. This entire thing has been a complete roller coaster. Well, I want off the ride, God. Get me off the ride safe and sound, Lord. Tell me what to do. Tell me what to say. Let everything that is about to take place be directed by the Holy Spirit. Protect me right now, Father God. Protect me from the enemy, even if the enemy is me. Keep me covered in the blood. And above all, Lord, as you remove the covers off of this situation, provide a blanket of protection upon all those affected, so that they will be covered by your love, warmth, and comfort. Only you know the outcome, God. And in the end, let me be mindful to give you all the honor, all the glory, and all the praise. I love you, Lord. In Jesus' name I pray. Amen."

With shoulders relaxed and putting all her trust into the Lord, Lorain made her way back into the living room where Broady was seated. When he noticed her return, he stood.

"Is everything okay? Are you all right?" Broady asked her.

"Yes," she assured him. "I haven't really been feeling myself these days, you know." Lorain went and took a seat on her couch, which was catty-cornered from the chair Broady was sitting in.

"That's, uh, kind of why I'm here." Broady took a deep breath and sat back down. "I think I kind of know what's going on here, Lorain."

"*Do* you? Do you *really*?" Lorain saw an opportunity where she could take possession of the ball. But she didn't want to make a move too soon. She didn't know what kind of grip Broady had on it.

"It's about me and you."

Chills shot through Lorain's body. She had to coach herself. *Stay calm. Relax. No weapon formed against me shall prosper.* "Me and you?" Where was his head at? Lorain needed to know.

"Exactly, and I owe you an apology, Lorain; a long, overdue apology." Broady's eyes looked downward with regret. "And all I can do is just pray that you can find it in your heart to forgive me."

Was this the moment? Was this the moment he was going to turn the ball over?

"It seems as though you and I never really got a chance to hit it off," Broady continued, looking at

Lorain. "You don't really know me, and what you do know . . . well . . . I can't say it's something a girl would want to know about her stepfather." He shook his head. "Whew, that day in the church when you stood up and called me out about my past conviction as a pedophile . . . umpf, umpf, umpf, but God is good. Because He gave me the opportunity to clear the air with you right then and there. But as you know, what I said in the church wasn't everything."

Now this is when Lorain thought she wasn't going to be able to control herself. She had her game face on tough as she nodded for Broady to continue.

"God wanted me to do more, to say more. He wanted me to take it to another level. But instead, what did I do? I ran off and married your mother. And by doing so, I failed you and your mother." He paused for a moment. "She doesn't even know I'm here now saying what I'm about to say. I . . . I had overheard her talking to you this morning. From the gist of things, I concluded you were home from work ill today. I decided to seize the moment to come over here and say what I needed to say."

Lorain couldn't take it any longer. She needed for Broady to say what was on his mind. In turn, she could then say what she needed to say; that he needed to divorce her mother and leave their lives just as quickly as he had entered it. "So exactly what is it you came here to say, Broady?"

He stood and ran his hands down his pants as if his palms had been sweaty and he needed to dry them off. "I know I can't turn back the hands of time, but I can move forward. And I'd like to move forward by getting to know you better. It's been you and your mother for quite some time, so I had no business just coming into her life and taking her away from you like that. I know it had to hurt you. And maybe you thought by putting me on blast like that in front of my church family was a way to hurt me back. But I forgive you and hope we can—"

"*You* forgive *me?*" Lorain exclaimed in disbelief. That's it! She'd had enough. She'd heard enough. There was no way she was about to let Broady dunk on her. So she decided to muster up all the strength she had and block the shot. It was time she took back what was hers: peace of mind.

The clock on the scoreboard was ticking away. If Lorain was ever going to make her move, she had to do it now. Time was running out.

Chapter Twenty

"Aren't you the least bit nervous? I mean, you are about to see your mother again for the first time after all these years," Paige asked her husband as they walked hand in hand toward the elevator.

This time, instead of meeting at the court building, the plaintiff, defendant, and their attorneys were meeting in the conference room at Ms. Turner's office. It was supposed to be sort of like a pre-deposition, where Blake would disclose his financials dating back to when his father received a settlement up until now. The only thing Blake wanted his mother to disclose were her whereabouts for the last three decades.

"Trust me, wife, nervous is the last emotion that's running through my veins," Blake replied as he hit the arrow pointing up for the elevator. "I can't believe this woman has the nerve to come back into my life after she left my father and me for dead when I was only three years olds. She doesn't come back into my life because she wants to apologize or start up a relationship with me. She comes back into my life to sue me. Are you *serious*?" Blake's temper was starting to flare.

Knowing getting him all fired up wouldn't be a good idea, so Paige gently rubbed the back of Blake's hand in order to calm him down. Blake could go into that meeting and jeopardize everything—not only the money, but their house and cars as well. The last thing she needed was for him to catch a case . . . another one.

"Where in God's name is this stupid elevator?" Blake stated as he pressed the button repeatedly, his aggravation evident.

"Baby," Paige said, standing in front of him and wrapping her arms around his waist, "relax. Think about the time we just spent together this morning." A mischievous grin spread across her lips. "That ought to settle you down a little. Besides, after all that work you put in, seems like you wouldn't have the energy to be all wound up," she teased.

"Put in work was exactly what I did. Maybe if you lost a little more weight, then you could get on top, and I wouldn't have to work so hard."

Paige couldn't believe her husband was using her insecurity against her, the fact that she felt she was too big, too jiggly to mount her husband. Her arms fell to the side as if made of stone. Talk about her self-esteem shrinking down to nothing. Just that morning as she slipped on her size fourteen pants, she'd felt good about herself. Down two sizes and feeling healthier than she'd ever felt in her life, she thought she was the stuff. The five minutes of quick lovemaking with Blake before they had to hurry out the door had made her feel good inside. The way Blake had made her feel in only five minutes, he had just destroyed with his words in only five seconds.

"Finally!" Blake huffed as he moved Paige aside and walked into the open elevator.

Paige just stood there, not wanting to take that first step into her reality; that the person who could make her feel whole was the same person who could break her down to nothing.

"So are you coming or not? Or are you going to make me late again so that I might as well just turn over my checkbook to the woman?"

Even though the words had stung her, had cut deep, Paige knew Blake hadn't really meant what he'd said. He'd never had an issue with her weight before. When he first met her, she was a size sixteen. Well, she wore a size sixteen, but truth be told, a size eighteen is what she should have been wearing. Nonetheless, Blake had loved it. Now she was smaller and healthier, so he should have loved it even more. Once again, Paige surmised that this change in her husband's attitude had nothing to do with her and everything to do with the stress his mother's lawsuit was putting on him. Once it was all said and done with, he'd go back to being the man she fell in love with. So Paige made her mind up that she was along for the ride through thick and thin. Not just the ride on the elevator, but wherever else her marriage took her.

"No, uh, I mean, yes, I'm, uh, I'm coming. I'm coming," Paige said in a soft voice.

She hopped into the elevator just before the doors closed and stood by her man.

"Good, you're here. I was just about to call your cell phone," Blake's attorney, Randall, said, relieved. He'd nearly pounced on Blake as he and Paige exited the elevator. "The plaintiff is already here. Everybody's waiting in the conference room. It's right this way." Randall began leading the way to the conference room. "Oh, excuse my manners," he said, still keeping up a good pace as Blake and Paige trailed behind him. "You must be Mrs. Dickenson." He turned slightly to extend his hand to Paige, but still kept it moving.

"Yes, I am. Pleased to meet you." Paige shook his hand while she tried to keep up with him.

"It's great that you could come. A supporting wife is always a good look," Randall stated as they arrived at a door with a sign on it that read CONFERENCE ROOM 2. "So are you ready for this?" Randall asked Blake as he put his hand on the doorknob.

"Are *you* ready?" Blake shot back at him.

"Look, I know I mainly deal in real-estate law, but trust me, I got this. From what you've told me, this woman hasn't got a chance at getting her hands on one red cent of your money."

Paige ran her hand up and down Blake's back to reassure him that she was there to support him. "Are you ready, sweetheart?" she repeated Randall's initial question.

"As ready as I'll ever be," Blake replied. "Let's do it."

"Mrs. Dickenson?" Randall looked at Paige for her reply. She simply nodded that she was ready. "Alrighty then. Here we go."

Randall gave the door two small knocks while putting his hand on the knob and opening it.

"Come on in," the three could hear a female voice order from the inside. "If your client is here, then we're all set."

Neither Blake nor Paige had any expectations about what Blake's mother would look like; what she would be like. In all actuality, they hadn't even shared a conversation on what his moment would be like. Blake hadn't wanted to talk about the woman he couldn't even remember, let alone meet her. But now, regardless of whether he liked it, he was standing in the very same room with her.

Four women were already seated at the conference table. Upon Blake, Paige, and Randall entering the room, one stood. Automatically Paige and Blake knew it was Ms. Turner, his mother's lawyer. She was dressed in a fire-red pants suit with her hair in a bun. To top off the look, glasses with black frames shielded her thin, slit, slanted eyes. Being a female attorney, Blake surmised that she was more than likely going for the look of strength, power, and domination in an effort to be intimidating. After all, he'd never seen a male attorney in a fire-red pants suit.

Next to Ms. Turner sat a woman who, without a doubt, was the stenographer. Her fingers rested in place on the machine in front of her like a cop's would rest on the trigger in the middle of a shoot-out. A frail little thing with stringy dirty-blond hair, she looked as though she probably lived vicariously through the words she sometimes pounded on that machine.

Then there were the two other women. They looked like sisters. Each had café-au-lait skin that was a shade or two lighter than Blake's. One had weaved microbraids with golden blond streaks down her back, while the other simply had golden blond weave straight down her back. Blake couldn't tell which one was wearing the most makeup. Between the two of them, there was a Mary Kay representative somewhere who had just earned a pink Cadillac.

"Is that him, Mama?" one tried to whisper into the other woman's ear, but the entire room could hear her. Her hand was up to her mouth and cupped around the other woman's ear. One couldn't miss the two-inch colored acrylic nails or the rings resting on each finger. "Too bad he's my brother. He's kinda fine."

"Hush now," the older woman chuckled and playfully smacked her daughter's leg under the table. She then flipped her golden blond weave over her shoulder.

Ms. Turner nearly broke her neck to interrupt the embarrassing actions of her client. "Hello, I'm, uh, Ms. Turner." She extended her hand to Blake and Paige and greeted them with a handshake. She then looked at Randall. "You and I know each other." Turning toward the older woman and her daughter, she stated, "And this here is my client, Barnita Dickenson, and her daughter, Sharlita Dickenson."

Barnita stood. She stared at Blake for a few seconds. "Oh, well, boy, I know we ain't seeing each other after all these years under decent circumstances, but what the heck." She opened her arms as if she expected Blake to come around the table and hug her.

Instead, Blake just nodded and said, "Miss Dickenson." He then immediately walked to a chair at the table.

Paige could tell he was holding back a raging fire. Without another word, he pulled her chair out for her first so that she could sit. "Thank you," Paige said softly as she sat.

"Oh, so you just gon' leave Mama hanging like that?" Sharlita jumped in, snapping her neck from side to side while her braids danced along.

"Shhh, don't worry about it," Barnita said as she sat back down.

"No, Mama, that ain't no way for a boy to greet his mother." Sharlita rolled her eyes so hard, everyone in the room thought her hazel contacts were going to pop out. "Shoot, I don't know who he thinks he is," she said under her breath as she too flung her microbraids over her shoulder.

Ms. Turner cleared her throat. "Why don't we get started here?"

"Uh, yes, that sounds good," Randall agreed.

"Well, first off—" Ms. Turner started before Paige cut her off.

"If no one minds, I was wondering if I could lead us in a really quick prayer," Paige requested.

Every eye shot at her like it was a dagger. Ironically, she felt like the Antichrist in a room full of saints.

"Honey, this isn't really the time or the place for that," Blake said under his breath while squeezing her knee.

"But, babe, God doesn't care about the timing or the place; He shows up and—" The added pressure on her knee halted further words.

"So this is the wifey, huh?" Blake's mother asked, giving Paige the once-over. "I see you're a chubby chaser just like your daddy was. I wonder what other traits of his you have," she said to Blake.

Paige's mouth flung open. Had this woman, her mother-in-law, just called her fat?

"Look, please, can we get started?" Ms. Turner begged, realizing that there was a possibility that the more her client talked, the slimmer the chances of them coming out of this thing with some type of settlement. "Mr. Dickenson, before we get started with the legality of everything, I know you've been estranged from your mother for quite some time. So, with that being said, is there anything you'd like to ask . . . anything you'd like to know?"

"No," Blake was quick to say. "I just want to get this over with."

"Very well," Ms. Turner stated. "I guess we can start with—"

"On second thought," Blake interrupted, "there is something I'd like to ask my . . . mother." He hated referring to the woman as his mother.

"Go ahead," Barnita said in gangsta mode, leaning back in her chair as she ran her fingers through her weave. "Bring it on."

Blake leaned in and glared his mother down. If only looks could kill . . . He then leaned back in his chair comfortably after asking, "Why did you leave me? And why didn't you ever come back?"

Chapter Twenty-one

"Son, please! Will you just come back down and talk to me?" Uriah pleaded as Hudson ran up the stairs, stormed into his bedroom, then slammed the door closed behind him. Hard. Then there was the clicking of the lock.

Uriah stood outside his son's door, hoping and praying that eventually he'd unlocked the door and let him in; let him in both his room and back in his heart. But he knew that wasn't going to happen, not right now, not anytime soon, for that matter. Feeling defeated, he retreated back into the living room to join his wife, daughter, and sister-in-law.

He'd shown up at the house an hour and a half ago and explained to the children why he allowed them to think he was dead. Why, for the past months, he'd practically lived as a vagrant, depending on the kindness of others in order to survive. In the split moment he'd decided to allow the world to believe he was dead, he never even thought about how he'd pull it off. How he'd survive without a place to call home. After all, ever since he'd started his trucking business, he'd pretty much lived on the road anyway. He'd been up and down the highway and streets more than he'd been in his own home, so what would be the difference?

There had been plenty of times he'd been out on runs and didn't have a dime to his name after making sure most of the bills at home were taken care of. But

God had kept him. God had shown him much favor by putting people in his path to provide for him exactly what he needed. And believe it or not, that is exactly what God had done for him these last few months. God had kept him, even while he was doing wrong. It was nothing but God's grace and mercy that even allowed him the opportunity to come back home and try to make things right. Even now it was hard for Uriah to conceive the fact that God had not forsaken him even though what he was doing went against man's law. Faking death so that his family would receive insurance money and Social Security benefits was against the law. Uriah would eventually have to turn himself in and face the music. He only prayed that once again, God's grace and mercy would get him through that ordeal as well. But for now, he simply needed favor with his own family.

"It's okay, Dad. He's just a little shocked right now is all," Sadie said, witnessing the anguished look on her father's face.

When Uriah had first walked in the door, Bethany had already set the stage for him by telling the children that he was alive; that it wasn't he who had burned up in the truck. That way, when he walked in the door, her children wouldn't think they were experiencing what that little boy in the movie *The Sixth Sense* was experiencing: that they could see dead people.

After hearing what her mother had to say, and then hearing her father's explanation, Sadie was a little on the fence. Of course she was glad to have her father back, but angry for the awful loss she'd felt—and all for nothing. But at the end of the day, her daddy was alive and she was grateful. She didn't want to think about the time she'd spent without him, but about the future she would now have with him.

Hudson was flat-out heated. There was no in-between mixed emotions, and he had no problem expressing to his father just how angry he was. "How could you do something so cowardly?" Hudson asked his father as he stood eyeball-to-eyeball with him. Ordinarily, this is something he never would have done, but right about now, things were far from ordinary. "You're no worse than a couple of my boys who turn to selling drugs on the street, talking 'bout so that their family can survive; so that they can put food on the table. That's a cop-out, Dad, and you know it."

At least the boy had still referred to him as "Dad." That meant light at the end of the tunnel as far as Uriah was concerned.

"Do you know the emotional strain you put on this family?" Hudson had asked. "It was far worse than the emotional strain of being broke. We thought you were *dead*. Yeah, we might have been able to pay some bills off, but at the end of the day, your life was far more important than any material thing."

"Look, son, I—"

"Don't call me son like you're my father or something," Hudson snapped. "My father's dead." And on that note, Hudson had run off toward his room.

Bethany had remained silent as her children expressed their different emotions and concerns. She didn't know what to feel besides feeling like she was in an episode of a soap opera.

Mother Doreen, being the peacemaker she always tried so hard to be, was there to support them all, including Uriah.

"Just give him some time," Mother Doreen told Uriah as he sat down in the living-room chair. "It's going to take some time."

"Yeah, I know," Uriah agreed. "It's just that I didn't take into consideration that anyone would be mad at me. I just thought everyone would be so glad to see me that the glory of it all would outweigh the suffering I put everybody through."

"I can't lie, Daddy," Sadie admitted, "there is a little part of me that is upset with you, but there is a big part of me that is just glad that you are alive."

"Thanks, daughter," Uriah replied. "But I guess it's just the opposite with Hudson. There's a little part of him that is glad that I'm alive, and a big part of him that is upset with me."

"Well, now that you're home, you two will have time to get things back to normal," Sadie reasoned.

Uriah and Bethany shot each other a look that didn't go unnoticed by Sadie. "What? What's going on? Why are you two looking at each another like that?" Sadie questioned.

"Baby, there is just so much going on right now, and so many more decisions that have to be made," Bethany started. "With that being said, honey, your father is going to be staying at Pastor Frey's for a little while."

"What?" Sadie said, shooting up off the couch she'd been sitting on like a shooting star streaking through the sky. "You mean to tell me that you're not going to let Daddy stay here but you let that jackleg pastor stay here when he didn't have anywhere to go? Giving us some story about not turning a man in need away because you never know when you could be entertaining an angel," she huffed. "Well, the last I checked the Bible, Lucifer had been an angel too." Sadie put her hands on top of her head to reflect how fed up she was. "I can't deal with this mess any longer. It's trifling and embarrassing." She stood up with her back straight and said to her mother, "So if Daddy goes, then I'm going with him."

"Hold on, Sadie," Uriah said, putting up both his hands. "It's not that your momma won't let me stay here. I just need to get some things together in my head is all. You know what I did is a crime. So we still need to decide how we are going to go about coming clean on this situation. And I kind of need Pastor Frey's spiritual guidance to get me through all of this. And your momma allowing me to stay here could put her in jeopardy. They might think she had something to do with it or she could become an accessory after the fact. I don't know," Uriah threw his hands up. "That's why there is just a lot to think about."

"So you could actually go to jail for this?" Sadie asked as she ran over to her father. "No!" She threw her arms around him. "We can't lose you again, Daddy. Don't turn yourself in. Just get a new identify or something. Repent to God. He'll forgive you, and then take care of everything."

Uriah smiled, warmed by his daughter's support. "It ain't that easy, Jellybean," he said, calling her by the special nickname he had given her. "Nothing is ever that easy. Every moment of your life has consequences. Well, this is one of those moments, and I'm gonna have to face the consequences."

Sadie just stood hugging her father and weeping.

"Come on, child," Mother Doreen said to Sadie. "It's getting late, and your father probably needs to go back to Pastor Frey's before it gets too late. Why don't you go upstairs and try to relax and calm down, and I'll warm up some sugar milk for you?"

Sadie released her father and nodded. She knew it would take more than sugar milk to make things better, but she appreciated her aunt's gesture. After kissing her father good-bye, she went to her room.

Mother Doreen let out a huge gust of air. "Whewww. Now *that* was tough."

"Who you telling? And it's only going to get tougher," Uriah agreed. "But I do need to get going."

Bethany had just remembered something. "But we didn't even get a chance to eat, and Doreen cooked a mess of—"

Uriah put his hands up, cutting his wife off. "I'm really not that hungry right now. Besides, it was nice of Pastor Frey to let me borrow his vehicle. I don't want to take advantage."

"Well, I'll just go fix both you and Pastor Frey up some to-go containers." Mother Doreen headed straight to the kitchen and began packing up food.

Bethany and Uriah stood in the living room with silence between them. "Oh, before you go," Bethany spoke up, "I brought up another box of your stuff I had packed away downstairs." She pointed to the cardboard box that sat by the front door.

"Oh, thank you, but I think I have plenty to tide me over." Uriah had already gotten some of his things the last time he was there.

"Here you are, brother-in-law." Mother Doreen returned to the living room and handed Uriah several bags of food. "You be careful driving home," she said, watching Bethany walk Uriah to the door.

Once the two got to the door, it was a very awkward moment for them. Mother Doreen could tell that they didn't know what to do. Should they hug or kiss each other good-bye like a husband and wife usually would? Eventually Uriah decided to simply extend his hand. Bethany grabbed it, but only to pull him in for a hug, almost causing him to drop one of the bags.

"I'm glad you're alive," she whispered in his ear.

Having his wife's arms around him, after months of being alone, almost erased all of her indiscretions. Almost. But there was still that matter of Pastor Davidson that had yet to be discussed fully. But for now, Uriah decided to just take in the moment of being in his wife's arms. "Yeah, me too," he smiled, feeling that perhaps there was a chance that things wouldn't be so rough after all. After pulling away from the embrace, he gave his final farewells to both Bethany and Mother Doreen and was on his way.

Bethany exhaled after closing and locking the door behind him. Then she leaned up against the door. "You know, watching him leave tonight, I have to admit that I kind of wish he was staying. I wish that things could go back to about three years ago, and we could start all over. Erase all of my wrongdoings with . . ." Bethany's words trailed off as guilt of her affair began to suffocate her mind. She had to admit, though, that since Uriah's return, her thoughts hadn't been much on Pastor Davidson. That undying, yielding love she'd tried to explain to Mother Doreen just days ago was now . . . well . . . dying.

"Look, it's all in the past now," Mother Doreen told her sister. "I'm about to warm Sadie some sugar milk. Can I get you anything?"

"No," Bethany said looking downward. "Just my old life back."

Chapter Twenty-two

Broady had been caught off guard by Lorain's sudden outburst. "Lorain, I didn't mean to upset you."

"*Upset me?* You did more than just *upset* me. You took everything from me—everything!" Lorain cried out. Her hands were trembling, and her eyes were filled with tears.

"I'm sorry, sweetheart. Really I am. I know your mother was everything to you, with your daddy leaving you two and all."

"Don't you put my father's name in your mouth!" she snapped, pointing at him. "He may have left me and Momma, but he took care of us. He still paid child support and alimony. He still made sure that when I was sick I could get medical care. But what he didn't do was take from me what you did—my innocence."

"Perhaps this wasn't a good idea, my coming by here." Broady stood to leave. "Which is why I didn't mention it to Eleanor; I knew she would have thought it was a bad idea too and would have tried to talk me out of it. Guess I learned the hard way." He nodded. "Good day, Lorain. I hope you get to feeling better."

"Oh, now that I bring it all out in the open, you just wanna run off," Lorain accused. "What, you going back to Phoenix? Where are you going this time when you run away from me? California? Yeah, you'll fit right in with all the freaks there. Or should I say with all the other *pedophiles?*"

"You've gone mad," Broady stated with a look of confusion on his face. "Perhaps you better go back to the doctor and get your head checked out, because you're talking real crazy." He walked to the door.

Lorain jumped in front of the door to block Broady from leaving. "No, you're just trying to make me *think* that I'm crazy. You're trying to manipulate me just like you did back when I was in middle school. But it's not going to work this time. I'm *not* crazy. I've got proof."

"What on God's earth are you talking about?"

"Don't play dumb with me. You know *exactly* what I'm talking about."

"Look, I'm leaving, and don't worry, I won't tell your mother about this little episode. It would break her heart to know of your actions."

"*What? My* actions? And you don't think it would break her heart to know about *yours* all those years ago?"

Broady's voice boomed with sternness as he walked up on Lorain and pointed in her face. "Look, I told your mother everything; she knows *everything* about my past, my conviction, and my jail time. More importantly, she knows about my deliverance and healing. I know what God has done for me, and I won't allow you or anyone else to force me to feel guilty or harbor on my past."

Lorain shook her head in disbelief. "This isn't an act is it? Neither is it some selective memory loss on your part either . . . is it? You honestly have *no idea* who I am, do you? Or what you did to me all those years ago." Before Broady could reply, Lorain was pushed forward by the opening door. The force landed her right into Broady's arms.

"Viola Lorain Waterson!" Eleanor shouted as she stood in the doorway carrying a pot of soup. She'd wanted to surprise her daughter by coming over to nurse her back to health. She surprised her all right. "My only daughter; my only child. Please explain to me what you're doing in my husband's arms!"

Before Lorain could reply to her mother, there was a loud thud. She didn't know at first whether it was her bottom hitting the ground, or Broady hitting the ground after he'd let her go.

"Mom, is he going to be all right?" Lorain asked Eleanor as she spotted and approached her in the ER waiting room.

Eleanor couldn't even look her child in the eyes as she spoke. "I . . . I don't know. It wasn't looking good. His heart stopped twice on the way here in the ambulance." Eleanor had ridden in the back of the ambulance with her husband after calling 911.

After finding out what hospital they were going to, Lorain drove over in her own car. Guess she wouldn't make it in to work after all. But her boss understood once she told him what had happened to her stepfather. Her concerns regarding Broady were genuine, but not because of him; because of her mother. She could see how torn up and scared her mother was. She didn't like seeing her this way. And she couldn't help but think that this might be the way her mother would react when finding out the truth about her and Broady.

Now Lorain was beginning to have second thoughts and regrets. She was having second thoughts about telling her mother the truth and regrets about rehashing the situation with Broady, although he was acting as if he were none the wiser. Lorain didn't know if it was just that—an act; the old man playing dumb in order to save face. But come to think of it, there was no way Broady would knowingly marry the mother of the girl he'd molested as a child. Would he? Could he? Only a monster would do something like that. But to Lorain, Broady was a monster. The Mr. Leary she knew was a monster indeed. If, as a grown man, he was capable of having sex with little girls, then he was capable of anything.

"Mrs. Leary," a voice called out. "Mrs. Leary. Mrs. Broady Leary."

"Oh, my, that's me," Eleanor exclaimed. She hadn't gotten used to her new last name. After all, it was the fourth time she'd switched last names. The name on her birth certificate is Eleanor Simpson. When she married Lorain's father, it changed to Waterson, but after the divorce, she switched it back to her maiden name of Simpson. And now it was Leary.

The doctor made his way over to where Eleanor was sitting and Lorain was standing. "Hi, I'm Doctor Healshire." The doctor extended his hand to both Eleanor and Lorain.

"Doctor Healshire, I just need to know if my husband is going to be all right," Eleanor said in a broken voice.

The doctor slowly closed his eyes, took a deep breath, and then opened them. "Mrs. Leary, I have to be honest. I don't want to give you false hope, but it doesn't look good. Your husband suffered a stroke. He's on a heart monitor, but we also have a nurse stationed in his room because his heart just isn't strong, and it keeps stopping on us. He's weak. I honestly don't know how much longer his poor body can handle it. Which is what I wanted to talk to you about."

Lorain put her arm around her mother's shoulder. She could tell that the doctor's report was only going to become grimmer.

Doctor Healshire inhaled, and then exhaled again before continuing. "I'm going to need you to decide whether you want us to continue to resuscitate your husband or place him on DNR."

"DNR?" Eleanor asked.

"Uh, yes, that means Do Not Resuscitate," the physician explained.

Eleanor jerked out of her daughter's arms. "Are you asking me whether I want to let my husband die?"

"No, Mrs. Leary, that's not exactly what we're trying to say."

"Who's 'we,' doctor? I only see you standing here asking me whether the next time my husband's heart stops I should just let him die. What kind of person would do that? What kind of wife would I be to stand here and tell you to instead of doing everything possible to save my husband, to restart his heart, that you just let him die? What kind of woman do you think I am, doctor?" By now, Eleanor was raging with tears streaming down her face.

"Mom, please." Lorain tried to grab hold of Eleanor's arm, but she jerked away once again.

"Look, Doctor Healshire," Eleanor stated matter-of-factly, "I don't know whether you believe in God, but I do. I'm a Christian. I ain't the perfect Christian, but I serve a perfect God. And my God is the author and the finisher. Not you, me, or anybody else is going to say when the end is for my husband. I don't care if his heart stops a hundred more times; if you can get it back to beating again, then by God, doctor, you better do it."

The doctor nodded his head in understanding. And he did understand. He dealt with these types of situations on a daily basis. But it was his job to provide the family of his patients with options. "Yes, ma'am, Mrs. Leary. We'll do everything we can." He turned to walk away.

"When will I be able to see him?" Eleanor asked before he could leave.

"Let us try to get him stable, and then I'll send a nurse out for you." The doctor gave Eleanor a reassuring smile, letting her know that her wishes would be granted. He was letting her know that he and his staff would do everything they could do to keep her husband alive . . . for as long as they could anyway.

Chapter Twenty-three

Things had gotten heated earlier that day in the conference room, so heated that both parties agreed to just see each another in court. It was obvious it would take a judge and a bailiff with a gun to keep the mother and the son, the daughter/sister, and the wife from strangling each other. Because that's just about what happened after Barnita took the liberty of answering her son's query.

After Blake asked his mother, "Why did you leave me? And why didn't you ever come back?" there was a moment of still, stiff, cold silence in the room.

In a *Lifetime* movie, this would have been the moment when the mother broke down with regret, giving her sad sap of a tale of how she felt Blake would have been better off without her. This would have been the part where the mother was overcome with emotion, realizing the error of her ways, then begged her son for forgiveness. This was the part when Blake would have broken down like the little boy he was when she'd left him and forgiven her, the two promising to make up for lost time. But that is not what happened.

Instead, a smooth, calm smirk eventually made its way onto Barnita's twisted lips before she spoke. "Iunknow." She shrugged as if she was answering a math problem in class. "I left you because I wanted to, and I didn't come back because . . . well . . . I guess because I didn't want to," Barnita had answered so heartlessly. It was a reply that infuriated Blake beyond measure.

"You low-down, selfish, gold-diggin' poor excuse for a human being, let alone a mother," Blake snarled through gritted teeth. "You should have done the world a favor and stayed gone; stayed put under the rock you slithered under all those years ago."

That's when Sharlita rose up out of her chair and began shouting out expletives toward Blake. She called Blake everything but a child of God. "Who do you think you are talking to my moms like that? I don't care how much money you and biggums here got." Sharlita nodded toward Paige. "She strolling up in here with you dressed in a Donna Karan suit, carrying a Prada bag with bangin' bling-bling rings while your mother is barely making ends meet."

"Hold on now, sweetheart." Now Paige stood. "My wedding ring set, yes, he bought, but the Donna Karan suit and the bag—all me, Boo. See, unlike you and your triflin' momma here, I don't have to run around suing people to get what I want in life. I gets mine on my own." Paige had no idea how long that ghetto seed had been being nurtured inside of her, but it fully bloomed today.

"Triflin'?" both Barnita and Sharlita spat.

"Oh, it's on and poppin' now!" Sharlita kicked off her shoes like she was Fantasia about to sing a song. She then started around the table, headed like a bull toward Paige.

Randall jumped up out of his seat and met Sharlita before she could reach Paige.

"Oh, let her go!" Paige shouted. "Please, let her go so she can put her hands on me, then let's see who's the defendant in a lawsuit."

"Baby, don't even stoop to their level," Blake said to his wife.

"Stoop?" Sharlita roared. "So you higher up than us? You think you better than us just because you got a little bit of ends? Well, we'll see who's better than who when this is all over." Sharlita looked at her mother. "Mom, sue the pants off of him." She then looked at Blake. "I was hoping, with us being brother and sister and all, that we could be cool. That you could put me on at your company or something so that I can be like you. You know, you be Puffy and I be like Li'l Kim." She then looked at Paige. "But I doubt that's possible with Piggy Smalls here."

Paige leaped over that table so quick and got a hold of Sharlita's weave, that no one saw it coming. Blake did manage to restrain his wife before she could do any real damage. But the damage had already been done as Paige held a handful of microbraids that she'd yanked out of Sharlita's head.

Paige couldn't erase the vision of looking down at her hand full of cheap, synthetic braids as she now sat at home thinking about it. "I'm sorry," Paige stated to her husband as she sat in the garden tub, bubbles surrounding her, with her arms wrapped around her knees. "I blew it. I might have ruined everything for you. Perhaps this is why I forgot about the first meeting; God didn't want me there. I should have just stayed out of it."

"No, it's not all your fault," Blake replied as he took the sponge and squeezed water down Paige's back. "I made a big stink about you being there, and I'm sorry. It was selfish of me."

Paige closed her eyes as the water drops drizzled down her back like honey glazing a ham. This was the Blake she knew and loved. This was the Blake she wanted to take up permanent residence in their home.

When Blake was on, he was on. It was that off switch she wished would deactivate itself forever.

"It's not selfish for a man to want his woman by his side," Paige begged to differ. "I'm supposed to be there for you, to have your back."

Blake chuckled. "And boy, oh boy, *did* you have my back." He began demonstrating Paige's earlier hand and arm motions. "I mean, the way you snatched that ghetto girl by her ghetto hair; that was—"

"Ghetto. That was *me* acting ghetto and shaming the Spirit man inside of me. I had no business putting my hands on that girl, no matter what she did or said." Paige looked over her shoulder into Blake's eyes. "No one has the right to put their hands on anyone." She hoped he was getting the message.

"Yeah, I guess you're right," Blake shrugged. "But sometimes folks deserve it."

Paige turned around again and leaned back against the tub. Perhaps both she and her husband had a point. Maybe sometimes she pushed Blake to the point of no-return, kind of like how Sharlita had done her. Paige had experienced firsthand how easy it was to set someone off. How could she look down on Blake for his actions when she herself was just as capable? Was God trying to tell her something, or was the devil trying to convince her of something? But she didn't want to dwell on that now. She wanted to soak up the tender, loving care her husband was showing her as he caressed her shoulders.

"Babe?" Blake stated.

"Yes," she replied, her eyes closed.

"I know I haven't really been myself lately. But this is rough for me right now. I'm trying to live up to my name at work, especially now that I've had media coverage. I'm trying to handle this lawsuit thing discreetly while at the same time try to keep our marriage intact. It's just hard for me sometimes, and sometimes I just lose it, you know?"

"Are you asking *me* if I know? The person who just lost it herself?" Paige certainly realized how easy it was for a person to just snap and do something they ordinarily wouldn't have. She'd done it, so that didn't make her any better than Blake for the times he'd snapped on her. She did not want to be the kind of person who threw stones while living in a glasshouse of her own.

"You did lose it, babe," Blake chuckled again.

Playfully splashing him Paige said, "Will you stop? It's not funny. I could have hurt that girl. What was she, a buck fifteen soaking wet compared to my—"

"Compared to your biggumness?" Blake laughed.

"Don't start," Paige teased. "You can get it up in this piece too. Besides, I lost another two pounds last week."

"I know, baby, I know. I'm just messing around with you."

"*Really* now?" Paige looked at her husband seductively. "Well, I can think of better ways for you to mess around with me."

Blake stared at his wife and shook his head. "My wife, the only woman I know who can take out a chick in one round and still have the energy to take care of her man."

"Is that what I do, take care of my man?" Paige asked.

Blake stared at her with eyes full of passion. "Yes, that's *exactly* what you do," he stated as he slowly leaned in toward his wife.

Paige puckered her lips, but before Blake could lay one on her, the doorbell rang.

"Are you serious?" Paige sighed. "Who in the world is ringing our bell this late, and without calling first?" Next came a loud pounding on the door.

"It must be an emergency." There was a worried look on Blake's face. "They knocking like the po-po." Paige had a look on her face that matched Blake's.

"I'll be right back," Blake said.

Paige sank back down in the tub as Blake exited the bathroom. She felt so awful about how she'd acted today. "God, I repent. Please forgive me," she prayed. "I know I grieved you today with my actions. I'm so sorry, and any punishment you deem fitting for me, I accept, God. But please, as in Psalm Fifty-one, 'have mercy upon me, O God, according to thy loving-kindness; according unto the multitude of thy tender mercies blot out my transgressions.'" Paige continued reciting Psalm Fifty-one. ". . . I sinned, and done this evil in thy sight: that thou mightest be justified when thou speakest, and be clear when thou judgest—"

"You can't go in there! She's in the tub, for Pete's sake." Blake's yelling interrupted Paige's prayer.

Startled, she stood up, climbed out of the tub, and grabbed a towel to wrap around her. And thank God she did that when she did, because the next thing she knew, the bathroom door flew open and behind Blake was a police officer.

"What's going on here?" Paige panicked. "What are you doing to my husband? Leave him alone." Once again, Paige was ready to go into protection mode. She wasn't sure, but she was certain this had to be what the streets meant by a "down chick; a ride-or-die chick," because that is just what she was willing to be when it came to her husband.

"Ma'am, we're not doing anything to your husband," the police officer spoke as another officer suddenly appeared behind them. "Are you Mrs. Paige Dickenson?"

"Yes, but what is—" Paige started.

"Then it's you we're here for," the police officer told her as he whipped out his handcuffs. "Paige Dickenson, you have the right to remain silent. Anything you say can and will be used against you . . ."

This had to be a nightmare Paige thought as the steel bracelets locked her wrists behind her back. The room was spinning. She could see the police officer's lips moving while her Miranda Rights. She could see Blake yelling at the officers something about at least allowing her to get dressed. The other officer appeared to be trying to settle both Blake and the first officer down. It was a mess. It was a nightmare, especially when Paige was ushered out of her home, barefoot, wearing nothing but a towel. At that moment, it surpassed just being a mess. It surpassed just being a nightmare. It was now officially a certified living hell.

Chapter Twenty-four

"So what time is this Justice supposed to be here anyway?" Mother Doreen asked Bethany as she sat down at the kitchen table with two cups of tea in hand. She placed one in front of Bethany, who was seated at the table. Then she took a sip from the other one. "And I still can't believe you're letting the child have a boy over for supper. Momma and Daddy would have never heard of such a thing when all of us were coming up. It didn't matter how many years apart us children were; the rules never changed. We were lucky if a boy could walk us home from school, stopping off at the malt shop for ice cream, let alone setting foot inside to break bread."

"Uh-huh, and that's exactly why we got mixed up with some of the boys we did back in the day," Bethany reasoned. "If Momma and Daddy had let us experience male-female relationships in high school, then we wouldn't have been so culture shocked once we were able to date. We wouldn't have latched on to just any ole everybody."

"Tuh, you the only one who dated everybody," Mother Doreen chuckled. "From what I hear, Pa was always chasing some boy out of your bedroom window with his shotgun."

"Oh, you think that's funny, huh? Well, you would have known firsthand if old Willie hadn't had your nose wide open," Bethany laughed.

Mother Doreen pointed. "Don't you go there, girl."

Bethany put her hands up in surrender. "Okay, okay. But you know what I'm saying. Anyway, Justice should be here around five. Sadie's coming straight home from school today. She's missing band practice and everything so that she can help out in the kitchen with dinner."

Mother Doreen couldn't hide the shocked expression on her face. "What? The child actually wants to *cook* for the young fellow? I need to take her back to New Day to teach those women a thing or two. Child, you should have heard 'em fussing one time when I suggested they do some cooking in order to get men folk involved in the Singles Ministry." Mother Doreen shook her head as she began to mock the women in the Singles Ministry. "I ain't cooking for no man unless he's my husband."

"Well, I guess they do have a point," Bethany reasoned.

"From the woman who fed her husband Beanie-Weenies and frozen dinners," Mother Doreen laughed.

"Stop it now," Bethany told her sister as she tried to hide her smile. "Uriah didn't marry me for my cooking. He married me because he loved me." The smile grew bigger as Bethany stared off.

Mother Doreen couldn't help but notice her baby sister's trip to La-La Land. "What you thinking about?"

Bethany coyly put her head down. "Nothing."

"That look on your face wasn't from thinking about nothing," Mother Doreen pressed. "You were thinking about you and Uriah, weren't you?"

Bethany's eyes watered as she nodded. She didn't want to speak because she didn't want her emotions to get the best of her.

"Oh, now, now." Mother Doreen slid out of her seat and went over to comfort her sister. "It's going to be all right," Mother Doreen assured Bethany as she rubbed her shoulders. "Y'all just going through right now, but trust in the Lord. He'll bring you out. You know that."

Tears fell from Bethany's eyes. "I can't even be mad at him, 'Reen," she sniffed. "I mean, I complained so much when our mortgage kept going up. I was worried we were gonna lose this house. Yet he was so bound and determined to do whatever he had to do to take care of us. But me, not only back then didn't I trust God the way I needed to, but I didn't trust my own husband either." Bethany allowed herself to collapse down on the table. "Oh, Sis, what did I do? What have I done?"

Mother Doreen squeezed her tighter. "Nothing that God can't fix. You didn't do nothing that God can't fix." Mother Doreen held Bethany for a moment before she spoke again. "Beth, can I ask you something?"

"Sure, sure," Bethany said, sitting upright and wiping her face.

"Are you still seeing, you know, Pastor Davidson?"

Bethany shook her head. "No. I haven't seen him since he left here."

Mother Doreen stopped rubbing Bethany's shoulders and made her way back over to her seat. "Do you *want* to see him?"

Bethany thought for a moment. She took a sip of her tea, then she thought for another moment. "You know what? I honestly haven't thought about the man. My mind has been too stayed on Uriah and this entire death-faking thing, and now him being back again. Then I have my new grandbaby . . . it's just so much. I mean, when I first saw Uriah that night he came home, I was stunned; shocked. I didn't really get the chance to examine how I felt about it at the moment because I was too riddled with shame. I mean, it wasn't much of a homecoming for him to find another man standing in his living room, hearing all those details. It just made me feel . . . it made me feel . . ."

"Convicted," Mother Doreen helped her find the right words.

Bethany once again nodded her head. "I hate to admit it, because I've tried to justify my actions for so long. I tried to blame it on love instead of just blaming the real guilty party—me."

Mother Doreen could finally exhale about the situation regarding her sister having an affair with Pastor Davidson. For months, Bethany had walked around as if she'd done no wrong. As if the entire world, including God, was supposed to understand her infidelity. Mother Doreen knew better though; she knew that until Bethany confessed her wrongdoing and asked for God's forgiveness, then she and Uriah could never really move on in their marriage.

"I know that was hard for you to confess," Mother Doreen told Bethany. "But now you have to repent to God and seek His forgiveness, then your husband's."

Bethany let out a chuckle. "It's funny, I can sit here and finally confess it to you, but I feel too ashamed to confess it to the two men who really need to hear it." Bethany wiped a lone tear, then looked up at Mother Doreen. "Come with?" Bethany asked her sister.

A confused look covered Mother Doreen's face. "Come with" is what Bethany used to say when she was younger and wanted to go "bye-bye" with Mother Doreen.

"Come where?" Mother Doreen asked.

"Come with me to the throne." Bethany extended her hand. "I'm sure God won't mind if I bring along a little company. I don't need you to pray for me or for my forgiveness. I know that's something that I need to do. I just need you there holding my hand. It's like when

I was younger and would do something wrong and Momma would make me tell Daddy what I did when he got home. I always wanted one of my sisters to come with me. I always needed one of my sisters." Bethany stared Mother Doreen in the eyes. "I need you, Sis. I've always needed you, and I'm so glad God sent you here to Kentucky. I appreciate you so much, and I appreciate everything you've done since coming here. And I mean, everything. I know a lot of times it didn't seem like I wanted you here, but that was because I wanted to do bad all by myself; I didn't want anyone around to witness it. But I don't know what I would have done had you not been by my side . . ."

"Uh-uh." Mother Doreen shook her index finger as if she was disciplining a child. "Who did I tell you them words are for?"

Bethany thought for a minute back to when she was in the hospital and what Mother Doreen had told her. "You said, 'Them are words for Jesus only.'"

"So you do listen." Mother Doreen winked.

"Yes, I really do, and I'm going to start listening more, to both you and God. But right now, I need Him to listen to me." And on that note, both Mother Doreen and Bethany bowed their heads while Bethany prayed to God. She repented for her sins and asked for God to forgive her, and just like that, He did. He didn't make her jump through any hoops, and He didn't tell her He'd forgive her based on any conditions. He just forgave her just like that . . . because He's God . . . and that's what He does.

Chapter Twenty-five

The ringing doorbell made Lorain jump up out of her sleep. She hadn't been sleeping that well to begin with. For the last twenty-four hours, she'd been at her mother's side next to Broady, who lay unresponsive in his hospital bed. In those twenty-four hours, they'd had to resuscitate him twice. Lorain knew better than anybody that playing God was not an option; that He was the author of life and death, but she could now understand why some families chose for their love one not to be resuscitated. At some point, it just seemed like outright cruelty—having all the nurses and doctors running to Broady's aid, sending those waves of electric shock through him in order to get his heart back beating.

Every time Lorain envisioned his poor body, it sent chills through her. Those visions now covered and replaced the previous visions she'd been having of Broady before. It was now those visions that kept her up at night. It was because of those visions of a man she could clearly see slipping away from life that had her praying for him. Yes, that's right. She was praying for the man who'd molested her as a child. The man who had turned her life upside down and was responsible for her making one of the worst decisions of her life—throwing their baby in the trash can only minutes after she was born.

So much was going through Lorain's head now, things opposite of what had been going through her head before. At first, she'd been worried about how she was going to tell her mother that she was one of Broady's victims. Now, she worried about how she'd be able to go on with life not telling her mother the truth. It was no longer one of her ultimate missions. Right now, her only mission was to see her mother through this thing and hopefully see her mother happy again. Telling her the truth at this point would only break her mother's heart. She was not going to be responsible for that. Her mother was going through enough.

As a matter of fact, Lorain figured that was probably her mother at the door. Some of the congregation of the church she and Broady were members of had been coming up to the hospital trying to convince Eleanor to go home and get some rest. Eleanor refused. Lorain knew it was because she didn't want to go back home without her husband. Her church family had probably finally convinced her to go home, only now she was at Lorain's door because she didn't want to be alone.

At one point in the past, Eleanor had been home alone, overweight and depressed for years, triggered by Lorain's father up and leaving them. Eleanor had eaten her way through misery, gaining pound after pound after pound, never once thinking that she had a chance for life after divorce. Lorain, on the other hand, was young. She began seeking the attention of men, finally sleeping her way through life with men: married, single, and one gay one . . . Well, he wasn't all the way gay, which is what he'd told Lorain when she caught him with one of his boy toys. "Bi-curious" was the word he'd used. Bi-curious mixed with a few shots of Hennessy, to be exact.

Nonetheless, eventually mother and daughter were able to pick up the pieces of their past and throw it out with the rest of the garbage in their life. Eleanor ended up getting bariatric surgery, and Lorain ended up getting an HIV scare that ultimately gave her a religious awakening. Eventually, both had been led to God, and it was He who was helping them clean up their lives. So for now, Lorain just wanted to put all her mess aside and be there for her mother.

Grabbing her robe and house slippers, Lorain hurried to the front door. As she approached it, the bell rang again, twice . . . back to back. Then a third time.

Tying her robe around her waist, Lorain proceeded to open the door. "Hold on, Mom. I'm coming . . ." Her words trailed off. She was shocked to see who stood at her door. She frantically unlocked the screen and opened the screen door. "Come on in here."

After her guest was inside, she relocked her door. "Unique, what are you doing here this late? How did you get here?" Lorain asked.

Unique didn't look like herself. She looked worn-out. Her shoulders were slumped. Her weave ponytail was lopsided. Her lipstick was smeared, and she stumbled trying to stand.

"Unique!" Lorain ran to her aid to catch her before she fell over. She still fell over, but onto the couch. "What's wrong?" Lorain looked Unique up and down. "Did someone do something to you? Did someone hurt you? Do we need to call the police?" With each question, Lorain's tone became more frantic. All she could think was that history was repeating itself; that Unique was right, she was part of a curse. Not the curse passed down from her foster mother, the one of having a bunch of kids with a bunch of different fathers. But the curse of being sexually abused. "Who did this to you,

Unique? You can tell me." Lorain had her hands rested on Unique's shoulders. That was, until Unique brushed them off her.

"No, ain't nobody done did nothing to me." Unique's words were slurred, and her head was bobbing on her neck like she was a Bobble head. "Nothing I ain't want them to do anyway, know what I'm saying?" Unique let out a laugh.

Now it was very apparent to Lorain what was going on here. Unique was drunk off her behind.

"Girl, you been drinking?" Lorain straight-out asked.

"I might have had a little somethin' somethin'," Unique admitted.

"Well, what you need now is some coffee," Lorain sniffed the air, "and a shower. Girl, have you been with a man?"

"What if I have? So what? So what if I have me a little drinky-drinky here and there. And what's wrong with a little male companionship? I'm stuck up in that house with nobody but my sister and all of our kids. Don't you think I need some 'me time' every now and then? What's wrong with me going out to make sure that a man still wants me? I just need to make sure of that every now and then, you know what I'm saying?" Unique gagged as if she was about to throw up but regained control.

"Yeah, I know exactly what you're saying," Lorain replied sympathetically, because she did. "But there's only one man that can validate you. I learned that the hard way. And that one man is God."

"Oh, here we go," Unique slurred, rolling her eyes up in her head. "Now you about to start preaching. Well, I don't need no preaching." Unique looked down as tears filled her eyes. "I need somebody to love me. To take care of me." She wiped the tears away, and then looked up with a mischievous grin on her face. "And one of my baby daddies just took care of me *real* good. Or should I say I took care of him?" She shrugged her shoulders. "I don't know. But either way it goes, I got this." She reached into her pocket and pulled out a wad of money.

"Oh, so you not only go out here and drink, but you tricking too," Lorain said. Her comment seemed to sober up Unique instantly.

"*What?* What did you say? Did you just call me a whore?" Unique asked, standing up, still with a slight wobble.

"If it walks like a duck and it talks like a duck . . ." Lorain smelled the air. "And if it smells like a—" She broke off her sentence, dodging Unique's swing. Lorain felt the wind behind Unique's blow and knew that if she hadn't ducked in time, Unique probably would have knocked her head off.

Missing her target, Unique did a full spin and fell backward, right into Lorain's arms. They both hit the floor. Unique struggled to turn around and at least get one lick off on Lorain, but Lorain managed to pin Unique's arms behind her back. The two lay squirming on the floor for what seemed like hours to Lorain. She made a mental note to break out her treadmill so that she could get her stamina up for the future.

"Get off me!" Unique yelled. "Get your dang on hands off me."

"*Dang on hands?*" Lorain repeated. "Shoot, you doing everything else you big enough to do. You might as well go ahead and curse too."

"Get off!" Unique spat as she squirmed, finally wearing herself down, both physically and mentally. The next thing she knew, she was crying, shoulders heaving up and down, in Lorain's arms.

"It's okay," Lorain whispered in her ear as she rocked her. "It's okay."

For a minute there, Unique seemed to be enjoying Lorain's loving and motherlike embrace. It appeared to be just what she needed, just what she'd been searching for. And sitting there holding Unique in her arms was like a dream come true for Lorain. Ever since she realized that Unique was the daughter she'd thrown away, she'd wanted to do nothing but just hold her in her arms and never let go. She'd prayed for that very moment. It looks like her prayers were coming true. But it was short-lived as Unique abruptly pushed away from Lorain's arms.

"I said get off of me," Unique fussed.

"It doesn't have to be this way, Unique," Lorain told her, rubbing her arm. "You don't always have to wear this hard exterior. You don't always have to fight."

Unique jerked away. "That's all I know how to do is fight. All anyone ever wants to do is fight. All my babies' daddies fight. The only time we ain't fighting is when we're sexing." She shot Lorain a glare. "Not tricking, just making each other feel good. That's how it is when you from where we from. Besides, it ain't nothing but the child support he owed me anyway."

"Yeah, but when you gotta sleep with your child's father in order to make him come up with money for your child to eat, then let's call it what it is."

"Okay, fine. Call it what it is. So you saying I'm a whore? Fine, I'll be a whore. What you gon' do? Run and tell Pastor so I get kicked out of my position from the Singles Ministry?"

"No, I'm just going to pray for you, daughter." This time when Lorain called Unique her daughter, she didn't mean it in the biological sense. She meant it in the spiritual sense.

"Stop it," Unique gritted through her teeth. "Stop calling me your daughter. You ain't none of my momma. I don't have a momma. My momma threw me in the trash, and the women who raised me only did it for a monthly check from the government, not because they loved me. Real love doesn't exist, so I take what I can get."

"Oh, baby girl, if you didn't believe in real love, then you can't possibly believe in God. God is love, Unique. Please listen to me when I tell you that. Please listen to me when I tell you that I'm not on the outside looking in at you making judgment. Little girl, I was you," Lorain said. She began to breath heavily while tears fell from her eyes. "I was that girl whose daddy left her when she was a little girl. I was that girl who spent the rest of her life trying to find that daddy kind of love that was void in my life. I slept with more men than Wilt Chamberlain did women. I slept with the married ones, the gay ones, the young ones, the old ones . . ." Lorain's words trailed off; her fleshly words. They were wiped out by the words which the Holy Spirit was now dictating to her.

"The old ones," Lorain continued. "In middle school, I slept with an older man. Thought I was doing something. Thought I was grown. Thought I was in a relationship." Lorain sniffed back some tears. "He showed me attention that I perceived as love. I perceived it as what I'd been seeking for the past few years. That wasn't it, though. So even after that, I spent years going from man to man. But not before I had ended up pregnant by that older man when I was in middle school."

Unique's ears were fully tuned in. Any high she'd had left was now gone.

"Yeah, that's right. I got pregnant by this man. Had a baby when I was thirteen. Thirteen! I didn't know what to do. I didn't tell anybody, not even my momma. I didn't have any girlfriends to tell because I never really got along with girls. Most of their mommas wouldn't allow them to hang out with me because I was *fast*." Lorain snickered. "So I had that baby all by myself on the cold, nasty, dirty floor in the bathroom stall of my school," Lorain cried. "And I didn't know what to do. I didn't know what to do with no baby. So I put it in my book bag."

Lorain was crying uncontrollably because this was the first time she'd ever vocalized what she'd done. "I put the baby in my book bag, and I walked out to the school dumpsters and threw the book bag into the trash."

Now it was Unique who was trying to comfort Lorain as she crawled over to her on the floor and rubbed her hand up and down Lorain's back.

"I threw my baby away and left, knowing it was going to die."

"You mean you let your baby die?" Unique said sadly.

"Yes." Lorain shook her head and wiped her runny nose. "That's what I thought for years; that the baby had died." Lorain looked up at Unique and stared at her with telling eyes. "But then I found out that the baby didn't die."

"Oh praise God!" Unique stated.

"Yes, I praise Him for that every day now."

"What happened to your baby?" Unique was so fix-ated on Lorain's story that not once did her thoughts jump outside the box and begin to piece their two life stories together.

"A man found the baby. I think he was a janitor at the school or something. Anyway, the baby was taken to the hospital. It was in all the newspapers and on the television stations. I remember sitting down after sup-per one day and watching the news with my mother. If I wasn't a Christian I would tell you all the names she called the woman who would throw her baby away like that. Little did she know she was talking about her own child. The little girl sitting next to her. I was so ashamed. I hurried up and changed the subject, talking loud over the news reporter so that my momma didn't have to hear all the details. So that I didn't have to hear all the details. I didn't watch the news for months after that. I could hardly live with myself."

"But you were so young. You didn't know any better. Besides, you said you were sleeping with a man, a grown man. He should have had to take some responsibility, right after he served his time in jail."

"Nobody would have seen it that way. That's why I've never told anyone." Lorain , still looking into Unique's eyes said, "Not until now."

"Don't worry. I won't tell your secret," Unique promised.

"Oh, but it's not a secret anymore. Not now. A secret is something you keep inside of you. Something that belongs to just you. Usually something that burns a hole through your very being. Once you tell even one person, it's not a secret anymore. I told you. So now it's not a secret anymore. It's a testimony."

There were a few seconds of silence. "Look, I'm sorry I came here tonight. It's just that I didn't want to go home and have my babies see me like this. And I didn't have anywhere else to go. So I had my oldest son's father drop me off here. But I can catch a cab home or something." Unique went to stand up.

"No." Lorain grabbed her by the arm. "You can stay. You don't have to leave. Besides, I'm not finished giving you my testimony yet."

"There's more?" Unique stayed put, never one to walk out on a juicy story.

"Yes," Lorain said, "there's more; more than you could have ever imagined . . ."

Chapter Twenty-six

"And again, Mr. Dickenson, we apologize for the actions of our overzealous arresting officer. He's a rooky. It was his first bust. I guess he'd watched *Training Day* one too many times." The police sergeant tried to make light of the situation with a little joke, but Blake wasn't laughing. He was embarrassed; humiliated. It was almost four o'clock in the morning, and he was tired; tired, embarrassed, and humiliated.

Even at first when Blake had thought only some of his neighbors had seen his wife being marched out of the house wearing nothing but a towel and handcuffs, he was mortified. But that wasn't enough. Someone had to record the entire episode with their cell phone and turn it over to the media. Now there was probably even a link of the footage on the Internet. The entire world could possibly see his wife half-naked. His real-estate accolades would be eaten alive by this story just like that. This was the type of stuff the world flocked to: drama . . . reality drama. People would care even less now about his cover story in the magazine.

"Anyway," the sergeant cleared his throat, "your wife should be out in just a few minutes. Can I get you anything while you wait?"

"Yes," Blake replied before answering sarcastically, "you can get my attorney on the phone."

"Not that I was eavesdropping or anything, but didn't you already call your attorney?"

"Yes, but that was for my wife," Blake stated. "Now I need to call an attorney for when I sue the pants off this place for dragging my wife out of the house buck-naked." Blake's tone was low, but menacing nonetheless. Then he pulled out his cell phone just to let the officer know that he didn't need their phone to make any calls. He'd just been forewarning the sergeant of his intentions.

"Where is she? Where's Paige," Tamarra inquired as she approached Blake.

"She was in a holding cell," Blake answered. "The good officer here . . ." he pointed at the sergeant, ". . . says she should be out in just a few minutes."

"I can't believe she's in jail."

"That makes two of us," Blake said as he took a seat. "By the way, thanks for coming."

"No worries," Tamarra replied. "Today had already been one of those days. I had a flat tire this morning. Some of my supplies that arrived today were put on back order, and then one of my employees didn't show up for a catering event. Now this! But at least this time, it's not about me." She replayed the last words she just said through her head. "I mean, not that I'm glad it's Paige in jail and not me. Although there is no way I'd ever want to go to jail. But I'd never want Paige to go to jail either . . ." Tamarra was glad when Paige came from around the corner. She was running out of formulas to clean up her words.

"Paige, honey!" Tamarra exclaimed, then ran over and gave her best friend the biggest hug she could muster up. That's the good thing about having a friend both in the church and outside of it. For some Christians, after they fellowship within the four walls, it ends there. But not for Paige and Tamarra. Even after Tamarra left New Day, she and Paige still remained just as close as ever, if not closer. It felt good for both of them knowing that their relationship was not based upon their attendance together in a building. "Are you okay?"

Wearing state-issued garb because that's all she had besides her towel, Paige returned Tamarra's hug. "Honestly, friend, I can't say that I am okay." It was evident that Paige was still a little shaken up, still in disbelief.

Tamarra could feel Paige trembling, so she held her tighter. "It's okay now. You're out here with us."

"I . . . I'd . . . I would rather die than ever go back to a place like that again." Paige could barely keep her voice from cracking up completely. "I was in there with criminals, Tamarra. *Real* criminals. Prostitutes, thieves, violent women. One woman still had blood all over her. I don't know if it was hers from where the police tried to take her down or the person's she'd assaulted." Paige began to cry and sniff.

"I'm here," Tamarra reminded her as she hugged her even tighter. "I'm here."

Blake watched as the two women embraced. He watched through the slit in his eyes before calling a time-out, stating it had been a long day and it was time for everyone to go home.

When Paige and Blake walked through their front door after leaving the jail and driving home, Paige wanted to kiss the ground. That's how good it felt for her to be home—like an astronaut returning to Earth. And she thought returning home after a week in Jamaica felt good. . . . "I can't tell you how good it—" Paige started before Blake abruptly cut her off.

"Oh, so *now* you want to talk to me? *Now* you want to acknowledge my presence?" he fumed.

"Babe, what—"

"What am I talking about?" he mocked sarcastically. "I'm talking about the fact that I had to do back flips, as well as threaten to sue the entire police force to get you out of there without first having to see a judge. And what do you do? You turn that corner and run right into Tamarra's arms; not *my* arms—your husband's— but some woman's."

Paige didn't feel like going there with Blake, not now. Not after feeling so violated with the cavity search inflicted upon her after she was booked. She couldn't dare put herself in a position to feel violated in her own home.

"I'm sorry, Blake," she simply stated before turning to go to her room. The next thing Paige felt was as though her arm were being ripped out of its socket. It felt like that because that is *exactly* what Blake did when he grabbed her and jerked her around to face him. A screeching yelp filled the air. It was so painful that Paige began to float in and out of consciousness. The next thing she remembered was doing ninety down the highway in the passenger seat of Blake's car, and then him guiding her into the ER.

Yes, she'd surmised properly earlier—this really was hell.

Chapter Twenty-seven

"How does it feel to have your house all to yourself now that Uriah is back at home with his family?" Mother Doreen asked Pastor Frey as she stood in his church office doorway with an armful of clean, folded towels.

"I kind of miss him," Pastor Frey admitted. "I enjoyed the company. But I believe a man's place is at home with his wife and family."

"Yeah, but after he turns himself in on Monday, let's just hope the courts believe that same thing." Mother Doreen looked down at the towels and, changing the subject, asked, "Since when did I become your unofficial aide?" She'd taken it upon herself to bring home and wash the little hand towels Pastor Frey used to wipe away his perspiration that sometimes formed when he was giving the Word.

"Well, nobody asked you to gather all the laundry around here and wash it," Pastor Frey told her in a playfully sarcastic tone.

"Humph! I didn't figure I had much of a choice when last Sunday you had to use tissue to wipe your forehead. The congregation didn't know whether to keep their eyes on Jesus or those pieces of tissue scraps on your face. Then there were those wondering if God had dropped manna from the sky and it landed on your face."

Pastor Frey couldn't help but laugh. "Woman, you are something else."

Mother Doreen blushed. "No, I'm just a woman; a woman doing the things she does for her m . . . a . . ." She caught herself before getting the "n" sound out. ". . . her man of God, you know, when the woman is a pastor's aide," Mother Doreen rambled.

Pastor Frey stood. "Nuh-uh, woman. You know that's not what you meant."

"Uh, I need to go put these towels up." Mother Doreen made an attempt to leave Pastor Frey's presence.

"Not before you say what you were really going to say." He had stopped Mother Doreen from walking away. Each of his hands now rested on her arms as he looked her in the eyes.

Mother Doreen tried to stop those batting eyes of hers, but they were on autopilot, just flapping away. "I don't know what you're talking about, Pastor."

"Don't play with me, woman." Pastor Frey was intense. "You know what you meant. You were going to say that you are a woman doing the things a woman does for her man."

Mother Doreen coyly looked down. She couldn't lie, especially not in the house of the Lord. Pastor Frey stood correct; that is exactly what she was going to say.

"Let's be real with each other for a moment," he continued. "You and I both know we've been spending a lot of time together." Pastor Frey paused for a minute. "And I've enjoyed every single minute of it. But what I want to know right here and right now is if you've been doing those things as a woman of God just helping her pastor out or—"

"Oh, so you're *my* pastor now?" Mother Doreen asked, knowing she'd not yet joined Living Word, Living Waters.

"Orrrr," Pastor Frey stretched over Mother Doreen's attempt to change the subject, "are you doing those things, spending time with me, as a woman—a woman taking interest in a man?"

Mother Doreen bent her head down so low, her face was nearly buried in the towels she held. She was hoping to bury the expression on her face, the one that showed her true emotions. The emotion wasn't solely embarrassment due to Pastor Frey putting her in a position to have to reveal her true feelings toward him. Not just that, but to reveal her feelings about him *to him*. The last man whose eyes she'd looked into and shared her feelings with was her late husband, Willie. And to do that with any other man, well, a piece of her felt like she'd be cheating on Willie.

Perhaps that's why ever since Willie's death, Mother Doreen had never thought twice about remarrying. She never thought twice about even having another relationship with a man, let alone remarrying. She figured that's why God had placed it in her spirit to start the Singles Ministry back at New Day. She felt it was God confirming that she'd be single the rest of her life. But Pastor Frey was stirring something up inside of her that she didn't know could be stirred up in an older woman like herself. She thought those senses and sensations had been buried with her Willie. Pastor Frey had resurrected them from the grave, and honestly, Mother Doreen didn't think she could pass up on this opportunity for love again.

"Okay, Pastor," Mother Doreen said with authority, "you wanna know what I'm really trying to say here?" Pastor Frey nodded. "Well, I like you, man. I like you a lot. And if I were your . . . woman . . . I wouldn't be ashamed about it."

At first Pastor Frey just stood there, still holding Mother Doreen's arms and still looking deeply in her eyes. She was feeling kind of awkward standing there.

She felt like she'd just told her new boyfriend that she loved him for the first time, and now she was waiting for him to say it back; only he couldn't get the words out.

Finally Pastor Frey spoke. "You don't know how it makes me feel right now to know that your feelings about me are mutual to how I feel about you."

Mother Doreen exhaled and smiled. Only Pastor Frey was still as serious as a heart attack.

"So what do we do about it, Pastor?" she asked.

"We seek God and let Him direct our paths." Now he smiled. "And prayerfully our paths will join. But until then . . ." Surprisingly, he leaned in and placed a nice, soft kiss on Mother Doreen's lips. It was one that sent sparks through both their veins. "I'll leave you with—"

Pastor Frey's final words were interrupted by someone clearing their throat and then saying, "Excuse me. I'm Bishop Klein."

"Bi-Bi-Bishop . . . *the* Bishop Klein?" Pastor Frey stuttered as he gave the larger-than-life man the once-over. Pastor Frey had only seen a picture of him, an outdated picture at that. He couldn't believe he was standing before the man himself, the man he'd only heard wonderful things about. He'd heard how he had whipped sister churches back in shape and kept others on the straight and narrow, but not once had he'd been assigned to Living Word since it started twelve years ago. Pastor Frey couldn't help but wonder what had now brought Bishop Klein their way. Perhaps he was just passing through. Perhaps.

"Oh, well, I don't mean to be rude," Pastor Frey stated. "Just a little surprised to see you here is all." He extended his hand. "I'm Pastor F—"

"I know exactly who you are, Pastor Frey," the bishop stated, totally ignoring the outstretched hand extended to him.

Pastor Frey allowed his hand to drop slowly. He then looked at Mother Doreen. "Oh, and this is—"

"Uh-huh, I'm quite clear on who she is as well," the bishop said in his deep baritone voice. His voice was even larger than his persona. If anyone was to ever make a movie and needed the voice of God, this is the voice they would choose.

"So, what brings you by?" Pastor Frey asked, failing miserably at his attempt to hide his nervousness.

"Actually, Pastor, I've been in town for a bit now," the bishop informed him.

"Really?" Pastor Frey was surprised. "How could I not have noticed you?" He chuckled. Bishop didn't. Neither did Mother Doreen.

"Anyway, I've seen enough," Bishop Klein continued. "Actually, after what I just witnessed, I think it's safe to say that I've seen *more* than enough." He looked from Mother Doreen to Pastor Frey. "Pastor Frey, we need to talk."

Chapter Twenty-eight

Lorain sat in Broady's hospital room next to her mother. In just the past few days it looked as though her mother had lost more weight than when she'd had the bariatric surgery. Getting her to leave her husband's side was not an option. Getting her to go down to the cafeteria to grab a bite had been an unsuccessful task as well. The salad Lorain had carried in from a local deli two hours ago was dry and wilted. Eleanor had picked at it, but never once took a bite.

"Mom, you really need to eat something," Lorain said to her mother.

"I'll eat when my husband eats," Lorain told her only child.

"Come on, Mom. It's been four days. Please eat something, or I'll be up here visiting Broady *and* you."

Eleanor looked away from a near lifeless Broady and into her daughter's eyes. "Why are you here anyway?"

Lorain was shocked by her mother's ice-cold tone. "Wha . . . what do you mean, Moth—"

"Just what I said," Eleanor spat. She turned her body toward Lorain. "You didn't even like him. You've been jealous of the man ever since the day you met him. Don't think just because I didn't say anything that I didn't notice the look in your eyes that first day you met him. It was that day he came to my house for dinner. The day you played sick and ran off like Snow White at the ball."

"It's Cinderella, Ma," Lorain said in a hushed tone.

"Huh?" Eleanor snapped.

"It was Cinderella who ran off away from the prince at the ball. Snow White ate the poison apple and . . ." Lorain's words trailed off once she saw her mother could really care less about the technical details of a couple of Disney princesses.

"You know what I mean," Eleanor said, rolling her eyes and turning her attention back to Broady. "You know, Broady didn't have a regular heart attack." She rested her hand atop of Broady's, which were folded across his chest. "His heart broke."

"I guess you could say that," Lorain agreed. "When your heart stops functioning right, I suppose one could say it is broken—"

"No, I mean it *really* broke." Eleanor was defensive. "The doctors said it's called Broken Heart Syndrome. That's what gave Broady his heart attack. They said with a classic heart attack, a blood vessel that feeds the heart muscle is blocked. The heart muscle is rendered helpless and can't pump blood through the body. But with Broken Heart Syndrome, the damage comes from a surge of chemicals released by a strong emotion."

"Huh? What?" Lorain began to get nervous and fidgety. "A strong emotion? Like what?"

"Like anger, sadness, or fear even," Eleanor answered so technically, as if she'd memorized word-for-word the report the doctors had given her. For a moment there, Lorain felt as though she was listening to someone with a Ph.D. explain Broady's condition to her.

Once again, Eleanor turned and faced her daughter. "So let's not dance around the giraffe in the room any longer."

"Elephant," Lorain said with eyes cast down.

"Huh?"

"It's elephant in the ro—never mind." Heavy silence blanketed the room.

"Well?" Eleanor almost shouted, causing Lorain to jump in her seat.

"Well, what?"

"Well, what did you say to my husband that broke his heart?"

This was all too much for Lorain as the room started spinning. Technically, the room wasn't spinning, but her mind was. Yes, this was all too much. She was hoping that her mother's concerns would be so fixated on Broady that she wouldn't even be worried about why Broady had been at Lorain's in the first place, what they had been talking about when she arrived at the condo. Why did her mother have to bring it up? If she told her about Broady, then she'd have to tell her about Unique. Wasn't that too much for her mother to handle all at once? She didn't want the shock of it all to land her mother in the empty bed across the room from Broady's. She didn't want to be responsible for causing her mother that broken heart syndrome stuff, her death certificate reading: "Cause of Death: Viola Lorain Waterson."

A glaring light bulb went off in Lorain's head. That was it. *Viola Lorain Waterson*. It was those words that had landed Broady in that hospital bed. The light bulb, still flickering, shone its light on the day Eleanor had stormed into Lorain's house.

"Viola Lorain Waterson!" Eleanor had shouted. *"My only daughter; my only child . . ."*

As an adult, Broady had only been introduced to and knew his wife's daughter as Lorain. As a young girl back in middle school, he knew her as Viola. And that last name. He'd probably assumed, since she wasn't married or anything, that she carried the same last name as her mother; Simpson. Eleanor's maiden name was Simpson. She'd abandoned the last name of Waterson after the divorce from Lorain's father. It all made sense now.

Lorain looked over at Broady. "He really didn't know who I was," she mumbled under her breath.

"Who? What are you talking about? Don't try to change the subject. You answer me what I asked you, girl. Why was my husband at your house? And more so, why were you in his arms like some damsel in distress?" Eleanor sneered at Lorain. "Wait a minute. You were jealous all right, you were jealous of *me*. You wanted my husband. My own daughter wanted my husband!"

Lorain had almost forgotten that her mother was there . . . waiting. Waiting on answers. Answers that Lorain now had. There were so many answers now. So many pieces to the puzzle. Broady . . . Unique . . . the connection . . . the final fit. What had once been a bunch of scrambled pieces now looked just like the completed picture on a puzzle box; what it's suppose to represent when it's been put together correctly. Was now really the time to share the picture with her mother? Wasn't it all just too much, too much for Lorain to share with her mother? Yes, it was. Lorain knew this because it was all still too much for her.

It was just two days ago when Lorain had sat on her living-room floor and told Unique who she really was— that she was the horrible witch of a mother that Unique had hated all her life. The mother who had thrown her away like trash and left her for dead. Lorain had hoped— no, she had pictured, envisioned, and imagined a thousand times since learning that her baby was alive—how the reunion might take place. But nothing she had thought up in her head came close to Unique's reaction.

Just a few minutes before telling Unique the truth, Lorain had urged her to curse since she appeared to be doing every other work of evil, like drinking and fornicating. Unique finally did take her up on the offer by calling her every curse word she could think of. She cursed Lorain all the way to her sister's house. Not riding in the passenger seat of Lorain's car though. She stormed down the sidewalk while Lorain drove slowly next to her, trying to convince her to get in the car so that they could talk things out.

"Talk things out?" Unique had shouted. "What's left to talk about? *You* are the trifling, no-good whore of a tramp who didn't have a problem spreading her legs to make me, but couldn't bother to raise me."

The words didn't even anger Lorain. She deserved them, and much more. What she had done all those years ago was heinous and incomprehensible. She felt as though she even deserved the wad of spit Unique shot in her face the moment she'd let the words, "I'm your birth mother," escape her lips. She felt Unique needed to get it all out. Holding it inside wouldn't do anything but make it worse. Lorain knew that from personal experience. She'd held in so many secrets for so long. The one she'd finally shared with Unique was just the tip of the iceberg and it felt so good letting it go. Now it was time to let another secret go.

Lorain looked up into her mother's eyes. It was time for Lorain to introduce her mother to the giraffe in the room.

Chapter Twenty-nine

"I have to admit, Sister Paige, I was surprised when Pastor told me that you wanted to meet with me," Nita said as she sat next to Paige in the church sanctuary. They were the only two in the sanctuary, but not in the church. The pastor and the church secretary were back in their offices. The choir had just departed from their Saturday morning rehearsal.

"Uh, I know, I . . ." Paige's words trailed off. She felt so humiliated and so embarrassed. Right now, her throat felt dry as she nibbled on the crow she felt she'd been served up. "Sister Nita," she managed to get out, "I know you've only been trying to help me. And I know I haven't been the nicest person in the world to you. But right now, I'm . . . sorry. And right now . . . I need your help." Paige couldn't believe she was sitting there crying.

At first she didn't know if she was crying because of how bad she'd been treating Nita or how bad things were getting with her and Blake. She was out of excuses for that man. The other day when she sat in the hospital getting her arm placed back in its socket, wrapped, and put in a sling, she didn't want to make excuses for him; she wanted to hurt him back. She'd envisioned the next time him putting his hands on her she'd go to jail for real: arraignment, trial, and sentencing—probably getting life for premeditated murder in the first degree. It was as if everything bad that could happen as

a result of escalated violence in their home showed itself to Paige's inner eye. That's not the life she wanted.
That's not the life she'd intended when she said "I do"
to Blake.

On the drive from the hospital back to their home,
Paige had told herself that she was going to pack a
bag and go stay with Tamarra. But if she showed up
at Tamarra's doorstep in the middle of the night with
her arm in a sling, then she'd have to tell her why. She
didn't want Tamarra to see her like that. And although
she'd been devastated when Tamarra decided to leave
New Day, she was now glad that she no longer attended. That way, she didn't have to worry about Tamarra
seeing her injury at church.

Even though Tamarra and Paige talked quite a bit,
they didn't see each other a great deal. Tamarra's catering business was on fire, and so was her love for the
Lord. It was as if she'd fallen in love with Jesus all over
again and spent every minute she could in Him . . . in
the Word. Tamarra and Jesus were just like a couple
courting. Paige had been wrapped up in Blake, trying
to keep him happy and from losing it. And with all of
these thoughts going through her head, one person
popped up just as clear as day. And now she was sitting
in the church right next to that person.

"I accept your apology, Sister Paige," Nita told her.
"But I also understand."

"I was mad at myself, not you," Paige confessed. "I
was mad at myself because I could see where things
were going between Blake and me, but I didn't want
to face the truth. So I kicked truth under the rug and
walked over it. But then, here you come with your
broom and dustpan to sweep it up."

Both Paige and Nita chuckled at the analogy.

Paige turned to Nita. "So, how did it . . . you know . . .
the abuse . . . start between you and your husband?"

"Believe it or not, everything was fine while we were dating." Nita smiled as if recollecting back to the good times she'd shared with her ex-husband. "And our wedding, it was to die for; a true fairytale wedding. Our honeymoon was only two days long, but it was beautiful. We just flew to Chicago, 'bout an hour flight, and stayed in a really nice hotel. We got room service, spa treatments, carriage rides; the works. Those were two of the best days of my life." Now Nita's smile was replaced with a blank stare. "And it was the last two days of peace I can remember with him."

Nita paused for a moment, and then swallowed hard.

"You don't have to tell me if you don't want—"

"Oh, but I do have to tell you," Nita was quick to say. "I have to, and I want to." She turned and looked at Paige. "My testimony is my ministry."

"Okay," Paige said, relieved that Nita decided to continue. It wasn't that misery loved company; it was just that Paige needed to know that she wasn't the only one who'd gone through something like this. Not only that, but she needed to know that someone had made it out . . . alive. She knew the statistics. She knew that some abused women were eventually murdered by their partner. She knew that the abuse oftentimes started off verbal, that possessiveness was involved, that it turned to minor hits and jerks, but then escalated to something beyond control. She didn't want the kind of testimony Nita had. She wanted her own, of how God turned her marriage around before it could get to all that. But she needed both God and His vessels to help her achieve that testimony. And the way she saw it, Nita was one of His earthly vessels.

"Yep, two days of peace was all I ever had while married to that man," Nita told Paige. "It actually started the night we returned from our honeymoon.

His luggage didn't make it on the plane, so we had to go to the airline's baggage office at the airport. When the lady asked him to describe his suitcase, he gave her the standard description that a million other folks gave: black, medium size." She shook her head. "I'd told him to tie a bandanna or something around the handle because his suitcase looked like everyone else's and that someone might accidentally mistake his for theirs. When the lady at the office typed in a few things, she noted that his bag had, in fact, been placed on the plane. She went on to explain the likelihood that someone else had grabbed it, thinking that it was theirs and would hopefully return it.

"'See, I told you that you should have put a bandanna on it,' I said quietly to him. I knew something like this was going to happen." Nita sighed. "He didn't say anything at the moment, but if looks could kill . . . Anyway, we drove home. I tried to make small talk the entire way, but he wouldn't engage me. Then the minute we walked through the front door, BAM!" Nita made a smack on her hand that caused Paige to jump. "That's when it started. That was the first time he ever hit me. And he was screaming at me about how I disrespected him and made him look stupid in front of that woman and how it better not ever happen again."

"What did you do?" This was what Paige really wanted to know. Because whatever Nita did, she'd made up her mind that she'd do just the opposite. She did not want to experience what Nita had gone through. "What did you do after he hit you the first time?"

Nita looked at Paige and simply stated, "I stayed."

Chapter Thirty

Mother Doreen and Pastor Frey had been sitting at the restaurant table for half an hour. Their breakfast sat before them on top of the paper place mats that read "The Friendly Diner." Mother Doreen loved this place. It reminded her of the Family Café back in Malvonia.

Mother Doreen could count on one hand how many words she and Pastor Frey had spoken outside of ordering their meals. Although she had a gift of discernment, it didn't even take all that to see that something was going on with Pastor Frey. But enough had been enough. Watching him gobble down his food just to keep his mouth full so that he wouldn't have to talk to her was driving her crazy.

"Well?" Mother Doreen finally said, dropping her fork on her plate.

Pastor Frey looked up at her from his breakfast platter and shrugged. "Well, what?" He then turned his attention back to his mound of scrambled eggs and shoveled a forkful into his mouth.

"Well, what did he say?"

"He who?" Mother Doreen could barely make out the words that had squeezed around the eggs with cheese.

"The bishop," she said, trying to hide her frustration. "Obviously, whatever it was that he said to you the other day has really got a hold of your mind. Because trust me, your mind is certainly not here with me."

Pastor Frey stopped eating, the fork covered with hash browns paused midway to his mouth. Mother Doreen was right. His mind was not with her. Seems as though his mind had never really been with her from the time they'd met at the restaurant. He looked up at her, the woman who God had blessed him to be able to court. He looked at her like he was tired, though. Not tired of her. He was just tired of the games, tired of the secrets, and tired of the lies. It was the secrets, games, and lies that had prevented him from fully getting to know her better, sooner, in the first place.

He'd been so busy living two lives. On one hand, he'd truly been trying to be God's servant as the assistant pastor to his pastor, mentor, and friend, Pastor Davidson. On the other hand, he'd truly been trying to be too much of a friend to Pastor Davidson by covering up his affair with Bethany. Then, if he'd had a third hand, it would have been the fact that he'd been both attracted to and interested in Mother Doreen's spirit and was trying to see if she felt the same about him. Well, she had. And once they were able to focus on something other than Pastor Davidson and Bethany, they found the time to admit as much to each another, in hopes that next they could explore wherever it was the Lord wanted to take them. But now, it appeared as though there was still another chapter to the book they'd thought they closed concerning Pastor Davidson and Bethany. An epilogue, so to speak.

As far as Mother Doreen knew, all of that had been put out in the open, at least between the two families, anyway. The church body heard whispers and rumors. No one had anything concrete, though. Pastor Frey had tried to urge Pastor Davidson to go before the church and tell the truth to his congregation members, but he hadn't even told the truth to his wife yet, so he refused.

But whispers and rumors have always been the kindling in both the church and the world to cause people to form judgment. To cause people to turn their backs on someone. That had been the case with Pastor Davidson. So the congregation began to turn their back on him before he ever came forth with the truth.

But not Pastor Frey. No more than he'd want God to turn His back on him whenever he fell short of the glory, he'd refused to turn his back on his friend. So he continued, to some degree, covering for Pastor Davidson, but now, it could possibly cause him his position at the church.

"He wanted to talk to me about Pastor Davidson," Pastor Frey admitted to Mother Doreen.

"What about him? I mean, what's left to tell? He fell from grace, ungracefully, I might add." Mother Doreen lifted a forkful of food into her mouth. "So he stepped down. No need for the bishop to show up now. It's not like they need to come kick him out. He walked away on his own."

"He wanted to talk to me about Pastor Davidson and your sister . . . Bethany." Pastor Frey was more specific.

Still, Mother Doreen couldn't see why that would have Pastor Frey all distracted. "So what?" Once again she shrugged. "That's what's wrong with church folk versus Christian folk. See, Christian folk know how to forgive and move on. Church folk, like one of the apostles back home is known to say, play too much. And he ain't lying. Church folk like to keep things going. I mean, it's *old* news. Tell the bishop and whoever else to let it go and let God. And more importantly, let you do what God has called you to do without them coming here and butting their noses in your business."

After that long speech in support of Pastor Frey, all he could say was, "Not really." Now he looked away from Mother Doreen, as if he couldn't bear to face her.

Mother Doreen stopped chewing although she had food in her mouth. She sensed everything wasn't everything. Something, a piece from the puzzle, was missing; stolen even, and now the thief was about to return it. That thief being Pastor Frey. "What do you mean 'not really'? I was there that day in the sanctuary, the day Pastor Davidson said he'd be stepping down for a few months and asked you to be in charge of things."

"True. I mean, both you and I know why he stepped down, but the heads didn't know. Not everything."

And there Mother Doreen had it; confirmation that everything wasn't everything. "What do you mean 'the heads didn't know'?" she asked, pushing her plate away. All of a sudden she didn't feel like eating anymore. "Didn't you two have to tell them what was going on? Didn't they have to approve everything?"

"Well, yes and no," Pastor Frey admitted, now pushing his plate away as well. "We told them Davidson would be stepping down, but we didn't exactly tell them why."

"Why not? That's like lying by omission; omitting the truth is lying."

"Pastor Davidson just wanted to get through it on his own . . . and with God. We figured he'd only be absent two or three months. As you know, that first month was okay. He kept attending Living Word, but then there was all that gossiping, whispers, and rumors. And then Bethany and the kids stopped coming, which, in some folks' eyes, confirmed the gossip, whispers, and rumors. I think the kids might have told some of their friends at church some things, and then it just escalated from there."

"Oh, don't you try to blame my niece and nephew." Mother Doreen got defensive. "Pastor Davidson was a grown man in leadership. My sister was a grown woman. Those two made the bad choices they made."

Pastor Frey put his hands up in defense in an effort to calm Mother Doreen down. "Now, I'm not trying to blame your kin. I'm just saying that apparently all the gossip and whispering got back to the heads. That's why they sent Bishop Klein, to see what was really going on, to see if the secret sex scandal going on in Living Word, Living Waters was true. And then, of course, Bishop sees me planting one on you right there in my church office." Pastor Frey put his head down in shame.

Mother Doreen just sat there. She closed her eyes as her head slightly moved from left to right. "You didn't do it. God gave you the opportunity to right your wrong," Mother Doreen started, "but instead, you just put on your robe like it was a Superman cape and mounted the pulpit like you were here to save the world. Never mind all that was at stake by you just being honest about everything. What? Were you afraid that if you told the truth they'd take your cape and throw both you and Pastor Davidson out there on your butts? Then you wouldn't be able to supposedly save the world from evil—"

"I was there to save the world!" Pastor Frey stood as he shouted the words. "I'm here to save this world from the evil that walks the Earth seeking whom it can devour. I'm here to save the world from hell and damnation. I'm here to save the world's souls. Do you know how many souls the words I have delivered have saved in these last few months?" Once Pastor Frey realized that his abruptness had startled Mother Doreen and that he had the attention of everyone in the restaurant, he slowly sat in his seat.

After a pause, he spoke again. "I'm sorry. I didn't mean to get so upset. It's just that in spite of what you think and what things look like, I love the Lord. I love God with all my heart."

"But your love and your loyalty to man just keeps getting in the way of your love for God, huh?" Mother Doreen felt no pity. "Do you honor Pastor Davidson so much that you'd compromise the honor of God and His Word? Do you?"

Pastor Frey was silent as he thought about the words he was about to say. "I love no one before God."

"But yet, somehow, you're still under that man's thumb, looking out for *his* best interest while compromising your own walk with Christ. You could have told the truth, Wallie." This was the first time Mother Doreen had ever called Pastor Wallace Frey by the nickname she secretly called him in her mind.

"Wallie" was also the name that only his late wife had called him. He'd once told God in prayer that if God wanted him to have another wife, give him a sign and have her call him by that name. Mother Doreen had no idea of the confirmation that had just rolled off her tongue.

Pastor Frey always knew there was something special about Mother Doreen. She was everything he could ever want in a wife, in a first lady, as he knew in his spirit he'd been called to lead a church. And he had been leading the church, and now, Mother Doreen had jumped right in and started helping him. She was his helpmate. This was the woman he was going to marry . . . just as soon as he divorced the devil.

"You could have admitted your part in all of this," Mother Doreen told him. "And you could have trusted that if this was the position God had for you in the kingdom, leading the congregation at Living Word, that He would have moved the heavens and earth for you to do so. God would have touched Bishop's and whoever else's heart that has any say-so to forgive you. He would have given them the eyes to see that you were the chosen one to lead the church."

"But then it would have been as though I were throwing Pastor Davidson under the bus in order to take over his position," Pastor Frey reasoned.

Mother Doreen couldn't believe her ears. After all that had been said and done, Pastor Frey was *still* set on covering for his former pastor. She wiped her mouth with her napkin and with teary eyes stated, "It's time for me to go." Mother Doreen stood.

"Wait, I'll walk you to your car." Pastor Frey pulled out his wallet to leave some cash on the table for their breakfast.

"No." Mother Doreen held up her hand to halt him. "It's time for me to go back to Malvonia." She picked up her purse and turned to walk away as she whispered the words, "Good-bye, Wallie."

Chapter Thirty-one

"Code Blue!" the nurse shouted after entering Broady's hospital room as a result of Eleanor's panicking shouts and cries.

Other nurses and hospital staff began to run in the room in droves.

Lorain was trying her best to calm Eleanor down, but the moment Eleanor had heard the machine beep and saw the flat lines on the monitor, she lost it.

"There's something I need to tell you about—" Those were the only words Lorain had gotten out of her mouth. She'd been all set, all prepared to tell her mother the truth about the man she married; the truth about the man she married and her daughter. But the truth never even had a chance to escape her lips. The machine had interrupted her, almost deliberately.

Nurses and doctors came running from every direction, and there Lorain and Eleanor stood in the middle of it all. It was like they were caught up in a tornado.

"We're going to have to ask you two to leave the room," one of the nurses ordered.

Eleanor was frozen stiff.

"You're going to have to go wait out in the lobby," a second nurse stated.

Eleanor was still frozen, so Lorain had to guide her out of the room as if she were a mannequin in a department store. They remained in the waiting room for what seemed like forever. It was forty-two minutes. Well,

actually forty-one minutes and fifty-eight seconds. Eleanor had stood. Only Lorain sat. But as Doctor Healshire
made his way toward them, in slow motion it seemed,
both women stood. His lips moved. There was no sound,
but it was evident by the expression on his face what he
was saying.

All of a sudden there was sound, and the sound was
Eleanor crying out. She was crying out in pain, so much
pain that the yelp, the screech mirrored that of the one
Lorain had let loose that day in the girl's bathroom
years ago in middle school. It sounded like a rabbit's
cry out, but it was a woman's cry. It was the same cry
that so many women could relate to; could understand.
It was the cry of a woman in pain. The pain came from
loss; loss of a loved one, loss of innocence. Loss of
peace of mind. It was the cry of a woman who'd been
beaten, abused, molested, raped, and abandoned. It
was the cry of a woman who had lost her child, had to
bury her child. It was the cry of a woman who'd been
misled, mistreated, and misused. It was the cry of a
woman evicted from her apartment, having to take her
babies to a shelter, or to a friend's couch, or even to a
friend's basement . . . or on the streets. It was the cry of
a woman being delivered from the memory of some of
the things she used to do to eat, to pay the bills, to feed
her family, or to get her next high . . . or to get her baby
daddy to give her money for the kids. No matter the
woman, it was the same cry. It was a secret language
that only another woman could understand. Lorain
understood. She understood the pain. Although it was
a different kind than that of her pain, she understood.
She understood her mother's pain.

It was a secret language; a woman's cry.

Chapter Thirty-two

Paige sat on her living-room couch trembling in tears. She wasn't sure if Nita's testimony had helped her or hurt her more. Help in the sense that she needed to hear one of the worst-case scenarios possible when it came to domestic violence; enough to make her do something about it other than make poor excuses for her husband or hope that things get better. Hurt in the sense that now her heart was hurting, aching over a decision she might have to make, a decision she didn't want to have to make. She'd said going into her meeting with Nita that she was going to do just the opposite of what Nita had done in her abusive relationship. Well, Nita said she stayed in it. Did that mean that Paige needed to get out of it? Did that mean that she needed to leave her husband? And she asked Nita just that. That was a decision Nita refused to make for Paige, but she did give her something to think about.

"Sister Nita, are you saying that I should get a divorce from Blake?" Paige had asked her. "The Bible says that God hates divorce."

Nita shook her head. "No, I'm not saying you should get a divorce, but need I also remind you that it says in Malachi, chapter two, verse sixteen, that '. . . For the Lord, the God of Israel, saith that he hateth putting away: for one covereth violence with his garment, saith the Lord of hosts: therefore take heed to your spirit, that ye deal not treacherously.' Basically, God is saying

He hates a man covering himself with violence. God hates what your husband is doing to you," Nita told Paige, and then continued with, "First Corinthians, chapter seven, verse fifteen, says, 'But if the unbelieving depart, let him depart. A brother or a sister is not under bondage in such cases: but God hath called us to peace.' In other words, God is saying that a man or woman should not be bound in such circumstances; God has called us to live in peace."

As Nita spoke to her in the sanctuary, an internal struggle raged inside of Paige's head. The same internal struggle that was going on inside of her now as she sat on her couch. Did God want her to subject herself to Blake's abusive treatment? Would He want any of His daughters subjected to such abuse and harm? But what if she did leave? That would probably set Blake off even worse. He'd probably come after her and hurt her and anybody who tried to help her.

Nita had offered Paige her couch if she ever felt she needed to get away, but Paige couldn't see putting the poor woman in a position to get hurt by someone else's husband. Not after all the hurt her own husband had put her through. But what really surprised Paige was when she declined Nita's offer. She'd expressed the fact that she loved her husband and couldn't imagine ever being apart from him no matter what. Nita didn't think she was stupid. Paige felt bad because way back when she'd heard about the years of abuse Nita had suffered, the first thought that had come to her mind was, *She's stupid for staying that long. Her stupidity played a part in the death of her own children.*

Paige never thought she'd see the day where she felt so stupid. But Nita didn't make her feel stupid. And on top of that, Nita believed her. Nita believed her when she told her of the verbal insults Blake spun at her.

Nita believed her when she told her of the bruises she'd endured at the hands of Blake, and that Blake was responsible for her arm being in the sling. Paige might have lost a few pounds and went down a size or two, but she was still bigger than Blake. Some might believe that there was no way he could abuse her and get away with it as big as she was. But Nita had believed her.

"I hope you don't mind if I share our conversation with Pastor," Nita had told Paige. "As the shepherd of this house and our spiritual leader, Pastor needs to protect the sheep. And maybe Pastor or myself as individuals can't fully help, but together, we can at least make any necessary referrals."

Nita saw the skepticism reveal itself across Paige's face. "Don't worry, it's not like we are going to put you on blast to the congregation or anything. Trust me, you have my complete confidentiality when it comes to that. And I'm sure I speak for Pastor as well. But we won't use confidentiality as an excuse not to seek help for you. We won't use confidentiality as a means not to keep you safe." Nita was firm. Paige was confused.

Placing her hand atop of Paige's, Sister Nita said, "Look, I know you don't feel like Blake would ever do anything to the extremes of what my ex-husband did to me, but let it be known, you are still in danger of being hurt. Your arm being in a sling is confirmation. This is just the tip of the iceberg, Sister Paige."

Looking down at her arm now, Paige knew Nita was right. Paige had, at first, minimized the painful death grips and whacks Blake had subjected her arms and hands to, and now it had escalated to this: a sling.

"God, if you don't step in now and direct my path, I don't know what I'm going to do," Paige said as she sat on the couch holding her injured arm.

The sound of the garage door opening sent her heart racing. Blake was home. Paige never imagined the day fear would race through her body at the arrival of her husband to their abode. She'd imagined her heart racing, but for all the right reasons; her heart eager and anticipating, after being away from him all day, to be in his presence.

"It's done," was what Blake said. Paige could feel his presence standing behind her as she sat on the couch. "It's done and over. I gave her what she wanted. We can move on with our lives now."

Paige slowly turned around. "What do you mean it's over? What's done?"

"My mother. I had my attorney call her attorney up and settle."

Paige stood up. *"What?* You mean you *paid* that woman off? But she didn't deserve it."

"I just couldn't do it. I just couldn't have that hanging over my head any longer. I was so angry and stressed out by the pending trial. The continuances, testimonies, being in the same room with her. I couldn't do it. Not to mention having to relive the day she left me." Blake walked over toward Paige. "And look what it's doing to me. Look what it's making me do to you." He looked down at her arm. "When my mother left me, it didn't destroy me or my father. I couldn't allow that woman to come back into my life after all these years and destroy me now. You are my now. You are my tomorrow. She's yesterday; the past. Besides, it's just money. I can make it all back. Just give me a year; six months with God's favor."

"But that woman—now she's going to have it made in the shade." Paige was sick to her stomach at the fact that Blake was paying off that frivolous lawsuit provoked by greed. Why did that stupid magazine have to broadcast his business like that? Had he not been featured in that magazine, the woman would have never looked him up; that is, unless she got sick and needed him to donate a kidney to her something. She'd have just the guts and nerve to ask him for it too. And if he declined, she'd probably sue him for it.

"That woman, as much as I don't want to admit it, is my mother. The Bible says that a child is to honor his mother and father. She was also my father's wife. They never divorced. Legally, she was entitled to something. And she did give birth to me. She only took care of me for three years of my life, not counting my nine months in her womb, but she was good to me and Dad when she was there. I don't remember a whole lot, but I remember what Dad told me. I remember the photo albums too. She had a smile in every picture." Blake thought back for a moment of all of the photos his father had shown him of his mother. "Although sometimes it seemed as though she was hiding something behind the smile, she still had a smile nonetheless."

Paige thought about the words Blake had just spoken. Although she didn't agree with his decision to settle, she appreciated the fact that he loved her so much that he considered her more valuable than the money he'd worked so hard to earn.

"Oh, yeah, and as part of the deal, my sister is going to drop the assault charges against you."

"Now that's *priceless*," Paige said sarcastically.

"I'm just ready to move on. My attorney is going to draft the papers Monday morning and schedule an appointment for us all to meet up and sign the papers so that I can give her the money. Then she can disappear again for thirty more years."

Paige walked over to her husband and hugged him with her good arm. "Thank you, Blake. I'm not taking this gesture for granted. Not at all."

"Good, and I'm done taking you for granted." He looked down at her injured arm. "And I promise I will never put my hands on you again. You have to know that it wasn't me. It was just so much going on. I was so angry; so mad. That's why I made the decision to settle. It wasn't worth it. I'd rather lose the money than lose my wife." Blake caught the tear that was flowing down Paige's cheek with his thumb. He replaced it with a kiss.

Paige closed her eyes and took in the gentle kiss. She never knew a kiss could have so much meaning. That a kiss could mean I love you. That a kiss could mean I'm sorry. One little kiss.

Certainly Jesus felt the same way about Judas's kiss. Who knew a kiss could mean so many things?

Chapter Thirty-three

"He's gone! He went and did it without me! He's gone!"

Mother Doreen had already been exhausted from her conversation with Pastor Frey at the restaurant. When she walked through the door, she'd intended on telling Bethany that it was time for her to go back to Malvonia. That her work in Kentucky was done. There was nothing more she could do. No one needed her. Everyone had everything all figured out on their own. No one wanted to listen to God, let alone a little old woman being used by God; a mere earthly vessel. But somehow, with Bethany screaming and crying like a madwoman, she felt leaving Kentucky to go back to Malvonia wasn't going to be that easy.

"Calm down, Sis. Just calm down," Mother Doreen said to her baby sister. "Come on over here and sit down on the couch and tell me what's going on." Mother Doreen led a frantic Bethany over to the couch.

"He-he-he . . ." Bethany cried. "We-we-we . . . were supposed to do it together . . . on Monday." Bethany was absolutely beside herself.

"Please, Bethany, I have no idea what you are trying to say. You have to catch your breath and calm down."

"Okay. Okay." Bethany began to do as her older sister instructed. She sat on the couch taking one deep breath after another, looking at her sister for approval that she was doing it properly.

"Yes, that's it," Mother Doreen coaxed her. "Now tell me what's going on."

"Uriah. He turned himself in to the police today." The frantic screaming, crying, and tears started all over again. "My husband . . . he's in jail!"

Bethany sat in her bedroom in disbelief. Both she and Mother Doreen had been so certain that Uriah would be released from jail, at least until his sentencing. Pastor Frey had been certain as well as he'd stood in the back of the courtroom instead of the front with Mother Doreen and Bethany. He hadn't talked to Mother Doreen since she stormed out of the restaurant last week. She hadn't even shown up for church that following Sunday, which was the first Sunday of the month, which was also communion Sunday. That was usually when he needed her help the most, and she knew that. Still, she was a no-show. He could hardly preach the Word. Not because Bishop Klein was now sitting front and center, observing his pulpit teachings and etiquette, preparing to make his final report on whether Pastor Frey should remain as the interim pastor or if he himself should take over until a new pastor could be voted in. It was because he kept wondering if Mother Doreen was going to show up for church. She never did.

He tried to call her, but he never got an answer. He even tried calling Bethany's house. He reasoned that Mother Doreen, upon seeing his number on the caller ID, refused to answer the phone. She'd obviously given everyone else in the household those same instructions. He drove by the house a couple of times but didn't see her car. And now she'd missed church. Oh, she'd gone back to Malvonia all right, of that he was sure.

Needless to say, he'd felt relieved the next morning when he realized there was a chance that Mother Doreen hadn't actually packed up and headed back to Ohio. That she was still in Kentucky tending to yet new and unfolding drama in her sister's home. He realized the chances that she'd stayed were great when he'd read the morning paper. Buried within was a story about a man who'd faked his death to commit insurance fraud. The man had turned himself in to authorities. It stated that the man had a court hearing later that morning. Pastor Frey was quick to cancel his Monday morning appointments, something Mother Doreen typically would have done for him, and go show his support. He prayed the entire drive there.

Mother Doreen and Bethany had both prayed too. Nonetheless, they were all disappointed when Uriah was held in jail, considered a flight risk if let out on bail.

"After all, Your Honor," the prosecuting attorney had stated, "he managed to drop off from the face of the earth for months, with his wife not even knowing of his existence and whereabouts." The attorney had looked over his shoulder at a weeping Bethany. "At least that's what the defendant says. It's still yet to be known whether Mrs. Tyson will be a codefendant in this matter."

"My wife had nothing to do with this," Uriah had shouted out before the judge slammed his gavel down and demanded order in the court. "The insurance companies aren't the only victims. My wife and children are just as much victims, if not more."

Bethany's weeps grew louder as the judge ordered that Uriah be removed from the court and held in jail. He was escorted out before he could hear that the State was seeking jail time unless the defendant could pay restitution on the thousands of dollars the insurance com-

panies had paid out. Restitution, along with probation
and community service—that's what the State wanted
from Uriah. Bethany knew that would be impossible;
the money part of the deal anyway. She'd spent ninety
percent of the money paying off the house and all the
overdue bills. The rest she'd invested to grow interest.
Between the disability check she received for her medical condition and the Social Security money she and the
kids received as a result of Uriah's alleged death, she
figured she could maintain. But everything had changed
now, and of course, Uncle Sam wanted his money back
too. Unless God had something in the works, Bethany
knew that her husband would be spending the next few
years in jail. Perhaps he would have been better off dead.

"Can I come in?" Mother Doreen asked after tapping
on Bethany's bedroom door.

"It's open. Come in," Bethany called from the other
side of the door.

Mother Doreen entered the room and noticed that
Bethany's face was buried in the Bible. She couldn't
remember the last time she'd seen her sister taking
time out to seek God's Word. It made her heart smile,
but she knew not as much as it was making God's heart
smile. "Whatcha doing, Sis?" Mother Doreen walked
over and sat on the edge of the bed next to Bethany.

Closing the Bible, Bethany replied, "Doing something I should have never stopped doing." She held
the Bible up. "Do you know I used to read this thing
religiously every day?" She let it drop to her bed. "God's
got a way of drawing you back to Him."

"Ain't that the truth?" Mother Doreen stated.

"Are the kids home from school yet?" Bethany asked.

"You know Hudson is over there seeing that grandbaby of yours."

"Yes, I miss my grandbaby. Haven't seen her in three days. I can't wait for her to come spend the weekend with us."

"Me either," Mother Doreen agreed.

"Is Sadie over there too? I figured her having a baby niece to tend to will keep her busy enough so she won't get the notion of having one of her own anytime soon."

Mother Doreen chuckled. "Actually, Sadie's downstairs watching television. CNN."

Bethany looked shocked. "My baby is watching CNN and not that *Teen Nick: Degrassi* stuff?"

"She said it's part of an extra credit assignment."

"She's been doing a lot of extra credit assignments lately," Bethany analyzed. "She's probably just trying to keep her mind off everything going on around here. I wish I could figure out a way to keep my mind off it." Tears filled Bethany's eyes. "I just can't believe Uriah's in jail. And the bad thing about it is that a part of me wishes he'd never turned himself in. But I know we have to live by man's laws too."

"I know, sweetie, but even though Uriah has to pay a debt to man for what he did, God still has the final say. God's got a way of turning things around that would blow your mind." Mother Doreen leaned back to get comfortable. "I remember one time—" Before she could proceed with her story, an ear-deafening scream resonated throughout the house.

"Mom! Mom!" Sadie's scream pierced through the silence.

"Oh my God! Did you hear that?" Bethany jumped up from the bed. "That was Sadie."

Without saying another word, both Bethany and Mother Doreen ran toward the direction in which Sadie's yelp was coming from.

"Mom! Mom!" Sadie continued to yell.

Finally Mother Doreen and Bethany made it to the television room where Sadie stood up next to the TV.

"Honey, what is it? What's wrong?" Bethany asked her daughter as she walked over to her and immediately began examining Sadie's body for some type of injury.

"Look! Look!" Sadie pointed the remote to the television DVR. She hit a button to rewind what she'd just seen on the television. "It's about Dad. Watch."

All three women stood in the room as a CNN Newsroom reporter spoke.

"It's said that the auto dealer is going to announce a major recall here in the U.S. in the morning," the reporter said. "At the time, the supplier of the brake hardware had only been in business six months and was offering a major discount to both auto dealers and auto supply stores. Not only did they manufacture hardware for automobiles, but some semi trucks as well. So far, seven major accidents have been reported, three of them including fatalities. The manufacturer is asking that anyone whose vehicle has its product, cease use immediately."

The reporter then stepped to the side as words scrolled next to her on the green screen. "This is a preliminary list, so far, of the various makes, models, and some store locations that have sold the product. There are also a few garages listed where the owners have used the products on some of the vehicles they've repaired."

"Look! Look! Watch! This is it!" Sadie shouted as she stood by the television and pointed.

Mother Doreen and Bethany watched the words scroll.

"See there? That's it!" Sadie paused the television. "*That's* where Dad gets his truck worked on."

"She's right," Mother Doreen agreed. "I remember the paperwork from when we planned the funeral. That is the name of the company."

"So y'all think they might have put faulty brakes on Uriah's truck?" Bethany asked.

"Yes, Mom. So, you see, Dad is not going to have to do all that time in jail."

"Honey," Bethany told her daughter, "even if that supplier is responsible for the brakes going out on the truck, that has nothing to do with the decision your father made to fake his death. That still leaves the fact that he owes a lot of money to the insurance companies and the Social Security office."

"Exactly!" Sadie said with excitement, and then hit PLAY on the DVR.

"One of the largest and most successful law firms has already started the Class Action lawsuit," the reporter continued. "It's reported that millions will be paid out to victims. Visit our Web site for more information."

Both Bethany and Mother Doreen stood there with their jaws dropped.

"See? See? Everything is going to be all right," Sadie told her mother and aunt with teary eyes. "We're about to get paid! Daddy can accept the offer for restitution and pay back the insurance companies." She walked over to her mother. "God worked it out, Mom. God did it." Sadie hugged her mother as she began to cry.

"Yes, He did, honey," Bethany agreed as tears streamed down her face. "God worked it out."

Chapter Thirty-four

Was this déjà vu? Lorain had to ask herself as she, still half asleep, opened the door at three o'clock in the morning to find Unique standing on the other side.

"Can I come in?" Unique stood there with her arms folded.

Lorain looked hesitant.

"Don't worry, it's not like last time," Unique quickly explained. "I know it's three o'clock in the morning on a Tuesday, but I haven't been out drinking or backsliding or anything." Unique looked over her shoulder at the car parked outside at the curb. "My sister let me use her car. I told her it was an emergency."

Lorain still looked hesitant. She didn't know if she could trust this girl. For all she knew, she had a knife or gun or something in her purse and had come over to get revenge for what Lorain had done to her as a baby.

Unique, once again, detected the hesitation in Lorain allowing her inside. "Look, I just want to talk. Tomorrow's Wednesday. I didn't want to have to see you in Bible Study and act all funny or trip or anything. I just want to come in and talk, that's all."

Finally, Lorain moved to the side to allow Unique to enter. She closed the door and locked it behind them. Turning, she saw Unique getting ready to sit on the couch. "We need to go in the kitchen. My mother's sleeping here tonight, and I don't want to wake her. She

probably won't wake up considering the doctor had to
give her Valium, but I don't want to take that chance."

Unique followed Lorain into the kitchen. Without
even asking Unique if she was interested, Lorain prepared each of them a cup of hot chocolate. It only took
a couple of minutes because she nuked the milk in the
microwave instead of waiting for a pan to boil on the
stove. After adding the powered Swiss Miss with itsy-
bitsy marshmallows, she stirred, then placed the two
cups on the table.

"Be careful. It's hot," Lorain warned Unique.

Unique was silent. She simply embraced the mug
in her hands, blowing on the chocolate, creating small
ripples. "You know, I once had a dream," Unique started. "Or maybe it was a fantasy . . . or just pure wishful
thinking. But it was of my mother and me. Not the
foster mother, not the mother who raised me, but my
mother; the one whose veins pumped the same blood
as mine. The one I never knew. Anyway, it was in the
middle of the night. I'd had a nightmare or something,
and to sooth me, I guess, she fixed me a cup of hot
chocolate. She watched me drink it and told me that
everything was going to be all right. It was like the life
I'd lived had been nothing but a nightmare. I hadn't
really lived that life. I woke up from it with her there
to tell me that everything was okay. That she loved me.
That I was her little girl. Hers." Unique fell silent, sipping some of her hot brew.

"Well," Lorain decided to speak. Her tone was low
and gentle. "I don't know what you want me to say."

"Say it's all been just a bad nightmare." Unique
slammed her cup down, gobs of chocolate spilling
onto the table, some even spilling on Unique's hands,
scorching her. But she seemed so unfazed, like the blis-
ters that would form would be far less painful than the

things she had endured in life. "Pretend I'm just getting up from a bad nightmare." Unique squeezed her eyes closed tightly.

Lorain didn't know if it was so that she could have complete darkness, providing a canvas to paint the picture she wanted to see. Or if it was to lock in the tears that wanted to burst out. If it had been the latter, she failed.

"I wish I could, Unique," Lorain said. "I wish with every ounce of my being this wasn't our reality, but it is. I'm so sorry for the decisions I made, for the choices I made. But I can't take them back. If I could, I would. But right now, all I can say is that I'm sorry. God, I'm so sorry."

There was more silence.

"I'm so mad at you." Unique said the words through clenched teeth. "I've hated you ever since I could remember. My hate for you is what kept the hurt away, kept me from not caring anymore. And now I'm madder than ever because I want to keep hating you."

"I don't blame you for being mad, for being hurt, angry, feeling hate, or whatever else you've thought about me all these years," Lorain said.

"Can I ask you something?"

"Baby, you can ask me anything you want," Lorain said sincerely. "I want you to know that. And I want you to know that I promise you that I will answer any and everything openly and honestly."

"Why? Why didn't you want to keep me?"

Lorain swallowed. She knew that question was coming eventually. She'd expected it the night she told Unique that she was her mother, but at the time, all Unique wanted was proof. The night Lorain shared the truth with Unique, she'd gone to her computer room to retrieve the folder that held all the proof. She'd removed the documents that related to Unique only and placed the folder in the top drawer of her desk. She gave the documents pertaining to Unique to the young woman in order for her to take them with her. She didn't really need them anymore; she knew the story by heart. She was careful not to display to Unique any of the documents that had to do with Broady. One thing at a time. But after scanning the papers, reading about how she'd been left for dead in a trash can, that's when Unique had gone totally ballistic. She never really gave Lorain a chance to say much of anything besides "I'm sorry." So Lorain knew eventually the questions would come. As the two sat at the table sipping warm cocoa, they were joined by the questions.

Openly and honestly, Lorain reminded herself of the promise she had just made to Unique. It was the very first promise she'd made to her daughter. She had to keep her promises, so she told Unique why; why, not that she didn't want to keep her, but why she didn't. Lorain proceeded to explain to Unique how an older man had taken advantage of her. How she was so young, so scared, and how she hid her pregnancy. She had to relive the horrific experience with each word she spoke, but Unique deserved to hear it. She deserved to know.

By the time Lorain finished her story, both woman were in a tight embrace, crying a river. Each tear carrying away years of pain, losing it forever in a flowing stream of forgiveness. Of course there was still some pain and definitely still some bitterness on Unique's part. But after talking for almost three hours, both women concluded that it would take some time to build a healthy relationship. Right now, they just wanted to work on their relationship before Unique told her boys and Lorain told her mother. Besides, presently, Eleanor was dealing with so much herself.

Lorain walked Unique to the door. Before saying good-bye, she wanted to hug her again. Tight. She didn't want to let her go for a really long time. But she knew that was too much too soon. Earlier, Unique embracing her had been because she was caught up in Lorain's emotions as a friend, not as a mother. But Lorain would pray that one day soon she'd receive that loving hug that only a daughter can give her mother.

"So I'll see you in church tomorrow?" Unique asked.

"Actually, I'm probably going to have to stay here with my mother. It all depends."

"Guess I didn't have to waste my time coming over here then, trying to avoid that awkward moment in church tomorrow."

"No, but I'm glad you did," Lorain smiled.

"Well, I better get going. I told my sister I'd only be a minute, and here it is almost six o'clock in the morning. She probably done called the police and reported the car stolen. She funny acting like that sometimes."

"Well, then, I guess you better get going. One New Day member on television getting dragged off to jail is enough." Lorain was referring to Paige.

"Yeah, you know . . ." Unique began. She paused. Lorain sensed she was stalling for some reason. She was. "Before I leave, I just want to know one more thing; something we didn't talk about . . . something you didn't even mention."

"Sure," Lorain said. "You can ask me anything."

"Where's my father?" Unique just came out and asked.

Wow. Lorain wasn't expecting that. She'd been far too focused on just her and Unique. She hadn't even thought to bring Broady up in the equation. But a few hours ago, she'd told Unique that she wanted an open and honest relationship with her as they attempted to form a mother-daughter bond. No secrets and no lies. So she fixed her lips to tell Unique the truth about her father. "He's dead," Lorain said sadly. "He's dead."

Chapter Thirty-five

Paige opened the door, and before she could even greet her best friend, Tamarra fell into her arms.

"She's in heaven," Tamarra cried. "She's in heaven. She didn't kill herself, Paige. She's in heaven."

Paige was confused, but could see that her friend was emotional, so she just held her until Tamarra could calm down long enough to tell Paige who and what she was talking about. "It's okay, honey. It's okay."

"I know it's okay. She's in heaven. Raygene is in heaven." Tamarra was just one big pile of mush; happy mush-tears of joy and relief. After a few more moments, she was able to regain her composure.

"Can I get you some water or something to eat or anything?" Paige offered.

"No, I'm too much in awe to drink or eat anything right at this second," Tamarra stated as she headed for her regular spot on Paige's couch. "Hallelujah!" Tamarra shouted out of nowhere. Then came a "Praise God!" Followed by an "I love you, Lord." Then finally a, "Thank you, Jesus!"

Paige, dressed in a chocolate-brown pants suit, walked over and sat down next to her best friend. She waited a few seconds to see if Tamarra was going to have any more sudden outbursts unto the Lord. Once she saw that she wasn't, curiosity caused her to speak. "You wanna tell me what's going on now?" Paige asked.

"I wanna shout with you."

Tamarra looked at Paige and burst out laughing. "Oh, I'm so sorry. You have no idea what I'm even talking about." Tamarra cleared her throat. "You know how my brother's daughter died?" Tamarra asked Paige. She then caught herself and made the correction. "I mean, you know how my daughter died." A proud smile spread across her face like jelly being spread on toast.

It had taken Tamarra years to claim her only child, Raygene, and Paige knew this. Tamarra had shared it with her after returning from Raygene's funeral. And even though she was leaving New Day for good, she'd shared it with the pastor as well. And she didn't even feel as though she was sharing a secret at that point. Some things aren't secrets; some things are just skeletons . . . bones the devil likes to dangle over a person's head like puppet strings, controlling their life on Earth. No longer was Satan Tamarra's puppet master, and Paige couldn't be more proud of her.

The fact that Tamarra could finally claim Raygene as her daughter was a significant hurdle she'd jumped over. She'd been so ashamed of having given birth to the girl after she was raped repeatedly by her own blood brother. She'd been even more ashamed that when the girl showed up on her doorstep a few months ago, begging for a relationship with her, that Tamarra had turned her away. Then to receive a report that the girl had died in an accident—an accident later deemed suicide—had been devastating. So to see Tamarra rejoicing while saying Raygene's name at the same time, God had done something big. Real Big.

"Raygene, yes I know. What about Raygene?" Paige inquired.

"It wasn't suicide, Paige. She didn't kill herself. My baby didn't crash her car and kill herself because of me." That's another burden Tamarra was able to let go of; the fact that a small part of her felt partially to blame for Raygene wanting to kill herself. Being rejected by her own mother couldn't have been easy. Being the product of rape couldn't have been easy.

"It was faulty brakes or something like that," Tamarra continued. "My mom and dad were contacted by the dealership where Raygene had purchased her car. They wanted Raygene to bring the car in, saying that it had been recalled because of the brakes. That's why the police didn't see any tire marks or anything to show that she'd made any attempts to stop the car. She *couldn't* stop it. She couldn't." Tamarra keeled over in tears. She pictured Raygene in her little red car frantically pumping the brakes, trying to stop the car. Wanting to live; not wanting to die.

"It's okay now." Paige comforted Tamarra. "It's all okay. God has given you and your family clarity now. He has given you peace." Wrapping her arms around Tamarra, Paige felt guilty. She was jealous. She wanted peace. But then again, maybe in about an hour she'd have that peace. She looked at the clock on her living-room wall. It was eleven o'clock in the morning. She only had one hour. She had to go.

"You know what?" Tamarra said, wiping the last of her tears. "How about a drink or something to eat? Let's go celebrate. What do you say we go to the Golden Corral?"

"Actually, I'm not off work today," Paige explained, standing up straight and straightening out her suit. "I'm working the late shift because I have to meet Blake at an appointment. I don't think I had a chance to tell you that he ended up settling with his mother."

"Really? You mean he actually gave into that woman?" Tamarra, forgetting about her own situation for the time being, was now focusing on Paige's.

"Yeah. It was just becoming too much. Blake didn't want to keep fighting with m—." Paige caught herself. ". . . with Mother . . . his mother."

"Well, I guess it's like the Bible says: honor thy mother. Fighting with your mother is not a good thing. You and I both know that."

"Yeah, well . . . All this will be over soon. As a matter fact, in about an hour."

"Then I guess we'll have to celebrate another time," Tamarra stated, "but I just had to come over here in person and share the news with my bestest friend in the whole wide world who I love and trust enough to tell everything to, and who loves and trusts me enough to tell me everything."

Paige gave a smile. A weak smile. She hadn't been telling Tamarra everything. Sure, she'd told her the truth about the whole lawsuit thing, and the details of the arrest, but she'd also lied to her. She'd lied and told her that her arm had gotten hurt in jail; something about a guard twisting her arm too hard while she was being handcuffed. Tamarra had told her she should hire Blake's attorney to file a brutality suit against the department, but Paige refused.

There was more guilt. Paige remembered the big fuss she'd made when she felt Tamarra was hiding things from her. *I thought we were friends . . . best friends. I thought we could share any and everything with each other,* Paige had fussed at Tamarra. And now, here she stood being such a hypocrite.

What a fraud Paige thought she was. But she justified it by the fact that soon there wouldn't really be anything to tell. The weight of the world was about to be lifted off Blake's shoulders. The two would attend another counseling session or two, and then they'd live happily ever after. And all of this couldn't come soon enough for Paige. So after saying her good-byes to Tamarra, fifteen minutes later, she was out the door, headed toward her happily ever after.

Chapter Thirty-six

"Mom, thanks for inviting Justice's parents over for our celebration dinner tonight," Sadie said.

"No problem," Bethany replied. "Your daddy is coming home today, for good. I'd invite the whole world if I could."

"That's because you're not the one peeling all these potatoes for mashing," Mother Doreen shot from the kitchen table as she peeled a ten-pound bag of potatoes.

"Thank you, Aunti," Sadie said as she kissed Mother Doreen on the cheek.

"Anyway, you and Justice have been spending a lot of time on the phone lately. Seems you two are getting close. I figured it was about time I meet his mother and father so we can all discuss some ground rules."

"Mom, I told you, Justice's parents are all religious and everything," Sadie whined. "Trust and believe they've already set the ground rules. Oh, yeah, by the way, Justice says his pops is going to probably invite us to church on Sunday." Sadie looked at Bethany. "Mom, I know we haven't been to church since we left Living Word, but I think it would be nice." Sadie then looked at Mother Doreen. "Aunti, I'd like it too if you would come. I'm sure Pastor Frey won't mind you making a visit to another church just this one time. He probably won't even miss you with how heavy he be into his sermons."

"You're right; he probably won't miss me." Mother Doreen's voice was low and sadness was etched across her face. Pastor Frey probably wouldn't miss her this Sunday like he probably hadn't missed her the Sunday before that. At first, after she'd left him in the restaurant that day, he tried calling her, but then the calls just stopped. If he really cared, she thought, he would have never given up. A part of her wished she'd taken his calls once she'd seen his number on the caller ID. A part of her wished she hadn't instructed the rest of the family to ignore them on her behalf.

Eventually, she surmised, he figured she'd gone on back to Malvonia just as she had threatened to. It had not been her intention, though, to shoot off idle threats. But her sister needing her again had kept her there, but now, everything really did seem like it was back to normal. God was in control. She was no longer needed, and just as soon as she could make the necessary arrangements and preparations, she still planned on going back home. But right now, she had a bag full of potatoes to peel.

"Anyway, I better go get ready," Sadie stated. "Daddy's coming home. For real. Forever. Yesss!" Sadie excitedly ran to her room.

Mother Doreen watched as Bethany just stood there with a smile on her face looking like she too was ready to burst with excitement.

"Well, go ahead," Mother Doreen said to her. "Let out that shout! Let out that praise."

Before Mother Doreen knew it, Bethany had begun to turn red and tremble. Her hands balled to fists, and her feet got to stomping. She bent her arms and started flapping like a bird ready to take flight. Face down toward the ground and eyes squinted, she got to moving faster; stomping and flapping, and then came the shouting.

Mother Doreen jumped up and walked over to Bethany. She spread her arms out as wide as she could as a barrier of protection for Bethany. Deep in the Spirit, Bethany danced, shouted, and praised unto the Lord like never before. She was thankful, she was grateful, she was blessed. That's what she was telling God. He was wonderful. He was altogether lovely. He was worthy to be praised. That's what she was telling God.

The joy of the Lord was finally and permanently etched across Bethany's face and embedded in her spirit. That's the look Mother Doreen wanted to see on her sister's face. The look that let her know for certain her job here was done. Her work was complete, her assignment was complete. It was a new day for Bethany and her family. And it would be a new day for Mother Doreen, literally, as she headed back to Malvonia, Ohio, to New Day Temple of Faith.

But first, Mother Doreen had to prepare what would probably be her last big dinner in Kentucky before she headed back. And a big dinner it was. Three hours later, Mother Doreen had taken the last part of the meal out of the oven. Just as soon as she set the homemade buttered rolls on the stove top, the doorbell rang.

"They're here!" Sadie could be heard shouting throughout the house. "I'll get it. They're here."

At first Mother Doreen didn't know who "they" were, as Bethany hadn't yet made it back home from the jail with Uriah. Then she realized they wouldn't have been ringing the doorbell to their own home, so it had to be Justice and his parents. She wiped her hands down her apron, and then removed it. She needed to go give her guests their proper greeting, but when she entered the living room, the guests weren't exactly who she'd had in mind.

"Pastor Frey," Mother Doreen said, surprised. She then looked at the man standing next to him. "Pastor Davidson?" She said this more shocked than anything. "What the—"

"I'm glad to see you two made it," Uriah announced, coming up behind the two men, Bethany next to him.

Bethany had an even more shocked expression on her face than Mother Doreen when she saw Pastor Davidson. "Uriah, wha . . . what's this about? What is *he* doing here?" The "he" she was referring to was Pastor Davidson.

"And since we're asking questions," Mother Doreen jumped in, "what's *he* doing here?" That "he" was Pastor Frey.

"I invited them," Uriah said without shame. "Now can we all go inside, or are we having dinner picnic style out here on the front lawn?"

Silently, not knowing what to say, everyone parted as Uriah made his way inside.

"Daddy, you're home," Sadie happily exclaimed, embracing her father.

"For good, this time," Uriah told her, then he looked into his daughter's eyes. "And I promise I will never do anything like this again. I really hope you'll eventually forgive me for everything."

Sadie squeezed her eyes tightly, trying to lock in the tears. Then she squeezed her father even tighter as she said, "I forgive you, Daddy." Whispering in his ear, she said, "Don't tell him I told you, but Hudson forgives you too. But you know Hudson; he only told me because he knew I'd tell you."

After holding on to his daughter for a few more seconds, Uriah stood up straight. "Good, because I learned in those couple of weeks in jail that not willing to forgive someone can ruin your life." He looked at Pastor Davidson. "Sometimes we have to forgive people even when we never thought we could."

Uriah thought about some of the jailhouse stories he'd heard. How some of the men were in jail because of revenge or crimes of passion. Some had never had as much as a parking ticket, but were now looking at life in prison. And for what? Because someone stole from them? Because someone did something to them they just couldn't let go? Because someone slept with their wife or girlfriend? No, Uriah was not going to be one of those men. Being hurt was a part of life, but letting go of that hurt and forgiving the person that caused it was a part of enjoying life. Uriah had been given a second chance with his wife and children, and he wasn't going to waste not one part of it harboring any type of anger toward Pastor Davidson. Yeah, maybe some might think that breaking bread with the man who'd slept with his wife and impregnated her was a bit much. But tell Jesus that about Judas.

Uriah extended his hand to Pastor Davidson. "Glad you could join us."

Pastor Davidson shook his hand. "I'm glad God put it on your heart to allow me to join you. You are a good man, Uriah. A darn good man. And about that money still owed from the loan, forget about—"

"No, sir," Uriah stated, cutting him off. "We shook hands like men when that money exchanged hands. We had a deal. You're going to get back every dime, with interest." And Uriah meant it. He'd made up in his mind that since there was a part of him that felt Pastor Davidson had tried to buy his wife by loaning him that money, then he was about to buy her right back. "Besides, that company is already offering money to settle out of court. It will just be a matter of time before we get—"

"I know you're good for it," Pastor Davidson inter-rupted. "Besides, if the State of Kentucky and Uncle Sam are confident that you'll pay them, then I guess I can trust you enough as well."

Both Uriah and Pastor Davidson chuckled. Some-how they were able to get past the past. No, not *some-how*; it was God. God had shown Uriah favor. Unmer-ited, undeserved favor on top of both His grace and mercy. So much favor that his defense attorney made a plea with the courts, after convincing them that Uriah wasn't a flight risk, that restitution payments could be set up and that with the windfall coming Uriah's way, the insurance company and the government would be paid back. No one from the insurance company or the government showed up to argue against the court's de-cision. So it was done.

"And thank you for coming too, Pastor Frey," Uriah said, shaking Pastor Frey's hand. "You've always been such a great support to me and my family. That's why I wasn't surprised to see you in the courtroom at my initial hearing."

The look of astonishment that covered Mother Do-reen's face went unnoticed. He *did* know she was still in Kentucky. He had to know because he would have seen her in the courtroom. Besides that, he would have known that she would not have left her sister at such a difficult time. Yet, he hadn't reached out to her; hadn't tried to stop her from returning to Ohio. A part of Mother Doreen had secretly wanted just that to take place. After all, that's how it usually happened in mov-ies, on soap operas, and in romance novels. But this was none of those, that much Mother Doreen was sure of.

Uriah looked at both Mother Doreen and his wife. "Is everything okay?" He wanted to make sure the extra guests wouldn't be a problem. Before either of them could reply, footsteps were heard coming up the walk.

"What's *he* doing here?" This time, it came from Pastor Frey. The "he" Pastor Frey was referring to was Bishop Klein.

Everything was not okay.

Chapter Thirty-seven

"I'm glad you could find the time to squeeze me into your life, into your schedule."

Lorain detected far more than just a hint of sarcasm and bitterness in Unique's tone. She'd thought when Unique had called her up and asked if she could come get her and the kids and go to the park, that things would be pleasant. Lorain needed a breath of fresh air. The last few days had been consuming and rough.

"Yeah, well, I know we haven't talked in the last couple of days—" Lorain started before Unique cut her off.

"Forty-six hours, three minutes, and twenty-two seconds, to be exact," Unique rattled off. "That's how long it's been since we last talked."

"Wow, I guess time flies," Lorain said. In all honesty, trying to comfort Eleanor in her time of bereavement had drained Lorain.

"Yeah, I guess time does fly when you're having fun. I suppose you've been having lots of fun."

Lorain had no idea what Unique was getting at; what her problem was. "Let's sit on this bench right here where we can still see the kids playing."

At the park Unique and Lorain were at, the playground sat in the middle of a mile long circular walking trail. Benches and exercise equipment were scattered around the trail every twenty to thirty feet or so.

"Fine," Unique agreed, and then sullenly flopped down on the bench.

From how Lorain saw it, Unique was acting like a teenager throwing a temper tantrum. Was *this* what she'd missed out on? Lorain glanced over at the boys. "I can't believe I'm a grandmother," she smiled.

"Slow your row. You're barely my mother, so don't start acting all sappy with my kids. We agreed I wouldn't say anything to them until you and I got things situated and on one accord."

"Yes, I know," Lorain affirmed. "It's just going to be so hard not being able to be granny; you know, to do things grannies do."

Unique let out a harrumph. "You mean as hard as it was not being able to be a mother; to do things mothers do?"

Lorain was reconsidering whether it had been a good idea to accept Unique's invitation to the park. She thought it would be a chance for them to talk and bond, not for Unique to beat her upside the head with slick comments, reminding her of her mistakes. "Yes, it is going to be just that hard." Lorain turned to face Unique. "Had I known my baby was alive somewhere, it would have been hard to go through life without being able to—"

"Who are you kidding?" Unique interrupted. "Had our paths not crossed the way they did, you would have never thought twice about me. I know your story and all, but I've had some time to think. Yeah, you might have been just a kid yourself when you had me, and you probably didn't think about the consequences or the possibility that I was still alive. But once you got older, didn't you care? Didn't you even think to find out what happened to the baby that got thrown in the trash? Where it was buried so that you could at least come put flowers on my grave?"

"I did wonder, for a minute. I was even wondering the day I saw on the news when the reporter said that someone had thrown their newborn baby in the trash. My mom just started talking and cursing the woman who did such a horrific thing. And I started talking over her about something else. Neither of us even heard what else the news reporter said. We didn't hear whether the baby was dead or had been found alive. I just assumed—"

It was clear that Unique was not going to let Lorain finish a complete thought. "But couldn't you *feel* it? Wasn't there something, an instinct, a sixth sense, that told you that your baby was alive? Like that *Lifetime* movie they show during Latino month. That one where the Hispanic woman is told that her daughter died in a fire, but she never believed it. She felt in her soul, in her heart, that her daughter was alive. She even recognized her daughter when she saw her years later. Some mothers say that they even know the *moment* their child has died." By now, Unique's angry words had turned to tears. "Didn't you feel *anything? Anything* at all?" she cried.

Lorain inhaled. A part of her wanted to make up something, something Unique wanted to hear; something that would make her feel better; take away more of the pain from past years. She couldn't. *Open and honest.* So she opted to remain silent.

"I didn't think so," Unique said, drying her tears. "And you don't really feel anything now. If you had, then you would have at least picked up the phone and called me these past days. But you don't really care. I'm grown now. I don't *need* you."

"Unique, my mother's husband just died. His funeral was yesterday, you know that. Not that you showed up to support me."

"I had a really huge catering affair to attend," was Unique's reason for not going.

"And I had to help my mother make the arrangements and everything, so it seems we've both been busy. I haven't had a moment's rest since . . . since the last time I talked to you."

Unique felt bad. She felt selfish. "I'm sorry." Now she felt sad, but then, a sudden thought occurred to her. "Was *he* my grandfather? Your mother's husband, was he also your dad? Was he my grandfather?"

Lorain shook her head. "No . . . no, he wasn't your grandfather." That wasn't a lie. Broady wasn't her grandfather. "He was someone my mom had just recently married actually." She said a silent prayer that Unique wouldn't ask her anything else about him. "Look, Unique, I do love you. I loved you before I even found out you were my daughter. It's just that—"

"I'm pregnant." Unique said it as if she was giving Lorain the weather report.

"Huh? What?" Lorain didn't know what to say.

"That's why I really asked you here. I'm not mad at you. I'm mad at myself." Unique closed her eyes and shook her head in dismay and disgust at her condition; a condition she knew all too well.

"My God, Unique. How could this have happened? I mean, why? What about you wanting to break the family curse of having babies with all these men and not having a husband?"

"I messed up, all right?" Unique cried.

"I'm . . . I'm sorry. I didn't mean to upset you. I'm just . . ." Lorain was at a loss for words.

"Shocked? Well, that makes two of us. Make that three of us."

"Three? You mean the father?"

Unique nodded.

"Who is it?"

"Remember that night I came over to your house drunk? That night you told me about . . . Well, you know."

"Yeah."

"Well, turns out that one little slipup got me knocked up."

"So it's your son's father? He's the father of this baby too?"

"Yeah, my oldest boy's daddy."

"Well, at least it's not a different man. I guess the upside to all of this is that at least two of your four children will have the same father."

"Tuh," Unique spat. "Four kids? I'm not keeping this baby."

"What do you mean you're not keeping the baby?" Lorain asked sternly. "Young lady, I'm not allowing you to get an abortion. I won't hear of it. I'd rather you—"

"You'd rather me *what?*" Unique snarled. "Give birth to it, and then throw it away in the trash like you did with me?" Just as soon as Unique uttered those words, she wished she could take them back.

Lorain sat there as the words went through her. The bullets Unique had just spit didn't penetrate her. She didn't allow them to. Instead, they zipped in and out, missing her main organ, her heart. There was nothing anyone could do or say, including Unique, to make her feel guilt and shame about her past; not any more. She'd repented, and God had forgiven her. She'd apologized to Unique as much as she was going to.

"I'm sorry." Unique's sudden apology shocked Lorain. But it pleased Lorain more so.

"Apology accepted."

"It's just that you haven't even been my momma for that long, and already you're trying to step in and lecture me."

"No, that's where you're wrong," Lorain corrected her. "I've been your momma for all your life. Now I can't make up for all those years where I didn't play the role of your mother, but I can promise you that moving forward, I'll be the best at it that I know how to be. That's if you'll let me."

Unique sighed. "To be honest with you, I'm so confused I wouldn't care if Mary Jones from the movie *Precious: Based on the Novel Push by Sapphire* was my mother."

Both Lorain and Unique began to laugh. It was better than crying. And the situation Unique had put herself in by turning up pregnant was indeed worth a few tears.

"I know you don't want me preaching to you, acting like your mother, but, sweetheart, I am your mother. And you talking about not keeping the baby and getting an abortion is not going to fly with me."

Unique put her hand up to stop Lorain from continuing. "Hold up, wait a minute. I ain't said nothing about having no abortion. I'm a Christian. Now I know a sin is a sin, but a fornicator, okay, I'll take that title, but a murderer? Please. I ain't killing my baby. Now that's one thing the women in my family don't do; abortions. As you can see, we have our babies," Unique clarified. "I was thinking about giving the baby up for adoption."

"Adoption?" Lorain allowed the word to fall off her lips in a whisper.

"Yeah, I mean, I was watching this reality show marathon the other day," Unique started, then looked at Lorain. "You know how I am about my marathons," she continued. "And there was this couple who gave their baby up for adoption. They were only like sixteen. So if a sixteen-year-old girl had enough wisdom to, first, realize that she couldn't provide for that baby like some other couple could, and second, to have the strength to go through with it, then I think I can do it too. I'd like to think I'm pretty strong. Granted, I didn't use wisdom when I laid down, had unprotected sex by a man who was not my husband, and got pregnant, but there's no better time to start using wisdom than now." Unique paused while she looked at Lorain, whose thoughts appeared to be wandering off somewhere. "So, what do you think?"

Lorain just remained silent for a minute with a serious faraway look on her face. Then suddenly her eyes locked with Unique's and a smile spread across her face that was so huge it lit the entire park up brighter than the sun could have. "I think it sounds like a wonderful idea," Lorain told Unique as she threw her arms around her daughter and hugged her tightly. She then pulled back and looked Unique straight in the eyes. "And I know just the person who'd love to adopt your baby."

Chapter Thirty-eight

Half an hour after Tamarra departed, Paige left her house and found herself back downtown at a familiar place. Standing hand in hand with Blake and escorted by Randall, the three of them entered the conference room of Ms. Turner's office.

Blake's mother and sister were already waiting, sitting beside Ms. Turner. They each wore victory smirks on their faces. The smirks made Paige want to snatch the papers from out of Randall's hands and rip them to shreds. But it was too late. Before the three of them could even sit down, Randall was already handing Ms. Turner the paperwork.

"I've already sent drafts back and forth to your paralegal, so I'm sure that everything in the contract will be to both your and your client's satisfaction," he stated. "Still, we'll give you all a couple of minutes to look over it." After handing Ms. Turner the paperwork, Randall sat down and began to converse with Blake in a whisper.

"I don't understand all that legal mumbo jumbo," Barnita said to Ms. Turner as she tried to go over the documents with her. She then looked over at her daughter. "Sharlita, didn't you take a couple of legal assisting classes over at the community college?"

"Yeah, but that was just so they wouldn't cut off my benefits," Sharlita answered. "But then when I got pregnant with Rahtekia, I knew they was gonna have to give me a check anyway, so I quit."

"Oh." There was a slight disappointment in Barnita's tone. "Oh, well, I'm sure you still learned in those classes more than I know." She stood up. "Here, trade places with me. You sit by Ms. Turner and go over this with her. I gotta go pee."

Paige, as a black woman, was just outright embarrassed. These two belonged in a *Wayans Bros.* movie as far as she was concerned. She rolled her eyes as Barnita exited the conference room after being given directions to the ladies' room.

As Paige sat there watching Blake and Randall hold a private conversation and then Ms. Turner and Sharlita going over the legal documents, she felt useless. There was only one other person she could have a conversation with, and she knew exactly what she wanted to say.

After excusing herself from the conference room, Paige made her way into the women's bathroom. She'd hoped to catch Barnita in there alone. Her wish was granted as she pushed open the bathroom door to find Barnita at the sink washing her hands and the two bathroom stalls empty.

Barnita glared at Paige as she snatched a paper towel from the holder. "The one on the left doesn't have any toilet paper." She nodded in the direction of the stalls.

"Thanks, but I didn't come in here to use the bathroom," Paige shot back.

"Oh, I see." Barnita balled up the paper towel, and then threw it way. "I can see you got a lot on your mind; some things you probably want to say to me. So let's do this." She said it as though she were challenging Paige to a brawl.

"Okay," Paige accepted the challenge. "Let's do this then." And without biting her tongue Paige did it. "What kind of sorry excuse for a mother are you? What kind of lowlife woman runs off and leaves her flesh and blood for dead, then comes back all these years later and sues him? Seems like this entire lawsuit should be offset by the back child support *you* owe."

Paige threw a few more not-so-nice shots at Barnita. Surprisingly enough, Barnita didn't even try to interrupt her. She didn't roll her eyes, snap her neck, put her hands on her hips, or anything. She just stood there and took it until Paige ran out of insults or ran out of breath to say anything else; one or the other.

"You finished?" Barnita asked calmly.

With her lips pinned tightly together, Paige stood silently.

"The same way you just laid it out there, I guess I owe you the same courtesy. So here it goes." Barnita threw her arms up, and then let them drop. "You wanna know what kind of woman I am?" She walked in close to Paige. "I'm the kind of woman who takes in her husband's whore's son. I'm the kind of woman who stood by her man affair after affair, and then when he knocked up one of his concubines, I wrapped the little bastard in a blanket and took him home from the hospital like I'd just pushed him out myself."

Paige thought she could just fall out on the floor right then and there, and it wouldn't have had anything to do with low sugar this time.

"I'm the one who was young, dumb, and stupid enough to allow my husband to convince me to legally adopt his whore's son, change his diapers, feed him, and clothe him." Barnita paused when her voice cracked, bound and determined not to break down in front of Paige. No, she was not about to give Paige the pleasure of knowing how much it had hurt her back then . . . how much it was hurting her now. "It was some type of private, closed adoption that Blake's father managed to work out through an attorney.

My name is even listed on the birth certificate as his mother. Go figure. But I didn't care about no adoption. Blakey was mine as far as I was concerned. I came so close to taking him just to spite that no-good daddy of his. I wanted to pay him back so bad it wasn't funny."

In spite of Barnita's attempts, Paige could see the hurt and pain written all over this woman's face. "So *that's* why you're doing this? To get back at your late husband?"

Barnita folded her arms and turned away from Paige. She couldn't face her. She couldn't face the words of truth Paige had just spoken. "Think what you want about me, Miss Thing." She whizzed the words over her shoulder at Paige. "I was a darn good woman to do all those things. But I wasn't doing it because I wanted to. I was doing it because I loved him; I loved my husband and would have done anything for that man."

Although Paige couldn't see her face, she could tell Barnita was crying.

"But then I just couldn't take it no more." Barnita began reminiscing back. "That day—the day I left—it wasn't planned. It was just a regular day. I'd gone about my regular duties that day. Prepared breakfast. Cleaned the house. Did laundry. Fixed lunch. And it was while I was fixing lunch that I realized, 'Barnita, you can't do this anymore, girlfriend.'" Barnita sharply turned to face Paige. "I couldn't do it anymore." Her eyes were full of tears. "And I remember right then and there deciding that I didn't have to do it anymore, so I left." Barnita shook her head as tears finally won the battle and burst forth, her nose running. "I bet you think I just took my baby girl 'cause she was mine out of my womb, but that ain't true. I loved Blakey like he was my own."

"Blakey?" Paige stated.

"Yeah, that's what I called him." She smiled. "I got to name him, you know. I gave him that name; Blake." Her smile grew wider. "Called him Blakey, and he loved it." Her smile faded. "The day I left, Blakey was sleeping. I went to his room to give him a kiss good-bye, but when I put my hand on the doorknob I stopped. I couldn't go in that room. I knew if I went in there I'd take him with me. And that wasn't right. He was his daddy's blood, not mine. And although I loved him like he was my own flesh and blood, I couldn't take that boy from his daddy." She pointed a stern finger at Paige. "And I don't care what you or anybody else thinks. I loved that boy and took care of him like he was my own. I never treated him any differently than I did Sharlita."

Strangely enough, Paige believed her.

"Besides, I couldn't take him with me even if he had been my flesh and blood. A boy needs a man to raise him. And no matter what his daddy did to me, he had good in him. More good than bad. I knew he'd raise that boy to be something special. So when I was standing in the grocery store line and saw his picture on the cover of that magazine, you don't know how much I rejoiced. Standing right there in the grocery store I acted a fool. Sharlita thought she was going to have to commit me to a crazy house. 'Cause see, she didn't know nothing about it. I might not have carried Blakey outta that house with me that day, but I carried a heap of shame. And it was that shame that had prevented me from telling Sharlita the truth—until that day in the store anyway.

"While I was telling Sharlita why the tears of joy were pouring down my face, the tears of joy turned into tears of anger. It was like I was having to relive the entire thing over again. Me in the middle of cooking

dinner and Blakey's daddy calling and telling me there
was an emergency and I had to come up to the hospital.
I thought something was wrong with him. I thought
something was wrong with my man. The entire drive
to the hospital I kept praying to God, 'Please don't
take my husband away from me.'" A gloomy, sicken-
ing look came across Barnita's face. "But he took him
anyway. That man was so wrapped up in his firstborn,
his first and only son, that I didn't even exist anymore."
She smiled. "But I really couldn't blame him, though.
Blakey had that 'something' about him even as a baby."
She looked over at Paige. "You know that something
I'm talking about? It's probably why you married him
in the first place."

Paige smiled, although her mind was filled with so
many questions. "So why hurt Blake? Because that's all
you're doing with this lawsuit, hurting him. His father
is six feet under now; it's not going to hurt him."

Barnita shrugged. "Maybe so. But at the time I was
just so . . . I just kept seeing Blake's picture on that
magazine, and eventually, all I could see in his eyes was
the sin of his father. I couldn't see past the sin of adul-
tery that turned our lives upside down. Mine anyway.
Blake and his dad were happy. And I was happy seeing
them happy. But then there came a time when I needed
to feed off of my own happiness. That time came the
day I left 'em."

Exhaling, Paige couldn't believe all Barnita had just
shared with her. But what truly baffled her was why
she'd shared it with her. "You do know that all I have to
do is go out there and tell Blake what you just told me
and this whole lawsuit thing could possibly go away. I
mean, yeah, you legally adopted him, and you were his
father's wife, whom he never legally divorced, but . . ."

"Yeah, I know," Barnita acknowledged. "And there's
no way I'd want all that dragged out in the open." She

chuckled. "I actually never thought the lawsuit would hold water anyway. But now seeming it did, I'm still not worried about it. Because I know you are going to go out there and do anything but tell your husband the truth." Barnita looked into Paige's eyes. "See, I know you. I used to be you. You love that man out there far too much to ever do or say anything that would hurt him. Because just like I needed for Blake's daddy to be happy, you need for Blake to be happy. Whether that man is happy or not defines your life right now. Am I right about it?"

Paige remained silent. Barnita was right. The last thing Paige was going to do was to run out there and tell Blake news that would destroy the man he was. It would tear him apart to know of the sin, the manipulation, the lies his father committed. After all, his father was the man whom he looked up to and admired. The man who made him persevere in life. Finding out that his father, his mother—his life—wasn't who or what they claimed to be would rock Blake's world. And Paige knew what that would mean for her.

"Well, I guess I better go out there and sign them papers. I got a whole new life ahead of me," Barnita stated.

"Yeah, you finally got your own happiness, but I guess it still ain't your own after all, huh?"

"Touché," Barnita stated before she moved toward the door.

"Wait!" Paige stopped her. There was still one thing she needed to know. "Did-did—I mean, besides cheating on you—did Blake's father ever hurt you in any other way?"

Barnita thought for a moment with a confused look on her face. "What do you mean . . . Oh, you mean like hit me or anything?"

Paige nodded.

Barnita laughed out loud. "Heck, no. That man wouldn't hurt a fly. He was big and gentle." She smiled as if reminiscing on his touch. Then she turned serious. "Blakey ain't putting his hands on you, is he?"

Now Paige feigned a laugh. "Oh, no," she lied. "I was just wondering, you know, if that was something I had to worry about in the future. You know they are doing studies that show violence can be inherited, passed down in the genes or something." Paige was lying through her teeth while at the same time asking God to forgive her.

"Harrumph. If you say so." Barnita didn't believe her. "I ain't never heard about that study. But if it's true, if that type of thing can be passed down, then you better leave Blakey now, because that mother of his was a beast." And on that note, Barnita exited the bathroom, leaving Paige alone with a million thoughts two-stepping through her mind.

"Oh, God, tell me what to do?" she prayed, but closed her mind to any answers He might have given her. In all honesty, she'd already made up her mind what to do. She'd already made up her mind not to go into that conference room and stop Blake from signing those documents. Doing so would mean having to tell him the truth about his father, about his real mother. She feared their marriage wouldn't be able to survive the breaking of that dam. So she opted to keep quiet and do what Barnita had done and was about to do again: live off of Blake's happiness.

When Paige returned to the conference room, she made eye contact with no one. The scribbling of the signatures onto the legal document that would transfer most of Blake's life savings over to Barnita sounded like nails scratched down a chalkboard to Paige. She cringed in torment in her seat, but still she said nothing. If Blake had been willing to let go of the money for the sake of their marriage, then why couldn't she? Paige was doing this for the sake of their marriage as well. Just as long as Paige could keep that thought at the forefront of her mind, everything would be okay.

"The funds will be transferred by the close of business today, tomorrow at the latest," Randall told Ms. Turner before he escorted Paige and Blake out of the conference room.

Paige couldn't help but look back at Barnita and Sharlita sharing a hug. Over her daughter's shoulder Barnita gave Paige a wink, as if the two of them shared some secret bond now, some special connection.

Not being able to get out of that conference room soon enough, Paige was grateful that she would never see the likes of Barnita again. But as she rode down the elevator arm in arm with Blake, her head resting against his shoulder, she remembered that there was one last question she had not asked Barnita, and that question was, who, in fact, was Blake's biological mother.

She looked up at Blake as he just happened to look down at her and smiled. She smiled back. And it was then that Paige realized she didn't need to know who his real mother was. None of that mattered now. All that mattered was that they were happy, and like Barnita had called it, Paige would do and say any and everything to make Blake happy. But it was what she wouldn't say, what she would never tell him, that she intended to do to keep them happy.

Chapter Thirty-nine

"Justice!" Sadie exclaimed happily as she made her way through the adults all the way to Justice, who stood behind his mother and father. "I'm so glad you made it." Sadie really was glad that Justice had arrived, so her greeting was genuine. But she was also making a big scene about him being there in order to simmer down the brewing storm. The tension among the adults may have been invisible, yet it could be felt.

"Me too," Justice stated with a shy grin and just enough pimples to show that he was heading toward the finishing stages of puberty.

"Mom, Dad," Sadie said to her parents, "this is Justice. Justice, this is my mom and dad, Mr. and Mrs. Tyson." Sadie looked at Mother Doreen. "Oh, yeah, and this is my Aunti Doreen I be telling you about." Next, Sadie looked at Justice's parents. "Hello, Mr. and Mrs. Klein. This is my mom, dad, and my—"

"Oh, I know *exactly* who Justice's father is," Mother Doreen said, giving Bishop Klein the look. "And I think it's a shame that this man used his son to help him do his dirty work."

"Aunti, what are you talking about?" Sadie was really confused as she stood next to Justice.

"This bishop has been snooping around the church trying to get the dirt on Pastor Frey and this family," Mother Doreen stated. "And it looks like he used his son here to get close to Sadie so he could do the same."

A hurt look came across Sadie's face as she inched away from Justice.

"'Reen," Bethany stated, seeing the disappointment in her daughter's eyes. "That can't be true."

Mother Doreen hadn't mentioned the incident involving Bishop to Bethany because she felt it was church business. So Bethany was doubtful of her sister's accusations. But now that Bishop Klein had stepped foot into their home and was using his son to infiltrate the family's affairs, it was anybody's business who Sister Doreen felt it should be.

"Well, there is some truth to it," Pastor Frey stepped in. "I can vouch for that much."

"Oh, please," Bishop Klein stated. "I'd never use my son to do my dirty work."

"So you *do* admit that you played dirty?" Mother Doreen stated to Bishop. "You laying low just waiting to catch somebody doing wrong? If you were here because you thought there was some wrongdoings going on up at Living Word, Living Waters, then you should have come in the name of Jesus, showed yourself, and nipped it in the bud. Pardon me if I'm overstepping my boundaries, Bishop, but God don't play, so neither should His vessels."

There was complete silence in the room, all eyes glued to Bishop for his comeback.

Relaxing his shoulders and letting out a gust of air he stated, "She's right," in reference to Mother Doreen. "She's absolutely right."

Now Sadie completely inched away from Justice and went to her mother's side. "Justice, I can't believe this. You *used* me."

Justice went to open his mouth, but it was Bishop's voice everyone heard.

"What I mean, sweetheart," Bishop said to Sadie, "is that your aunt here is right about me going about this entire thing the wrong way. But what she's not right about is me using my son's aid in my efforts. Justice had no idea about my assignment here in Kentucky. He had no idea of the church or the players in the game."

"So this was just a *game* to you?" Now Pastor Frey stepped in. He'd been biting his tongue. He respected his elders and leaders in the ministry, his dedication to Pastor Davidson making this very obvious. But what Pastor Frey was sick and tired of was his leaders playing games. Ministry was not a game, and he was tired of feeling like a pawn.

"No, Pastor," Bishop replied. "I take the ministry very seriously, but sometimes, just like everybody else, I do what I want to do, what I think will work, instead of what God knows will work." Bishop continued. "I apologize for the way I went about handling this situation. You should have been notified that I was coming here and why. You should have been able to prepare and cover yourself with prayer the same way I was. You should not have been a victim of my sneak attack."

"Thank you, Bishop. I accept your apology, and I'm glad you see it that way." Pastor Frey calmed down. "And, uh, like Sister Doreen, I'm sorry if I overstepped my boundaries with the way I just spoke."

"I think we both might have overstepped our boundaries to some degree," Bishop admitted. "Apology accepted." He then extended his hand to Pastor Frey.

Pastor Frey looked down at Bishop's hand, and then shook it.

"Praise God," Uriah expressed, throwing his hands in the air. "Now, can we eat? I passed up cold oatmeal for breakfast and spoiled egg salad sandwiches for lunch in order to save room for this meal."

There were several chuckles.

"And, Justice," Sadie spoke, now inching her way back in his direction, "I'm sorry I doubted you."

Blushing, Justice stuck his hands in his pocket and replied, "Aw, don't worry about it. It ain't nothing. But like your dad here stated, can we eat? The way you talk about your aunt's cooking, I don't know how much longer I can just stand here smelling it without getting my grub on." Justice rubbed his hands together as everyone laughed.

"Yeah, my aunti is the best cook in the world," Sadie confirmed.

"Good, 'cause it's been a minute since I've had a meal where I can throw down."

Both Uriah and Bishop cleared their throats. When their children looked over at them, they each nodded at their wives. That's when both Sadie and Justice realized while complimenting Mother Doreen's cooking, they weren't saying too much about their own mothers' skills in the kitchen.

"Oh, but my moms can throw down too," Justice added, receiving a bright smile from his mother. "She makes the best Beanie-Weenies in the world."

"Oh, I beg to differ; *my* moms probably got *your* moms on that," Sadie said confidently. "She can make it with her eyes *closed*."

"Okay, okay, that's enough," Bethany stated. "I think Mrs. Klein and I get the point."

"Yeah," Mrs. Klein smiled.

"So like my husband asked," Bethany said, "can we eat now?"

"Yes, indeed," Mrs. Klein stated, "but only if you all agree to have dinner with us next week."

"How about we make it a joint effort?" Bethany stated. "A Beanie-Weenie cook-off. Then we'll *really* be able to decide who makes the best in the world."

"Deal," Mrs. Klein agreed as she and Bethany shook on it.

"Now, right this way," Bethany instructed as she led the hungry mob into the kitchen, not even realizing that the crew was one man short.

While everyone else enjoyed the dinner Mother Doreen had prepared, the cook herself spent her time packing up her things. It was clear that her tenure in Kentucky was over. Amidst the confusion that had initially plagued the dinner, God had managed to work everything out. Sadie apologized to Justice for accusing him of using her just to help his father, the bishop, do his dirty work. Justice accepted the apology. Bishop apologized to Pastor Frey for making him feel as though he were running a cathouse instead of a church, and Pastor Frey accepted it.

While having dinner, Bishop informed Pastor Frey of the recommendation he was going to make regarding the situation at Living Word. He was recommending that he, himself, pastor Living Word and that Pastor Frey co-pastor with him. Pastor Frey didn't hesitate accepting his offer. Bishop had said it was just to rebuild the integrity of the church, but he knew he was going to be permanently taking over the church when he relocated to Kentucky. Why else would he have uprooted his entire family? Nonetheless, Pastor Frey seemed fine getting back into his old position of co-pastoring the church.

The God in Uriah had really showed up and showed out by forgiving both his wife and her ex-lover. Hudson arrived later with his baby and expressed, with his actions, that he'd gotten over his anger toward his father faking his death. His baby girl helped him with that. Knowing that she'd have her grandpa in her life to spoil her rotten and to raise her to love God, Hudson certainly saw the upside.

All was well.

"God don't need me here anymore," Mother Doreen said to herself as she zipped up her stuffed suitcase. "He's done everything Himself." It was bittersweet. A part of Mother Doreen wanted to stay in Kentucky, and that part was the part that cared deeply for Pastor Frey. But her interest in him had come with so much sorrow and confusion, and God was not the author of confusion. That was the reason Mother Doreen recited as cause not to pursue the relationship any longer.

Tired from all the packing, she sat on the bed and looked up. "Lord, you fixed everything. You brought everyone together but Pastor Frey and me. So if it was meant to be, surely you would have given me some sort of sign. And since you didn't . . . Well, I guess it just wasn't meant to be." Sighing, she stood up to begin filling her duffle bag with her toiletries. Ironically, she didn't know of any sign God could have given her when it came to Pastor Frey. He'd proved how great his loyalty was to his superiors. First, it was Pastor Davidson. Who was to say it wouldn't be the bishop next?

Even though nothing became of her and Pastor Frey, she had to admit that she was grateful for the feelings that man had brought out in her. "Lord, if I never feel that way again, I'm glad you allowed me to feel that way just one last time."

And with that, Mother Doreen finished packing. By the time she showered and got into her nightclothes, all the guests were gone. This gave her time to tell her family of her plans to immediately return to Malvonia. She'd probably stay in an extended-stay hotel until she could give her tenant notice. There were tears, but all understood. And even though they would miss Mother Doreen, Bethany, Uriah, and the kids looked forward to the opportunity of being a family again.

In bed, Mother Doreen lay down for a peaceful rest with dreams of heading back to her church. But her sleep was fitful. And although she was anxious to dive back into New Day Temple of Faith church business, something told her it was not going to be business as usual.

Chapter Forty

"Mom!" Lorain called out once she arrived back at her place. "Mom, I'm home, and I brought your favorite guilty pleasure—pizza!"

Eleanor had been staying with Lorain ever since Broady had passed away. She'd only left the house to take care of the funeral arrangements and to attend the funeral itself. Other than that, she'd stayed in her housedress that reminded Lorain of the old sitcom, *Maude*.

Figuring her mother might have taken Valium and was in a deep sleep, Lorain went and set the pizza down on the kitchen counter, and then walked toward the bedroom. With her mind fixed on her mother, she didn't even notice how spic-and-span the kitchen was.

When she cracked open the bedroom door, she was not only surprised to see that her mother wasn't in the bed they'd been sharing, but that the bed was made. The bedding had been changed and everything. Now that Lorain thought about it and looked around, everything was clean, much cleaner than any of her feeble attempts. She went into the living room and took notice of the shiny wood and the carpeted floor that didn't have a piece of lint on it. She peeked back into the kitchen at the sparkling stove and waxed floors.

"Mom?" Lorain called out again, now figuring her mother was somewhere cleaning. She checked the bath and the half bath. Her mother wasn't in either bathroom, but her cleaning touch was. "Wow, Mom," Lorain whispered to herself. She had to thank her mother. In all the years she'd lived there, it had never been that clean.

Moving onto the second bedroom, which Lorain had—turned into a computer room—she was certain she'd find her mother there. She was probably putting the finishing touches on some dusting or something. But to Lorain's surprise, when she entered the computer room, there was no Eleanor. Worry seeping in, Lorain went to the front-room window and peeked out. She let out a sigh of relief when she realized that Eleanor's car was no longer parked outside, something she hadn't noticed upon arriving home.

"Hmm." Lorain couldn't help but wonder where her mother had gone. Deciding to keep the pizza warm and then try calling her mother, she walked into the kitchen and placed the pizza in the oven, but not before taking a slice to tide her over until she and her mother could share dinner together.

Taking a bite of the pizza and then going back to her bedroom, she passed her computer room along the way. Glancing in, out of the corner of her eye, a blue blur caught her attention. A blue blur that sat on her computer desk. Lorain stopped in her tracks. Her stomach now turned as if it were full of a painful virus. The pizza made her feel nauseous. Having to take a step backward, Lorain pushed the computer room door open all the way and then began her trek toward the blue blur. The closer she got, the clearer it got. The closer she got, the clearer things became. The first time she'd peeked into the room, she'd been looking for one thing and one thing only: her mother. She hadn't even paid attention to anything else, especially *that*.

"MY LIFE," Lorain picked up and read the words on the folder, a folder that she was sure had been placed inside the desk drawer. But now it lay on top of the desk. Lorain pulled the drawer open. It was obvious her mother had run out of things to clean. The staples, paperclips, and rubber bands that had once been scattered about the drawer were now in neat, extra small plastic bowls. Her pens and pencils lined either side of the containers like soldiers keeping them in line.

Lorain's head started spinning when she realized what had happened. In her mother's cleaning efforts, she'd stumbled upon the folder. Surely she had read its contents. "Oh, God. Oh, God," was all Lorain could say while beginning to hyperventilate.

She dropped the folder and left the computer room. No longer having an appetite for the pizza, she hurried toward the kitchen to put it down the disposal. She wouldn't want it later. It was better off down the drain—just like she wished her life could be; anything to keep from having to face her mother. But it was too late. As Lorain cleared the living-room corner in order to get to the kitchen, Eleanor entered the front door.

Lorain just stood there silently as she watched her mother slowly close and lock the door behind her. "Mom, where have you been?"

Eleanor just stood looking at her daughter with puffy, red eyes. They'd been puffy for days from all the crying Eleanor had done for the loss of Broady. But they were puffier than ever today . . . and red; they hadn't been red before.

"Mom?" Lorain asked again when Eleanor didn't respond.

Eleanor snapped out of her daze. "Oh, I had to go home and get this." She held up something that, from where Lorain was standing, looked like a notebook.

Eleanor walked over to the couch. "I had to look in the garage and all over the attic before I found this thing." She laid it on the table.

Lorain approached the table. "Wha-what is it, Mom?" she stammered as she sat down next to Eleanor.

"It's your middle school yearbook," Eleanor stated, smiling. It was a forced smile. A smile that screamed, *"I'm here because I'm tired of crying."* Eleanor sniffled. "Did I tell you that I had to look through the garage and the attic in order to find it?"

"Yes, Mom," Lorain stated, confused. "But why did you need my middle school year. . ." Lorain's words trailed off. She knew exactly why her mom needed that yearbook—confirmation. It would be confirmation to what she'd read in the blue folder. As if what had been in the blue folder wasn't enough, Eleanor had wanted to connect all the dots, cure her suspicions herself.

Lorain closed her eyes, knowing that when she opened them, not only would she have to face her mother, but she'd have to face the truth as well.

"Right here," she heard her mother say. "I found it right here."

Lorain opened her eyes to see that her mother had turned to a page in the yearbook. Leaning forward, Lorain saw the page spread out that had her and her classmates' individual photos on it. Lorain's eyes landed on her own photo. She was smiling in the picture. But looking back at the picture now, it wasn't Lorain's usual smile. This one looked more forced. Her lips were smiling, but her eyes weren't. She was a child going through the motions.

"And then . . ." Eleanor flipped toward the front of the yearbook. "Here." She pointed. It was the page in the book that had photos of the staff. And there it was: a picture of Broady.

Lorain began to tremble. The memories were coming back. Way too many memories. The photo in the book; that's the exact Broady Lorain recalled. Not the man of God that had walked into her mother's life, her life, all these years later. Not the stepfather she'd just helped her mother bury. Lorain didn't know what to say. So Eleanor said it.

"You were one of his victims, weren't you?" Eleanor said the words as if she were describing the weather; cloudy with a high chance of rain.

Lorain affirmed with silence.

"When I found the folder, I couldn't understand why it had the words 'MY LIFE' on it, but yet, everything in it was about Broady. After reading everything in that folder, it didn't take much work to begin to put two and two together. Then I thought back to how you acted around Broady. How you reacted the first time you met him at my house . . . just everything. Ultimately, it was mother's intuition, I guess." Eleanor looked down. "Only the intuition kicked in years too late."

Lorain remained silent.

"I've been feeling real bad, daughter," Eleanor confessed as she slowly began rocking. "Real bad about Broady's death. And even had the nerve to be somewhat mad at God. I couldn't figure out why God had allowed me, in my late years, to find a man like Broady who treated me like a queen . . . who I was glad to have as a king, then take him away, just like that." She snapped her fingers. "Sadness, depression, anger, bitterness all rolled up inside of me like a ball of fire waiting to explode."

A tear fell from Eleanor's eye as she continued. "This morning I wanted to die. This morning I was gonna die. Didn't want to live anymore. I'd planned on taking all the Valium I had left. But you know me. Remember when you were growing up, what I used to say when I'd come into your bedroom?"

Lorain chuckled, and then replied, "Yeah. You used to say, 'Child, you better do something with this room. Tomorrow ain't promised. You could die in your sleep . . . and I wouldn't even want to be found dead in this room.'"

Eleanor let out a chuckle of her own. "Yep. And that's how I felt about your house."

Lorain looked embarrassed. "I know, and I was going to get around to cleaning up, Momma, it's just that—"

"It's just that you were too busy comforting me from mourning the loss of my husband; the man who ra-ra-raped you." The tears poured from Eleanor's eyes. "Your computer room was the last room I cleaned. And I'd only opened the folder because I was looking for a piece of paper to write you a note. A suicide note."

"Mom," now Lorain's tears started. Just the thought of her mother leaving her to join the enemy in the pits of hell tore her apart.

"I'm just telling you the truth here." Sadly, Eleanor looked at Lorain. "I think a mother and daughter need to be able to tell each other the truth. And I thought that's the kind of relationship we had." Eleanor began to cry even harder. "How could I not have known? How does a mother not know?"

Lorain embraced her mother. "Mom, please don't take the blame for this."

"I was a good mother. I was a *good* mother," Eleanor repeated over and over.

"Yes, you were, Mom. You were a good mother."

Eleanor pulled away. "Then why? Why didn't you tell me? Why didn't I know?" She pointed to the yearbook. "Why couldn't I have looked at that picture and seen it in your eyes?"

"Mom, please. It's over now. It's okay."

"It's not okay." Eleanor stood up in rage. She harshly wiped her tears away, then covered her mouth with her hand. "I'm sorry. I didn't mean to get upset."

"It's okay, Mom."

Eleanor closed her eyes tightly. "Will you please stop saying it's okay when it's not?" she shouted. "That man raped you. That son of a—" Eleanor balled her hands into fists. "He'd already killed a part of you—your innocence. After finding that folder and reading the papers inside, I wasn't about to let him take any part of my life, let alone my entire life."

Turning to her daughter as if she'd just had an epiphany, she stated, "So, ironically enough, the death of the man that had only moments earlier made me want to die, had, all of a sudden, made me want to live. The sorrow, the mourning for that man is no more. The anger and bitterness, especially toward God, is no more. Instead, I thank God for leading me to the truth. That truth; the truth in that folder and the truth right here in that yearbook, it set me free, girly. Yes, it did. There was no way I could feel that way about a man who did what he did to my daughter. No siree. I want to live. I want to live out every day God has for me hating that man. I want to make up now for all the years I should have hated him. I'm gonna hate him just as if what he did to you was yesterday."

Lorain sighed as her head turned from left to right. "No, Mom. That's not living. And I don't want to watch you spending the last of your days walking in hate instead of love. Is that any kind of way to thank God for setting you free?"

Eleanor remained silent, anger for Broady consuming her.

"Mom, don't take this the wrong way," Lorain started. "But you really don't hate that man. You really don't
want to walk around the rest of your days on earth hating him . . . when it's yourself you really hate."

Eleanor let out a wail. Her daughter's stinging words
of truth penetrated her soul. She keeled over as if in
pain. She *was* in pain. She was hurt, hurting for her
baby girl. There was that cry again. There was that
pain. And again, Lorain understood.

"I hated myself too, Mom, for years. And that's no
way to live. It ain't living."

"I just feel like the least I could do is hate him for
you. To hate him for us both," Eleanor cried. "My baby.
He hurt my baby," she screamed.

"But, I'm healed, Mom. Can't you see that? I'm delivered from all that hurt and pain and woe-is-me stuff
I used for a crutch for so long. Only a healed woman
could have stood by and supported you in that marriage."

"And that's what hurts even more. You were there
for me, but I wasn't there for you," Eleanor stated. "I
just started thinking about our conversations about
Broady. The times you tried to tell me; you tried to tell
me who Broady was and what he had done to you. Like
that day right here in your living room."

Lorain thought back to the conversation she and her
mother had had. It was when Lorain thought Broady
had told her mother the truth about them. She'd
thought that because that's what Eleanor's words had
led her to believe. *". . . Broady told me."* And Lorain
had taken those words and ran with them, running in
a totally different direction than her mother was going.

"And that day in the church, you really were starting
to remember things. And I just couldn't figure out for
the life of me why those things were coming to you;

why you were having visions of Broady. Heck, I was just glad you were getting your memory back." Eleanor began to weep at just the thought. "And I believed him. I believed he was healed and delivered. All that stuff about him making himself accountable to others. I mean, at first I had my doubts because I figured he didn't make himself accountable to the state board when he came back here. But he said that working with kids was his life, it was all he knew, and he knew if he disclosed that information to the board, no one would hire him. I should have reported him myself."

"But you didn't know everything, Mom," Lorain stated in an attempt to try to make her mother feel better.

"But I should have known." Eleanor grabbed her stomach as if she was going to be sick. "But *he* knew. He knew what he'd done to you, and then he turned around and married me. How sick! I guess since he couldn't have you anymore, he'd settle for me."

"No, Mom. That man loved you. I believe that with every being of my body. In all honesty, I don't think he knew who I was." Lorain went on to tell her mother about the day she'd come to her house, the day Broady had his heart attack. She told her how she believed it was then, when Eleanor had called Lorain by her full name, that Broady had remembered who she was; that ultimately caused his heart attack. Still, Eleanor couldn't get past her anger toward Broady.

"Mom, I know it's going to take some time, but you are going to have to ask God for healing and deliverance," Lorain told her mother. "And He will do it. If He did it for me, there is no reason on Earth He won't do it for you."

Eleanor looked into her daughter's eyes. "You make it look so easy."

Lorain hugged her mother. "And it is easy, Mom. Some Christians make it seem as though trying to stay saved, trying to get and stay healed, trying to get and stay delivered is hard work. But it's not. It's reasonable. God would never ask His people to do anything that wasn't reasonable; anything that He knew we couldn't do. All we have to do is make a conscious decision to say 'yes' to God and mean it. To want to be and stay saved; to want to be and stay healed; to want to be and stay delivered. Don't try to stay saved, just do it. Just stay saved. Just want it. And I wanted it!" Lorain began to shout. "My God, I wanted it. Hallelujah."

Eleanor began to watch her daughter dance in the spirit right there. And Eleanor swore she could feel the ground shake beneath her feet.

"Glory!" Lorain shouted. "You did it for me, God! Do it for my mother in the name of Jesus. I send up this plea on my mother's behalf, O God. Halleluiah!"

"Yes, Lord," Eleanor mumbled. Then again, "Yes, Lord," she roared. And before she knew it, her feet were dancing too. "I want it, Lord. O God, I want it."

And the two gave new meaning to Carole King's song that went, *"I feel the Earth move under my feet."*

The Earth *was* moving under their feet. Mountains were moving. Their shouts, the praise, the worship that followed. The devil wanted no part of it and had to flee. An hour later, Lorain and Eleanor were helping each other off the living-room floor from where the two had lay prostrate, communing with God.

It was something they had never encountered before. It was the best mother-daughter experience they'd ever shared in their lives. One they'd never forget.

"I feel born-again," Eleanor confessed. "Is this real?" she asked her daughter. "Is this feeling real? Can God *really* do that? Change a person instantaneously? Change their heart?"

With tears of joy flowing down her face, Lorain replied. "Yes, He can, Mom. God can do anything, and He just did."

Chapter Forty-One

"Pastor, I don't understand why you yourself can't continue to counsel us," Paige said as she sat in the New Day Temple of Faith's pastor's office. She'd shown up for her individual counseling session. Blake had been there for his session earlier that day on his lunch break.

"Like I told Brother Blake, I will still continue to provide the two of you general marital counseling, but I believe you both also need domestic violence counseling as well," the pastor replied.

"But I felt just fine speaking to you about . . ." Paige hated saying the words. She hated even thinking that she'd almost been a victim of domestic violence herself. "Almost" was her own wording. ". . . domestic violence. When you asked me how my family generally handles anger, I answered without hesitation. When you asked me if there was ever any domestic abuse in my home growing up, I answered honestly; there wasn't. Neither Blake nor I have been dishonest with you, Pastor."

The pastor gave Paige a discerning look.

"Okay, so at first I didn't just outright tell you that I hadn't really slammed my hand in anything, and that it wasn't that guard at the jail who landed my arm in a sling. But I eventually told you the truth, Pastor." Paige was becoming emotional. "I promise I won't lie ever again. Just help us. Please help us, Pastor. I know with just a couple more counseling sessions we'll be as good as new. Just these past few days, ever since Blake's mom left the picture again, things have been great. And he never actually hit me . . ."

"Sister Paige," Pastor managed to get those words in, "I'm not abandoning you. The church is not abandoning you. Please don't think that. It's just that, and I hate to say it, but the church does not have procedures in place to address domestic violence. And even so, I'm still just one person, and no one person has all the right answers. But now Sister Nita and I are working on finding as many answers, solutions, and resources possible." Pastor handed Paige a brochure from off the desk.

"Columbus Coalition Against Family Violence?" Paige read the front of the brochure out loud.

"Yes, it's an agency Sister Nita sought out in Columbus. The wife of the man who owns Victoria's Secret is the founder."

Paige just nodded, still not understanding why her pastor was sending her and Blake to someone else for counseling.

"I'm going to include teachings about domestic violence in my premarital counseling sessions from now on," Pastor told Paige. "And you know what? I'm going to start preaching about it from the pulpit. It should not have taken this situation to open my eyes and to realize that domestic violence is not just a problem; it's *our* problem. It's something the church needs to address. We have protocol for how to court first-time visitors and keep them coming back; how to increase membership; but we didn't even have something in place to help members in our church who are being abused."

"There's others?" Paige was surprised. "Here at New Day?"

"Perhaps. Sister Paige, there are millions of women going through what you are going through. But even so, whether those women are right here at New Day doesn't matter, because even if there was just one, then we need to be prepared to save just that one." Pastor smiled at Paige, letting her know that for now, she was the one that New Day wanted to help save.

Paige was starting to realize that Pastor wasn't just kicking her and Blake to the curb; Pastor really was trying to tap into every resource possible to help them . . . and perhaps those after them. "Thank you, Pastor. Thank you for caring. And Sister Nita . . . God bless her."

"Yes, she is going to be a big part of the changes and new things regarding domestic violence here at the church. She's already surfed the Web and found a site called www.swatcministry.com. SWATC stands for Sheltered Women and Their Children. They have a link on the site to assist others who want to start a SWATC ministry at their own church. Sister Nita is looking into it and has agreed to oversee a SWATC ministry here at New Day. Maybe eventually you can assist her."

"Yeah, maybe." Paige smiled and nodded. "Well, I guess I better get going. I'd just gotten off work before I came to see you. I need to go to the grocery store. Flo is off today, so I have to cook. I think I'll make Blake's favorite. I want to try to do everything I can to keep him happy, to do my part as a wife."

"That's fine, Sister Paige, but don't feel like you have to be perfect. Don't feel as though there was anything imperfect about you that might have caused Blake to act the way he did. All blame rests on Blake. And that's why I want you two to seek a domestic violence counselor. I'm not saying you have to. It's solely your decision. I'm not here to control your choices, but I do want you to know that you have choices."

"I understand, Pastor," Paige stated. And now, she really did understand.

"I don't want you jumping back into the groove of things prematurely without considering all your choices and options. And they are choices for you and you alone to make."

"But what about the Bible verse that says the husband is the head?" Paige asked. "And all the other scriptures, like Ephesians, chapter five, versus twenty-two to twenty-three?"

"I understand the scripture in Ephesians states that wives should be subject to their husbands as to the Lord. For the husband is the head of the wife as Christ is the head of the church, his body, and is himself its Savior."

The pastor paused, and then continued. "That scripture was not created to prescribe unquestioning obedience of a wife to her husband. But you know what I interpret the scripture as saying? It's telling the wife and the husband that their marriage should be based on Christ's relationship to the church. That relationship was sacrificial love and service, not intimidation and abuse."

Paige took in Pastor's words. She'd had to admit that just last night, she'd found scripture after scripture describing why she should stay in her marriage with Blake without ever even considering the option of leaving him if he continued to put his hands on her. And now Pastor had found scriptures stating why Blake's treatment of her wasn't right. It was at that moment that Paige decided that she didn't have to over think things, because she was going to take Pastor's advice and seek domestic violence counseling, but that was if, and only if, Blake was up to it.

Lord, let him be up to it.

"I understand what Pastor is suggesting," Blake stated as he and Paige prepared for bed. Paige lay in the bed while Blake slipped on his pajamas. "But I honestly don't feel we need to go to any special type of counseling. Besides, that would be labeling us—labeling me. What would people think if they found out I was going to a counselor that specialized in domestic abuse? I'd make the cover of a magazine for totally different reasons, that's for sure."

"I don't care what people think," Paige was quick to say. "All I care about is us being in a healthy, long lasting marriage."

"And we will be." Blake made his way over to the bed. "I mean, we are. Don't you agree? Now that the lawsuit is over and done with and that woman is out of my life," Blake stated, referring to his mother, "my stress level is way down. I'm working on building back up our nest egg. Life is going to be better, sweetheart. I'm going to be better, and our marriage is going to be better."

Before Paige could continue her fight for domestic abuse counseling, the kisses Blake began planting on her distracted her mind. Before she could even continue her efforts in convincing Blake that they should take Pastor's advice, he'd pleased her in ways that probably were a sin for even a married couple. But it made her feel good, happy. It made her feel better about, afterward, agreeing with Blake that they really didn't need counseling at all, not even from their pastor. That this was something they could work through on their own.

But after turning out the lights and bidding their evening farewells until morning, something inside Paige began nudging her mind. Yeah, maybe Blake was right. Maybe life was going to be better. Maybe Blake was going to be better. Maybe even their marriage would be better. But would Paige be better? More importantly, would she be better off . . .

She shook the negative thoughts away, not even wanting to think about living her life without Blake; not after all they'd been through and all she'd fought for. Paige closed her eyes and fell asleep knowing that deep in her soul, eventually things would get better. In the back of her mind, though, she couldn't help but question that if before things got better, would they get worse.

Chapter Forty-two

Lorain was surprised to find Unique sitting in a chair outside Pastor's office. "Hey," she greeted.

Unique stood, equally as shocked to see Lorain entering the doorway. "Hey, yourself." Unique began to grow a little nervous. Usually whenever Pastor had arranged for both women to meet at the same time it was because each had a complaint about the other. Typically it was a complaint regarding the Singles Ministry. But with the meeting before last being cancelled because Lorain was a no-show, and neither woman showing up at the last meeting due to all the drama going on in their lives, not much had been going on to complain about. So Unique's mind began to wonder about what Lorain could have possibly told Pastor about her.

"You here to see Pastor?" Lorain asked.

"Uhh, yes, but the secretary is in there with Pastor now," Unique replied. She swallowed hard, as if she'd been eating a tennis ball and was forcing down the last chunk.

Detecting her tenseness, Lorain said, "Don't worry, I didn't tell Pastor anything about you being my daughter."

Unique let out a sigh of relief, but then another thought popped into her mind as her eyes bulged.

"And don't worry," Lorain smiled. "I didn't tell Pastor about the baby either."

Unique closed her eyes, exhaled deeply, then sat back down.

"Why so worried?" Lorain asked. "I told you that no one would know a thing until you were ready," Lorain reminded her. "You do trust me, don't you? You do know that I would never betray your wishes. I know how hard this is for you, and I don't want to make it any harder." Lorain grabbed Unique's hands. "I do want you to know, though, that I can't wait for the world to know that you are my baby girl. I can't wait to tell the world that my baby girl is alive." Lorain looked down. "I know in doing so, that my testimony is going to have to come along with it."

"You don't mind telling your story?" Unique asked.

"If I don't tell my story, then how's God going to get the glory? And you know us—me and you." Lorain's eyes lit up. "My grandbabies." She then pointed at Unique's stomach. "My baby." She put her hand over her mouth to hold back the tears, forgetting the point she was about to make. "God is awesome."

Unique looked down at her belly. "Yeah, He is." She then looked up at Lorain with excitement. "And just think, if it's a girl it would be like you getting to raise me after all . . . a piece of me anyway, only through my baby instead."

"I know," Lorain agreed.

"Once she gets old enough though," Unique reminded Lorain, "once I've got my own place, my own car and a career, we'll revisit the idea of perhaps telling her the truth someday, right? And no matter what, she can still come stay with me and the boys sometimes, right?"

"Yes, just like we agreed. Like I said before and like I'm going to keep on saying, you can trust me."

Unique released the remainder of her tension by gently squeezing Lorain's hands. "I know I can trust you. And I do trust you . . . Mom." Unique barely knew where that had come from. Even though late at night while lying in bed she'd been practicing out loud calling Lorain, "Mom," she just had no idea she'd actually say it to her so soon.

For Lorain, it couldn't have been any sooner as she pulled Unique close to her and hugged her.

"Well, isn't this a sight for sore eyes?"

The pastor's voice caught Unique's and Lorain's attention. They quickly released each other, and then stood.

"Good evening, Pastor." Lorain was the first to speak, then Unique.

"Good evening, ladies," Pastor replied. "Thanks for coming. Sorry I'm running a little behind schedule, but there were a couple of calendar issues I needed to clear up with my—"

"Ladies." The church secretary came from behind the pastor and greeted Lorain and Unique. Lorain thought she detected a hint of nervousness in the secretary's voice, but figured it was just a rushed spirit.

"Hello," the women greeted her.

"I didn't mean to hold Pastor so long. But Pastor is all yours now." The secretary squeezed through everyone and headed to her office. "See you all in Bible Study."

After the secretary disappeared behind her own office door, Unique and Lorain entered the pastor's office.

"Have a seat, ladies," Pastor ordered. And after opening in prayer, Pastor got right to the point. "So I hear the Singles Ministry hasn't met in a couple of months." Pastor looked from Lorain to Unique. "Does anyone mind telling me what's been going on?"

Unique and Lorain looked at each other. Neither spoke.

"Well, don't you both go speaking at once," the pastor joked.

"You see, Pastor," Lorain started, "there's just been so much going on in the last two months that you wouldn't believe it."

"Try me."

Unique and Lorain looked at each other once more. Again, neither spoke.

Lorain cleared her throat. "I've just experienced so much family drama that I honestly have to say, the Singles Ministry has been the last thing on my mind." Lorain was ashamed to admit it, but that had been the truth.

"Yeah, same here," Unique admitted.

Pastor sat and thought for a moment. "That's odd, because from what I hear, you two have been spending quite a bit of time together. I guess I just assumed you were handling Singles Ministry business. I mean, it wasn't too long ago you two couldn't stand to stay in the same room together for the sake of Christ, and now you're best buddies. You were even hugging out there just a minute ago."

Unique and Lorain looked at each other once again, then back at Pastor.

"You both seemed so eager to want to take on the role of leader and co-leader of the Singles Ministry. But I guess that happens a lot of times in ministry. Folks are excited and on fire for the Lord. They have visions and ideas, but then somewhere down the road, they eventually lose their passion and—"

"I haven't lost my passion," Lorain interrupted. "It's just that, Pastor, there was so much going on, like I stated, stuff you wouldn't believe." Lorain looked at Unique and smiled. "Miracles even."

Unique smiled back.

Pastor's head was shaking from left to right. "I honestly think God gave Mother Doreen the vision to start the Singles Ministry. I just don't think the people are ready to see the vision through."

"I'm sorry to disappoint you, Pastor," Lorain started, "and as leader I take full responsi—"

"Allow me to stop you right there," Pastor said. "It's not me you're disappointing. It's the members who showed up at a meeting where neither the leader nor co-leader were present. And more importantly, it's God."

Lorain hadn't looked at it that way. For some reason she just thought God would understand. After all, He was the one setting up dominos, connecting dots, and helping her put together all these puzzle pieces in her life. Had He, on top of all that, expected her to continue on with the business of the Singles Ministry?

"I know you love the Lord, Sister Lorain." Pastor then looked at Unique. "And you too, Sister Unique." Pastor looked back at Lorain. "But you just said yourself that God has been performing miracles in your life. And I know that God continues loving us, blessing us, showing us favor, grace, and mercy whether we give Him anything back in return or not. But wouldn't it be nice if we just did?"

Lorain felt like sinking down in her chair. Just a minute ago she felt like she was on top of the world. Now she felt like the scum of the Earth. Both Pastor and Unique noticed her shift in demeanor.

"I'm not trying to make you feel bad," Pastor started, "but—"

"But you are," Unique interrupted.

Both Lorain and Pastor were caught off guard by Unique's sudden outburst. "And I don't mean any disrespect, Pastor. But I know what she's been through. I know what's been going on."

Lorain appreciated Unique's support, even though she really only knew half of what she'd been dealing with. She still didn't know the entire story about Broady being a pedophile, the older man who'd impregnated her, then turning around and marrying her mother. When Unique had asked about the man who fathered her, Lorain had simply replied, "He's dead," and left it at that. She honestly didn't plan on ever telling Unique every single, little detail. She didn't find it necessary. In her spirit, she felt Unique knew enough. Knowing only the half that Unique was now defending Lorain about with Pastor was enough.

"I think it's wonderful that instead of being against Sister Lorain," Pastor said to Unique, "that you are now with her. But we all have to be accountable for ourselves."

"And she is accountable. Where blame is due, she takes it." Unique's eyes began to water as she spoke of the woman she now knew to be her mother. "Had she not stepped up to the plate and been accountable when it was most important, that's when I think God would have been disappointed in her. But she did step up. And not only did she change my life, not only did she put a smile on my heart, but God's heart is smiling too." Unique wiped away her tears, and then sternly looked at Pastor and said, "So I can't just sit here and let you make my mother feel bad. She's been made to feel bad enough in life." She looked at Lorain with sympathy. "She's been made to do bad in life." It was obvious she was referring to Lorain's relationship with the man who fathered her. "You know what I've learned in my short life? That a person can feel bad and do bad all by themselves. But you know when God is really pleased? When God just really shows up and showers you with kisses? When you can do better all by yourself. I mean, 'cause anybody can do bad. There ain't nothing special about that. But giving all glory to God when a person can do better . . . my, my, my."

The room was dead silent.

"Well, hallelujah," Pastor said in shock. Pastor knew Unique had the Word in her heart and could pray the enemy away, but she'd just spoken as if she were standing behind the pulpit. "I like that, Sister Unique." Pastor stood and pulled the emotional Unique into a warm embrace. Noticing Lorain in tears, Pastor pulled her into an embrace as well. "I'm sorry if I've offended or made either one of you feel bad," Pastor apologized. "Just because I'm pastor doesn't mean I'm always right. Sometimes I steer away from what the Holy Spirit is telling me to do and say and allow my flesh to rise up." Pastor pulled away and looked at each woman. "The Holy Spirit might convict a person, but He is never into embarrassing folks, or like Sister Unique stated, making a person feel bad. And I'm sorry, daughters."

"Apology accepted, Pastor," each woman stated in between sniffles as the pastor pulled them close again. "The Holy Spirit also has good listening ears. And although you may have gotten it past me, it didn't get past the Holy Spirit." Pastor paused before asking. "Sister Unique, now what's this about referring to Sister Lorain as your mother?"

By the time Lorain and Unique finished telling Pastor about their recent discovery, Wednesday night Bible Study had already been in session for thirty-five minutes. As soon as Pastor had posed the question of why Unique had referred to Lorain as her mother, it was as if the Holy Spirit had touched each woman on her shoulder, nodded, letting her know it was okay to share their story with Pastor. Both women felt relieved. The spiritual guidance of their spiritual leader through all of this was something each woman needed, not saying that God would not have brought them through it Himself, seeing He'd brought them this far. But they both knew that sometimes God used a living, Earth-walking vessel, just like He'd used Jesus. Pastor was a welcomed vessel.

And although there were tears as the women told their story, at the end of the conversation, rejoicing, shouting, and praising could be heard from that little office.

"Oh, my goodness," Pastor stated after looking at the clock. "Look how late it is. We better go so we can at least catch the last of Bible Study. I'm sure Elder Johnston went on and started teaching when she saw I wasn't there."

"Thank you, Pastor," Lorain said. "Thank you for being the angel of this house. Thank you for being who and what you say you are. Thank you for being a soldier for the Lord, one that is always here for the saints, no matter the second, the minute, or the hour. I love you, Pastor."

"Amen to that," Unique agreed.

"Give all glory to God," was all Pastor stated. "To God be the glory."

Pastor ushered the women out of the office, then followed behind after turning off the light and closing the office door. "But, ladies, I have to let you know, and this was a decision I was in the process of making prior to my meeting with you two."

The women paused at Pastor's tone. It was the kind of tone that was a prelude to not-so-good news. "I'm going to be shutting down the Singles Ministry, at least temporarily until I can hear from God. Because as you know, if a ministry is not functioning in the spirit of excellence, then it ain't functioning up in New Day."

"We understand," Lorain spoke for both herself and Unique. Lorain thought about Mother Doreen and how she'd trusted her enough to turn the reigns of the ministry over to her. She wished Pastor would just assign someone else temporarily instead of shutting the ministry down altogether, but she understood.

As Pastor followed the women to the Bible Study classroom, although they'd just rejoiced something awful, there was a gloomy mood among them now. Whenever a ministry was dying, mourning took place. Pastor knew from experience that when ministries began to die off, eventually so did membership, and ultimately, sometimes, so did the church. Trying to stay saved was hard enough for a saint; the ministries and resources were there to assist in the battle. Whether the battle of maintaining New Day would be a win, lose, or draw, Pastor couldn't help but smile knowing that however it went, New Day and its members would be victorious in winning the entire war—because the Bible told them so.

Reader's Group Guide Questions

1) Do you agree that once the New Day Temple of Faith pastor suspected domestic abuse between Paige and Blake that they should have been counseled separately?

2) Do you feel Uriah had a right to be angry with Bethany's deception, considering he'd deceived her as well?

3) Nita seemed to always be around to witness incidents concerning Paige and Blake. Do you feel that was God positioning her, or was it merely accidental that she was in the right place at the right time?

4) Paige didn't want to give up on her marriage, but neither did she want to stay in a situation that was harmful. Do you believe she made the right decision?

5) Why do you believe Mother Doreen had such a difficult time hearing clearly from God?

6) How did you feel about the fact that Raygene, Tamarra's daughter, hadn't committed suicide after all? That it was faulty brakes that had caused her car to crash?

7) Do you find the New Day Divas series to be entertaining, ministering, both, or neither?

8) Have you realized up until this point that the gender of the pastor of New Day Temple of Faith has never been revealed? What sex do you think the pastor is? Does it matter?

9) At what point did you consider Blake and Paige's relationship abusive?

10) Quite a bit of turmoil and issues transpired between Bethany and Uriah. Do you think God had a plan in everything that took place? Do you think the enemy might have had something to do with it? If so, do you believe it might have been a legal assignment from God? Why or why not?

11) Do you think Mother Doreen hid behind church and assignments from God as an excuse to prevent her from finding love and happiness within her own life? Why or why not?

12) There is one more book to the "New Day Divas" series. Are you excited to read, after a four-book journey, the fifth and final installment? Or do you feel the series could have ended with this book, or any of the others?

About the Author

Blessed selling author E.N. Joy is the writer behind the five-book series, "New Day Divas," coined, the "Soap Opera In Print." Formerly writing secular works under the names Joylynn M. Jossel and Joy, this award–winning author has been sharing her literary expertise on conference panels in her hometown of Columbus, Ohio, as well as cities across the country.

After thirteen years of being a paralegal in the insurance industry, Joy finally divorced her career and married her mistress and passion: writing. In 2000, Joy formed End Of The Rainbow projects publishing company, where she published her own works until landing a book deal with a major publisher. Under End of the Rainbow, Joy has published *New York Times* and *Essence* magazine bestselling authors in the "Sinner" series, which include *Even Sinners Have Souls, Even Sinners Have Souls TOO,* and *Even Sinners Still Have Souls*.

In 2004, Joy branched off into the business of literary consulting in which she provides one-on-one consultations and literary services such as ghostwriting, editing, professional read-throughs, write behinds, etc. Her clients consist of first-time authors, *Essence* magazine bestselling authors, *New York Times* bestselling authors, and entertainers.

Not forsaking her love of poetry, she has published two works of poetry titled *Please Tell Me If The Grass*

About The Author

Is Greener and *World On My Shoulders*. Joy plans to turn her focus back to that genre one day. "But my spirit has moved in another direction," Joy says. Needless to say, she no longer pens street lit (in which two of her titles, *If I Ruled the World* and *Dollar Bill*, made the *Essence* magazine bestsellers list. *Dollar Bill* appeared in *Newsweek* and has also been translated into Japanese). She no longer pens erotica or adult contemporary fiction either, in which one of her titles earned her the Borders bestselling African American romance award at the Romance Writers of America National Conference. Instead, under the name E.N. Joy, she pens Christian fiction, and under the name N. Joy, she pens children's and young adult titles. Joy's children's story, *The Secret Olivia Told Me*, received the American Library Association Coretta Scott King Honor. Book club rights have also been purchased by Scholastic, and the book is on tour at Scholastic Book Fairs in schools all over the map. Elementary and middle school children have fallen in love with reading and creative writing as a result of the readings and workshops Joy performs in schools nationwide.

Currently, Joy is the executive editor for Urban Christian. When she's not adding her two cents to other authors' works, she's diligently working on her own. Joy's "New Day Divas" series is having greater success than she could have ever imagined. She is certain this project is the one that is going to afford her with the title of *New York Times Bestselling Author*. Until then, she doesn't mind the title of Blessed selling author.

You can visit Joy at www.JoylynnJossel.com and www.enjoywrites.com

Be sure to pick up Book Five of the "New Day Divas" series titled
I Can Do Better All By Myself

The series comes full circle as the New Day Temple of Faith's Single's Ministry begins to unravel. The New Day Temple of Faith pastor even considers dissolving the ministry. Some members believe the only way to hold it together is by getting their pastor to join the ministry. And why shouldn't their leader show support by joining, considering the pastor's own single status? Some church members support the idea, while others frown upon the fact that they are being led by a shepherd who is single in the first place. It becomes an all-out war with one side wanting the pastor to embrace singlehood, while others secretly play matchmaker.

Marriage has been the furthest thing from the pastor's mind. Not because there hasn't been an opportunity, but because there really hasn't been time. With a needy congregation facing trial after tribulation—namely Paige and the secret she's keeping from her husband, and Lorain and the secret she's keeping from her mother and Unique, not to mention the secret she and Unique are keeping from the world—Pastor has no time to play the dating game. And being a pastor on call twenty-four seven, who has time for a serious relationship, period, other than the one with God? But eventually, decisions have to made around New Day, and they will be, but will these decisions mend the ministry—or destroy the church?

Safety Plan Model for the Victim of Domestic Violence

Taken from *Turning the Tide: Charting a New Course Towards Safety,* Resource Guide
Columbus Coalition Against Family Violence
(Used with permission from the Ohio Domestic Violence Network, 4807 Evanswood Drive, Suite 201, Columbus, OH 43229)

Step 1. Safety during Violence

I Can Use the Following Options:

a. If I decide to leave, I will _____.

b. I can keep a bag packed and put it_____ so I can leave quickly.

c. I can tell _____ about the violence and have them call the police when violence erupts.

d. I can teach my children to use the telephone to call the police and the fire department.

e. I will use this code word _____ for my children, friends, or family to call for help.

Safety Plan Model

f. If I have to leave my home, I will go _____ (Be prepared even if you think you will never have to leave.)

g. I can teach these strategies to my children.

h. When an argument erupts, I will move to a safer room such as _____.

i. I will use my instincts, intuition, and judgment. I will protect myself and my children until we are out of danger.

Step 2. Safety When Getting Ready to Leave

I Can Use the Following Strategies:

a. I will leave money and an extra set of keys with _____.

b. I will keep important documents and keys at _____.

c. I will open a savings account by this date _____ to increase my independence.

d. Other things I can do to increase my independence are: _____
_____

e. The domestic violence hotline is _____.

f. The shelter's hotline is _____.

g. I will keep change for phone calls with me at ALL times. I know that if I use a telephone credit card, that the following month, the telephone bill will tell the abuser who I called after I left. I will keep this information confidential by using a prepaid phone card, using a friend's telephone card, calling collect, or using change.

h. I will prearrange with _____ and _____ so that I can stay with them and know beforehand who will lend me money.

i. I can leave extra clothes with _____.

j. I will review my safety plan every _____ (time frame) in order to plan the safest route.

k. I will review the plan with _____ (a friend, counselor, or advocate).

l. I will rehearse the escape plan and practice it with my children.

Step 3. Safety at Home

I Can Use the Following Safety Methods:

a. I can change the locks on my doors and windows as soon as possible.

b. I can replace wooden doors with steel doors.

c. I can install security systems, i.e., additional locks, window bars, poles to wedge against doors, electronic sensors, etc.

d. I can purchase rope ladders to be used for escape routes from the second floor.

e. I can install smoke detectors and buy fire extinguishers for each floor in my home.

f. I can install an outside lighting system that lights up when someone approaches my home.

g. I will teach my children how to use the phone to make collect calls to me and to _____ (friend, family, minister, etc.) if my partner tried to take them.

h. I will tell people who care for my children exactly who has permission to pick up my children and that my partner is NOT allowed to pick them up. Inform the following people:

Safety Plan Model

School _____

Day Care _____

Babysitter _____

Sunday School _____

Teacher _____

Others _____

i. I can tell the following people that my partner no longer lives with me and that they should call the police if he is near my residence:

Neighbors _____

Church Leaders _____

Friends _____

Others _____

Step 4. Order of Protection

The Following Steps Will Help Enforce the Order of Protection:

a.   I will keep the protection order in _____ (the locations). *Always keep a copy with you.*

b.   I will give my protection order to police departments in the area where I visit my friends, family, where I live, and where I work.

c.   If I visit other counties, I will register my protection order with those counties.

d.   I can call the local domestic violence agency if I am not sure how to register my protection order with the police departments.

e.   I will tell my employer, my church leader, my friends, my family, and others that I have a protection order.

f.   If my protection order gets destroyed, I know I can go to the county courthouse and get another copy.

g.   If my partner violates the protection order, I will call the police and report it. I will call my lawyer, my advocate, counselor, and/or tell the courts about the violation.

h.   If the police do not help, I will call my advocate or my attorney, AND I will file a complaint with the chief of the police department.

i.   I can file a private criminal complaint with the district judge in the jurisdiction that the violation took place or with the county prosecutor. A domestic violence advocate will help me do this.

Step 5. Job and Public Safety

I Can Do the Following:

a. I can tell my boss, security, and _____
_____ at work
about this situation.

b. I can ask _____
_____ to help screen my phone
calls.

c. When leaving work, I can do the following:
_____.

d. When I am driving home from work and problems arise, I can _____.

e. If I use public transportation, I can _____.

f. I will shop at different grocery stores and shopping malls at different hours than I did when I was with my partner.

g. I will use a different bank and bank at different hours than I did when I was with my partner.

h. I can also do the following: _____
_____.

Step 6. Drug and Alcohol Use

I Can Enhance My Safety if I Do the Following:

a. If I am going to "use," I am going to do it in a safe place with people who understand the risk of violence and who are committed to my safety.

b. I can also _____.

c. If my partner is using, I can _____.

d. I can also _____ _____.

e. To protect my children, I can _____ _____.

Step 7. Emotional Health

I Can Do the Following:

a. If I feel depressed and ready to return to a potentially violent situation/partner, I can _____ _____.

b. I can call _____.

c. When I have to talk to my partner in person or on the phone, I can _____ _____.

d. I will use "I can . . ." statements, and I will be assertive with people.

e. I can tell myself "_____" when I feel people are trying to control or abuse me.

f. I can call the following people and/or places for support:_____.

g. Things I can do to make me feel stronger are: _____.

Urban Christian His Glory Book Club!

Established in January 2007, **UC His Glory Book Club** is another way to introduce **Urban Christian** and its authors. We are an online book club supporting Urban Christian authors by purchasing, reading, and providing written reviews of the authors' books. *UC His Glory Book Club* welcomes both men and women of the literary world who have a passion for reading Christian-based fiction.

UC His Glory Book Club is the brainchild of Joylynn Jossel, author and Executive Editor of Urban Christian and Kendra Norman-Bellamy, author and copy editor for Urban Christian. The book club will provide support, positive feedback, encouragement, and a forum whereby members can openly discuss and review the literary works of Urban Christian authors. In the future, we anticipate broadening our spectrum of services to include online author chats, author spotlights, interviews with your favorite Urban Christian author(s), special online groups for *UC His Glory Book Club* members, ability to post reviews on the website and amazon.com, membership ID cards, *UC His Glory* Yahoo! Group and much more.

Even though there will be no membership fees attached to becoming a member of *UC His Glory Book Club,* we do expect our members to be active, committed, and to follow the guidelines of the book club.

UC His Glory Book Club members pledge to:

- Follow the guidelines of *UC His Glory Book Club*.
- Provide input, opinions, and reviews that build up, rather than tear down.
- Commit to purchasing, reading, and discussing featured book(s) of the month.
- Respect the Christian beliefs of *UC His Glory Book Club*.
- Believe that Jesus is the Christ, Son of the Living God.

We look forward to the online fellowship.

Many Blessings to You!

Shelia E. Lipsey
President
UC His Glory Book Club

** Visit the official Urban Christian His Glory Book Club website at www.uchisglorybookclub.net